T0244816

A great thriller with well-defined characters and a compelling plot. Hard to put down.

Jay (NetGalley Reviewer)

Put me in mind of Philip Marlowe, Jim Rockford, and the Jack Nicholson character in *Chinatown.*

MenReadingBooks Blog

Excellent . . . exciting to the last page.

WiLoveBooks Blog

It was refreshing to see a pure detective novel where the P.I. actually knows how to do a stakeout, research missing people, deal with others for information, and navigate a relationship with the police.

The setting was Los Angeles—and this was another strong suit of the author. The city was described well enough to be an additional character in the book without spending pages and pages describing it.

Lilac Reviews

. . . I would recommend the entire series from indie author Jesse Miles and am surprised that it hasn't been picked up by a major publisher.

Kelly (Well Read Reviews)

This reader got entrapped.

Schuyler (Kindle Reviewer)

This is a great first attempt at a novel, and . . . I'm really looking forward to the next one. If you like Robert Crais' character Elvis you'll undoubtedly enjoy Mr. Salvo. Do yourself a favor and check it out.

Nicholas (Kindle Reviewer)

DEAD DROP

JESSE MILES

ISBN 979-8-35094-050-3

ebook ISBN: 979-8-35094-051-0

1

I rolled down the San Diego Freeway that bright August morning, along with the usual commuters, truckers, and airport traffic. My destination was Culver Aerospace Industries, a little south of Los Angeles International Airport. In a telephone conversation the day before, the company's Information Technology Director, a woman named Darcey Mathis, had requested my help on a case of embezzlement.

In the Culver parking lot, I passed on two narrow, door-banging spaces and angled into the far corner, between a new Camaro and the fence. I got out and threw on my jacket. The sea breeze tossed me a bouquet of burnt jet fuel and salt air. The next thing to come out of the breeze was the labored whine of a jet climbing out of LAX. I craned my neck to see it, but the office buildings on Imperial Highway blocked the view.

The central Culver Aerospace structure was a towering monolith painted concrete-gray with blue trim. Employees passed back and forth through the glass lobby doors, their attire ranging from business suits to coveralls.

I announced myself at the front desk, and the uniformed security officer asked me to fill out a small form. He reviewed the form, looked at my driver's license, and handed me a temporary badge. As I clipped on the badge, a woman stepped into the lobby and smiled. She was in her mid-thirties, nice-looking but not enough to make you snap your head around. Her thick, light brown hair blended with her beige business suit.

She said, "Hello, I'm Darcey Mathis. Are you Mr. Salvo?"

"I sure am. Nice to meet you."

"Before we meet with the investigative team, my boss would like to talk to you."

She led me down a hallway, moving with a casual swing to her stride. She explained that her boss Del Hoffman, was a Vice President whose territory included Information Technology, Security, and Facilities.

I said, "By the way, should I address you as Ms. Mathis?"

She put a cheery smile in her voice. "My name is Darcey. You call me Ms. Mathis, and you're fired."

A minute later we were seated in Del Hoffman's office, and I had been properly introduced.

He was lantern-jawed, somewhere in his forties, wearing a dark suit. His dark hair was slicked back hard and shiny. A framed photo on the wall showed him wearing a cowboy hat, firing a Western-style revolver from the hip.

I pointed at the photo. "You shoot competitively?"

"I used to."

"Is that a Colt Single Action Army?"

"It's a Ruger, modified for fast draw competition. Have you ever done any competitive shooting?"

"Not really. I've had some tactical pistol and shotgun training. We had some informal competitions."

Darcey said, "I hate to interrupt boys' discussions of their toys, but the meeting starts in thirteen minutes."

Hoffman nodded. "Quite right, Darcey. Let me explain to Mr. Salvo our situation here. One of our employees got into our financial systems and sent checks to a fictitious vendor, a fake janitorial company."

I said, "That's a classic accounts payable scam. How much did they get?"

"In this most recent embezzlement, they got eighty-eight thousand and change. We also found two earlier losses, very similar to this one. They were back in 2009 and 2011."

"Sounds like the same embezzler."

"It looks that way. The fake companies were always janitorial or landscaping, supposedly working out of trucks, no real office. The limit for managerial approval of accounts payable disbursements is thirty thousand. The checks were always under that. It looks like they planned to keep a low profile and pull the scam every two years and hope nobody would ever catch it."

"And all of this was just recently discovered?"

"That's part of the embarrassment. If this becomes public, the negative publicity could impact our stock price."

"How did they get into the system?"

"We're not exactly sure, but we think they looked over the shoulder of a longtime, trusted employee named Mrs. Ito and stole her password."

"Is it possible Mrs. Ito is the embezzler?"

Darcey said, "Possible, but very unlikely. She's been a manager in the finance department forever, and she's what you call a solid citizen. Her husband is a retired dentist, used to be on the Gardena City Council. The only reason she's still working is to earn medical benefits for her and her husband when she retires next year. Mrs. Ito wouldn't be pulling a scam like this." She pulled a thin stack of manila folders from a leather portfolio. "But for the sake of due diligence, I included her in the files on the possible suspects."

She put the folders into my hand. "You can keep these. We're pretty sure the culprit is one of these four employees. We would like you to perform a detailed background check on them as the first phase in your investigation."

I said, "How did you narrow it down to these four?"

"They were the only ones who had inside knowledge of the accounts payable system and who were also in the office on all the days the fraudulent transactions were conducted. There were other employees who were capable of doing the transactions, but on at least one of those days, they were somewhere else . . . out sick, on vacation, jury duty, at another facility . . . whatever. The way our systems are set up, there was no way to conduct those transactions from outside this building. It's almost impossible for the culprit to be someone other than one of these four."

There were various possibilities. More than one of the four suspects might have been involved. There was probably an outside accomplice who rented a private PO box in the name of the fictious business. The accomplice would run the Culver Aerospace checks through an account at a bank in a neighborhood where he or she was not known. I doubted that there were more than two conspirators; splitting the take would be too painful if there was a third grifter. I kept those speculations to myself.

Hoffman gave a backhanded wave toward the folders. "Go ahead and take a look at our suspects. We have a couple of minutes."

Each folder contained a copy of the subject's employment application, Culver Aerospace work history, contact information, and a badge photograph.

Lucille Ito, sixty-one, looked like the president of the Fussy Old Women's Garden and Gossip Club. She had worked in the finance department at Culver for twenty-seven years, mostly as a manager. She lived in Gardena.

Joy Bodie, thirty-one, was cute with big eyes and a little button nose. She had been employed by Culver Aerospace for nine years in finance-related administrative positions. She was married, residing in Lawndale.

Oswald Pace, thirty, was round-faced with a wise-guy curl to his lip. He had been with the company for six years as a computer programmer. Single, he had a Brentwood apartment not too far from my office.

Derrick Jenkinson, thirty-three, had a thin face and a sullen smile. He had been with the company for five years as a systems analyst. Divorced, he lived in Manhattan Beach, near the water.

Darcey said, "It's not clear yet whether we will want to press charges. If there were a trial, details about internal company matters would be all over the news. I suspect that when you do your background checks and start turning over rocks and we zero in on the culprit, we will find things we do not want in the public record. Personally, I think we should just get rid of him . . . or her, as the case may be."

Hoffman said, "Mr. Salvo, in case you were wondering, our CEO Barney Xavier was the one who recommended you. He spoke with someone over at Dawson International in Torrance. They said you did a good job of breaking up a kickback scheme over there a couple of years ago. Now let's talk money. What do you charge?"

I pulled a partially completed client retainer contract from my briefcase and pushed it across the desk. "I get three hundred an hour plus expenses. I don't nickel-and-dime minor expenses such as local mileage, lunch, and shoe leather. In this case, I require a twenty-thousand-dollar retainer. The first meeting is a freebie, so you can assess me and decide if you want to hire me or give me the bum's rush. If you want to hire me, I need to have that contract signed. You get my final bill with the final report."

Hoffman studied the contract. "Doesn't sound like a bargain rate, but I guess it's in the ballpark. Cheaper than attorneys."

He pointed to the door and said to Darcey, "You can go ahead and take Mr. Salvo to the room. You and I have to drop by Barney's office and prep him for the meeting."

She led me down the hallway to an open door. "The meeting's in there. We'll be back in five."

2

The conference room had plenty of chairs, plenty of framed military aircraft photos, and a conference table slightly too small for launching and recovering navy jets. A notebook computer sat near one end, connected to a video projector aimed at a white screen on the wall. I took a chair directly across from the projector, but it wasn't the technology that pulled me in.

The only other person in the room was a young Asian woman leaning over the table and fiddling with a cable connection. Dark eyes lifted, swept over me, then went back to work.

In her twenties, she had black hair pulled back in a ponytail and wore a black long-sleeved blouse that could have been a half-size smaller and a maroon knit skirt that could have been a little shorter. No wedding ring.

She sat down. Now I could see her employee badge, which said Lilith Lin.

I said, "Hello, Lilith. I'm Jack Salvo. What kind of work do you do here?"

"Information security." She had a pretty voice, almost musical.

"Have you worked on many cybercrimes?"

"No." She typed in staccato bursts until she seemed satisfied with the results. She looked around at everything in the room except me.

I said, "Are you giving the presentation?"

"Yes."

"How do you think they laundered the money?"

"That will be in my presentation."

"How do you think they got the password?"

"That will be in my presentation."

"What's your sign?"

"What kind of sign?"

"Your astrological sign."

Now her voice had a fist in it. "What kind of education do you have?"

"I came close to a PhD."

"They probably kicked you out because you believed in astrology."

"They kicked me out for being an insensitive brute."

She nodded thoughtfully. "That was probably a sound decision by the college faculty. How long ago was that?"

"A few years ago."

"How many years?"

"Not too many."

"How many in numerical terms?"

"Have you ever considered the advantages of a dignified older man?"

"How old are you?"

"Thirty-seven."

"I am twenty-four. Pick on someone your own age."

"When do you get off work? Maybe we could go somewhere, and I could buy you an ice cream cone."

The corners of her mouth rose against her wishes. She got her mouth straight. "I suppose you are the hotshot private detective who came to save the day."

"What else do you suppose?"

"That you are overconfident."

"I have other qualities."

"Such as?"

"Toughness, chivalry, and dedication to justice."

She leaned forward and gaped in mock admiration. "Sir Galahad! I am so glad you finally arrived. I was beginning to think you would never get here."

People were starting to drift into the room, so I shut up. There were four I had never seen, two men and two women. Darcey Mathis and Del Hoffman came in behind them. Hoffman shut the door and took a seat, moving with the starched swagger that usually turns out to be driven by insecurity.

Darcey remained standing and took charge of the meeting. "I don't need to remind you that everything said in this room today stays in this room. This unfortunate event is not yet known by the rank and file employees, and we need to keep it that way." She took a chair next to Hoffman.

Darcey introduced me to the group. I produced a stack of business cards and dealt them out. Everyone except Darcey and Del pushed their card toward me. I organized the cards in an array reflecting the seating positions. The man from HR had a neatly-trimmed gray beard and a friendly, avuncular manner. The attorney from the legal department was a husky woman whose default facial expression was a tired frown. The auditor was a pear-shaped young fellow who was in a state of continuous eagerness. The public relations rep was a tall thirty-something brunette wearing black designer jeans and a black-and-white Louis Vuitton blouse. Lilith introduced herself to me as though she were meeting me for the first time.

A tall guy in his fifties came in, shut the door softly, and took a seat. He carried a little extra weight, and he looked like he knew how to throw it around. He had a large head, salt-and-pepper flattop, and a well-tailored light gray suit. Everyone in the room sat up a little straighter.

The newcomer said to Hoffman, "I'm going to watch and listen. I'll chime in when I need to."

Hoffman gestured toward him. "For those of you who haven't met him, this is my boss and our CEO Barney Xavier. He's taking a special interest in this matter."

Darcey dimmed the lights. "Okay, let's get going. Lilith Lin knows more about the details of this case than anyone else, and she has put together a presentation for us."

Lilith had already projected an image onto the screen: ACCOUNTS PAYABLE INCIDENT—CULVER CONFIDENTIAL. She ran her PowerPoint presentation, the main points of which had been covered for me by Del and Darcey, but there were other pieces of information that I found interesting:

- Four bogus checks totaling $86,600 were mailed from Culver Aerospace to a private PO box in the City of Commerce.

- The checks were deposited at a Southland National Bank branch in the city of Hawthorne, near Culver Aerospace. The account had been opened in the name of David Lopez, no doubt a false identity. The money launderer withdrew cash from the bank in amounts ranging from three thousand to forty-five hundred dollars and from ATMs in three-hundred-dollar increments. None of the amounts deposited or withdrawn would raise any eyebrows.

- The two previous embezzlements, in 2009 and 2011, were in the same modus operandi, using different private PO boxes and different banks.

Lilith did not list the names of the four suspects, but the team members knew who they were, and there was a spirited discussion regarding whodunit and how they did it. When Mrs. Ito was mentioned as a possible suspect, everyone laughed. The consensus was that Oswald Pace, Joy Bodie, or Derrick Jenkinson shoulder-surfed Mrs. Ito's password.

During the discussion I pulled out my iPad, accessed a subscription data service, and learned a few things. Lucille Ito and her husband were pillars of the community. Joy Bodie had a messy divorce in which she briefly lost custody of an infant son; she was solid since that time. Derrick Jenkinson ran a consulting business on the side and had no significant blemishes in his background; he had speeding tickets, but he would have to speed up to match my record.

Oswald Pace's background was more entertaining. He had fifteen different addresses in the past fourteen years, going back to an apartment in Orange County. In 2003 he was suspected of insurance fraud in a burglary claim and skated on a technicality. In 2005 he was evicted from an apartment after not paying rent for five months. One month prior to his eviction, he pulled a slip-and-fall in the carport and received a ten-thousand-dollar nuisance settlement. He had been sued in small claims court for unpaid bills on two occasions; he prevailed in one case and lost the other.

Lilith turned off the projector and handed out hard copies of her presentation. Darcey turned the lights back up.

Barney Xavier had shot some annoyed glances my way as I worked on my iPad and kept one ear on the meeting. His prominent jaw squirmed like a bulldog chewing tobacco when he spoke. "Mr. Salvo, if we decide to involve law enforcement in this matter, which agency would you recommend we contact first?" He seemed to think I hadn't been paying attention.

I said, "You start with your local police, then there are complications. The fraudulent data entry was committed here in El Segundo. The checks were mailed to a postal drop in the city of Commerce, where the fake invoices also came from. The checks were cashed in Hawthorne. That gives us a total of three cities and three different police departments, not to mention federal agencies for the mail and bank frauds. Also, I'm just talking about the most recent fraud. The previous scams probably involve other cities' law enforcement agencies."

Xavier kept going. "Twenty thousand dollars is a lot of money for background checks on four people and a brief investigation. Do you have any law enforcement experience?"

"No."

"Military intelligence?"

"No."

"What about your educational and professional background?"

"I've been a licensed private investigator with my own company for ten years. Previously, I worked for others, including Western Investigative Services, one of the larger agencies on the West Coast. I have a bachelor's degree in philosophy with a heavy minor in criminal justice and a master's plus more graduate work in philosophy. I teach a class at Coast College on Wednesday nights."

Xavier squinted and cocked his head. "Philosophy?"

I let the word hover over the table while I gave him my learned professor look. "It's a great discipline for people who want to learn how to form a complete sentence."

Everyone in the room froze except Lilith. She rested her fist against her mouth, the corners of which were again curved upward.

Xavier gave me a look that could have pinned me to the wall, but he spoke casually. "The CEO at Dawson International told me you were a wise-ass, and he told me you were very effective in your investigation. As far as I'm concerned, you can be a wise-ass all you want. I don't give a shit. What I want is results. What can you do for us?"

"For starters, I can do a detailed background check on the four subjects, much more detailed than your people can. If we identify the embezzler—and I'm assuming we will—and you decide you want to keep a low profile and not involve law enforcement, I might be able to persuade the swindler to voluntarily terminate their employment at Culver Aerospace and go quietly slinking away."

Xavier said, "And exactly how would you lean on the yet-to-be-identified swindler?"

"I can't give away any trade secrets, but I have a pretty good history when it comes to being persuasive with crooks, especially when I have them trapped like rats. I can get to work as soon as I get the banking and postal information."

Xavier looked at Darcey. "Let's do it."

She said, "Lilith can get that banking and postal info for Mr. Salvo right after the meeting."

Xavier looked around the room. "Does anyone have any questions for Mr. Salvo?"

Silence.

Then Lilith said, "Mr. Salvo, how many employees do you have at Salvo Investigative Services?"

"At the moment it's just me."

"Does that mean you are planning to staff up soon?"

"No. About seven years ago I went solo. I don't do a high volume of routine work such as pre-employment background checks like when I started out. In those days I usually had two or three employees."

"Would it be accurate to say that your private investigation business consists of just you and your office?"

"My business consists of me, my office, the investigative data services I subscribe to, and a network of other private investigators with whom I share information." I left out certain off-the-record sources, such as law enforcement agencies, utility and telecom companies, the Department of Motor Vehicles, and bartenders.

Lilith was starting to say something when Xavier looked at his watch and stood up. "I've got a conference call in three minutes. Thanks, everyone. I plan to see you in your next meeting." As he went out the door, he looked straight at me. "When you have some results."

The meeting sank into speculative chitchat and side conversations. The attendees started edging toward the door.

I walked around the table to Lilith and watched her shut down her computer. I said, "In addition to the banking and postal information, can we get together and compare notes?"

"What is it that interests you specifically?"

I thought, *Your spirit and your nicely shaped ass.*

I said, "The suspects' attendance records, card access inside the Culver campus, Internet history, and phone calls."

"I have already done much of that."

"Let's do the rest of it."

She thought it over for a moment. "We can go to my office."

Del Hoffman had been watching and listening. "Make sure we get our money's worth out of him, Lilith."

She gave me a skeptical look. "You can count on me, Del."

From across the room, Darcey caught my eye and made a "phone me" gesture, her hand to her face, pinkie extended.

I nodded.

Lilith led me through a maze of hallways and into her hard-walled office. She offered me a seat, but before I sat, I took a good look at three framed items on the wall: a bachelor's degree from UC Irvine, a National Taiwan University emblem, and a poster of the movie *Lilith.*

I said, "How long have you been in the USA?"

"When I was ten my family immigrated to the United States. My father worked for a company in Palo Alto that imports bicycle parts from Taiwan. He advanced through the management ranks and got a big promotion. We moved back to Taiwan when I was sixteen. He managed a factory there for two years. Then the family moved to back to Palo Alto for good, except I am in Los Angeles at the present time."

"Did you go to college in Taiwan?"

"For my final year of high school and first year of college. Then I went to a community college in San Mateo." She pointed to her diploma. "As you can see, I got my bachelor's at UC Irvine."

I looked again at the movie poster. The artwork featured a garish, contorted drawing of Jean Seberg's and Warren Beatty's faces. The poster's tagline: Lilith . . . her evil is in her innocence.

I said, "Cool movie poster. How evil are you?"

"Not as innocent as I look."

"Any chance I could get a look at our four subjects?"

She glanced at her wall clock, which said five minutes after nine. "Oswald Pace should be in the cafeteria now for his fifteen-minute break. He usually takes a half hour."

A few minutes later we were in the cafeteria, pouring coffee into paper cups. Lilith nudged me and whispered, "That is Oswald in the striped shirt, talking to the girl in the red dress."

Oswald Pace was comfortably arranged over a chair and a half, across the table from a younger female employee. He had a long, pointed nose that wasn't apparent in his full-face badge photograph.

I said, "Does he always have that smirk on his face?"

"Always."

"Makes me want to smack him."

"Please let me know when you do it. I want to watch."

We zigzagged through various hallways and into a large room divided into cubicles. In a far corner, Joy Bodie was talking on her phone. She sat facing away from us, wearing a long, loose-fitting dress. As we walked past her desk, I couldn't hear what she was saying. Her work area was brilliantly clean. The documents were in neat stacks, and Post-it notes were in perfectly straight lines.

Mrs. Ito was not in her office.

Lilith said, "It doesn't matter, because Mrs. Ito didn't do it."

Derrick Jenkinson was taking a vacation day, but we looked into his cubicle anyway and saw nothing worth looking at twice.

Lilith said, "We have come this far, so I might as well give you the standard tour."

She showed me a mainframe computer room, a mag tape library, and a room full of servers mounted on racks. On the factory floor, we put on plastic safety goggles and watched a milling machine cut intricate contours into a block of aluminum. We stood in the mouth of the Culver Aerospace Wind Tunnel while Lilith explained that they didn't use it much, since computer simulations were better and cheaper.

We climbed up to a raised walkway that crossed over a spacious room in the center of the building. We held on to the rail and peered down at a smallish aircraft resembling a cross between a prehistoric bird and a flying saucer. It had a wingspan of about thirty feet and a camouflage sky-blue paint job. A banner on the wall said PALADIN UAV.

Lilith said, "The Paladin is going to be the latest and greatest in unmanned attack aircraft."

"Can we see where they make it?"

She pointed down at a door near the Paladin display. "You cannot go into a classified area. You do not have the security clearance and access that you would need."

"But, now that I've seen the Paladin, are you going to have to shoot me?"

"What you can see here is no big deal. The real secrets are in the engineering design and the software."

"Why is it so great?"

"It will probably carry a new generation of very small missiles and drones that can seek out and kill people on the battlefield . . . or maybe in their beds. It could change the way wars are fought."

"How do the missiles tell the good guys from the bad guys?"

"Like I said, it is classified, and I do not know any of the details, but it would be something like this. The Paladin would look down and see someone. Let us suppose it sees you. Then the Paladin would take your picture and send it up to a satellite. The computers would identify you and send a message back that says, 'It is that wise-ass private eye Jackson Salvo. Shoot him!'" She poked me in the chest and smiled. She had a nice smile. Quick and spontaneous, as opposed to the more common plastered-on smile.

Back in her office, she gave me the banking and postal drop information Darcey had promised.

I said, "You work directly for Darcey?"

"She is my boss's boss. I have no immediate manager right now. The position of Information Security Manager is not filled, so I report directly to Darcey for the time being."

"Why don't you try for the position?"

"I have less than two years' experience, and I am starting an MBA program next month. After I get my MBA, I will have more employment options. And I think we should concentrate on our work now."

We reviewed the four subjects' telephone calls and Internet usage, and found nothing of immediate interest. Lilith found the descriptions and license plates of the cars they were parking in the Culver Aerospace lot: Ito drove a white Toyota Avalon, Bodie a red VW Jetta, Pace a blue Nissan 370Z, and Jenkinson a black Audi.

I was starting to squirm in my chair, anxious to hit the road and do some serious investigating. "Who do you think did it?"

"Mrs. Ito is too smart and too classy to have done it. Trust me on that one. Joy Bodie is not smart or creative enough to commit embezzlement and actually get the money in her hand. She used to be a floozy, and now she is a Bible-thumper. At lunch every day, she eats alone at her desk and reads passages with this faraway look on her face. I don't object to her reading the Bible, but she never reads anything else. In her defense, she is a good worker. The crook is either Derrick or Oswald, maybe a very slight chance of Joy Bodie. If it is Mrs. Ito, I will eat my shoes."

I said, "The embezzler usually turns out to be a trusted employee. Sort of like Mrs. Ito."

"Yes, I have heard that story many times. It is one of the clichés of the security world. In this case it will not be true."

"How about Pace?"

"He is a halfway decent worker, but he is mainly a talker. I have never heard anyone talk so much and say so little. He thinks he is much cooler than he really is. He is always hitting on the younger women, even the married ones."

"Did he hit on you?"

"Once. He will not try it again."

"I have no doubt. How about Derrick Jenkinson?"

She held her hand out flat, to designate a short person. "You mean Napoleon."

"A vertically challenged gentleman?"

"The little prick is at least an inch shorter than me. He makes up for it by being pushy and loud. He is also a parasite. He tries to get other people to do his work, and he takes his vacation days strategically, so he can avoid difficult assignments. In fact, he is on vacation today and tomorrow. Everyone else in his department is running around like crazy, preparing for a big quarterly review, so he took the time off. He said he had doctors' appointments. Everyone knows he works on outside consulting jobs, and sometimes he even works on them at his desk here at Culver."

A little after ten, Lilith walked me out to the lobby. I turned in my badge, and the security guard handed me an envelope containing my client retainer contract signed by someone in the procurement department. I was in business.

3

strolled out through the parking lot, calculating the odds on my four potential embezzlers. By the time my seat belt was buckled, my money was on Pace. Based on my initial research and Lilith's comments, he had an aversion to integrity and an affinity for easy money, but that was no reason to ignore the other three. Prior to their fall, white-collar criminals can be the most respected of citizens. The other three lived nearby, so it was time for a quick tour of the South Bay.

Mrs. Ito's address was a smartly painted tract home in a neighborhood of similar houses near Redondo Beach Boulevard and Western Avenue. A gray Lexus sat in the driveway. Three trash bins were evenly spaced at the curb: gray, green, and blue. The car and the bins all appeared to be recently polished and waxed. The dichondra lawn was perfectly manicured, with good reason. An older Japanese man, whom I presumed to be Mrs. Ito's retired husband, limped across the lawn, weeding fork in one hand, a plastic can in the other. The weeds didn't have a chance.

Joy Bodie's house was a mile to the west, across the street from a weedy triplex that may or may not have been vacant. Joy's house was of the same vintage as the Ito family's, but pride of ownership had fallen away somewhere along the line. A pair of little boys, about seven and nine, stood in the yard pushing each other. The front door opened, and a young Hispanic woman tossed out a small beach ball. The boys dove and wrestled for the ball, the older one gaining the advantage. The nanny screeched. The older boy let his brother out of a headlock. She gave me a good look as I moved past, so I kept moving.

I drove west on Manhattan Beach Boulevard, crossed Sepulveda, angled down toward the pier, and slipped into a feathery white cloud. White turned to gray, and the air temperature dropped off.

Derrick Jenkinson's condo was packed into a beach neighborhood where the grandmothers dress like teenagers and the teenagers don't acknowledge any life east of Sepulveda. There weren't any residential streets, but wide sidewalks separated the fronts of the properties. Garages and carports were on the alleys. I drove slowly up Jenkinson's alley and found his condo over an empty carport. A keypad at the rear gate would block access to his front door.

Across the alley, a black Mustang convertible was partially backed into an open garage. A thin young man with stringy blond hair bent over the hood and lazily sponged wax onto it. Another young fellow slowly rolled his skateboard down the alley toward us. His black stubble contrasted sharply with his sun-reddened face. From a distance, he appeared to be in his early twenties. At close range, he seemed to be at least thirty. With the slouch of a lackadaisical thirteen-year-old, he flipped the skateboard up into his hand and sauntered toward the other boy. They exchanged low-key greetings and pointedly refused to notice me as I eased my car past them. The first rule of beach etiquette is "always be cool."

I turned around at the dead-end and drove back down, trying to see what I could without being too obvious. All I could see of Jenkinson's condo was white stucco and covered windows. I parked on the cross street below and took the walkway that accessed the front of Jenkinson's building.

The houses and condos lining both sides of the wide sidewalk were mostly two-story, with big windows to capture the ocean view. The clapboard house on the west side of Jenkinson's building was an exception. Built back in the days when surfboards were ten feet of solid redwood, it was single-story and had small windows. External plumbing pipes were on the side adjacent to Jenkinson's residence.

The pipes were well-positioned for fence-climbing. I edged closer for a better view. If I were at Jenkinson's front door, there would be no direct line of sight between me and the boys across the alley. I calculated how many seconds it would take me to go over the fence.

A flicker caught the corner of my eye. The movement came from a deeply tanned woman who had too much bulk and too little clothing. She stood, garden hose in hand, at the corner of a house across the way. She turned off the water, stepped inside, and shut the door silently. Vertical blinds in the bay window shifted. If I went over the fence, I would soon be talking to a group of Manhattan Beach police officers, trying to justify my existence in their orderly little town.

A half hour later I arrived at Oswald Pace's residence. Brentwood Luau Apartments was a two-story building on the east side of Barrington Avenue, between Sunset and San Vicente. I backed my car into a visitor space in front.

A sign under the A-frame facade said something about gracious Hawaiian living. The derelict landscaping, tenuous paint, and rotting tiki poles said otherwise. The characters carved into the poles were all grimacing. Maybe they knew something I didn't.

One thing I didn't know was Pace's apartment number. It wasn't in the contact information Darcey had given me. I pushed through the lobby door, went past a pile of dusty rocks that had once been a fountain, and checked out the mailboxes. The tenant directory did not show the name Pace, but there were occupants named "tenant" in units 111, 209, and 211. A bin under the mailboxes held magazines, small packages, and large envelopes—nothing addressed to Pace. I still didn't know which apartment he was in.

A dark, narrow hallway went straight to the back. I walked softly on the stiff, industrial-grade carpet and kept my ears open. The building was curiously quiet. Out the back door, I found a row of electric meters on the wall. "Pace" was penciled on the meter for Apartment 211.

Outside stairs took me up to the second-floor hallway. The door across from 211 had a peephole and a slim gap at the bottom. I watched for a floor shadow. You never know when some nosy bastard might try to horn in on your personal business. My custom Swiss Army Camping Knife, with two of its foldouts somehow turned into lock-picking tools, easily defeated the cheap door lock.

Pace's living room had enough space for a black leather sofa, coffee table, television, and not much more. Magazines fanned out on the table. Magazines with titles referring to men's fashion and fitness, and articles advising how to get six-pack abs without exercising, a big Mercedes with no money down, and cheap dates with lingerie models.

A framed print hung over the sofa: the Magritte drawing of a tobacco pipe and the inscription *Ceci n'est pas une pipe*. I muttered, "Not a pipe, my ass. It's a pipe." Don't get me started on Surrealism.

The kitchen was offset to the left. The office consisted of a computer and a stack of papers on the kitchen table. There were few documents and no photos stored on the computer. I inserted a thumb drive and captured the documents, address book, appointment schedule, and e-mails. I photographed hard-copy bills, credit card statements, and bank statements.

In the hallway cabinets and drawers, I found nothing more incriminating than five reefers and what appeared to be a small quantity of cocaine. In California these days, you get a medal for taking drugs.

On the bedroom closet shelf were three new boxed pairs of Salvatore Ferragamo shoes from Saks Fifth Avenue. A heap of clothes piled up on the floor. On top of the dirty laundry was a Neiman Marcus bag containing two pairs of designer jeans and four Zegna shirts, all with the tags attached.

The bathroom had three drawers built into the wall. They came out quickly. I examined the enclosure using my penlight and Pace's handheld mirror. It almost went past me—a manila envelope peeking through a gap in the wood framing. I fished it out with my knife and thumbed through a stack of hundred-dollar bills. I peeled off what I estimated to be half, counted sixty-five hundred dollars, and multiplied by two.

I put the cash and the drawers back in place and went to my car. Twenty-five minutes later I was in my office, eating my recently purchased quesadillas and chips.

4

My office is on the south side of Pico Boulevard, between Bundy and Barrington. The twelve-hundred-square-foot building is one big room, except for the bathroom and kitchen at the back. When I bought it ten years ago, it was a shabby little dump that had seen better times as a barbershop, antique store, and insurance agency. I bought it cheap, but I had to invest in remodeling, plumbing, electrical, and a new roof. I always figured that if times got tough, I could live in it or rent it out.

A century-old wooden desk anchors the decor. My father inherited the desk from his father. Other furnishings: a writing table that almost matches the desk, a dark-gray Aeron chair for me, a cordovan leather sofa for clients, four vertical file cabinets, a supply cabinet, and a coat tree. Two wooden chairs move around the office on an as-needed basis.

My wall hangings include two framed college diplomas, my California Private Investigators Certificate, a canvas print by Gustav Klimt, and three framed photos: the original PI Allan Pinkerton, Ralph Meeker as Mike Hammer in *Kiss Me Deadly*, and The Three Stooges in *Who Done It?*

I worked on the information from Pace's apartment during my gourmet lunch. Nothing in his Word and Excel documents attracted my attention. The e-mails were the usual junk. The appointment schedule and address book were more interesting. Pace had listed four 8 p.m. meetings with someone named BV, from April through July. There was only one BV in Pace's address book, a Buddy Vega. Vega's phone number led to the fact that he was the owner of Celebrity Motors, a used-car lot out by Silver Lake, a neighborhood that sits about three miles north of downtown L.A.

Lilith's presentation had listed the dates of the illicit check deposits at the Southland National Bank branch in Hawthorne. Those dates aligned with Pace and Vega's four meetings.

Pace's canceled checks were mostly unexceptional: rent, car payment, utilities. The credit card payments were exceptional. He had a $20K Visa balance in March; he paid it down in three $5K increments from April through June. Those payment dates were also in alignment with the meetings.

After the fourth meeting, there was no credit card paydown, but there was a flurry of vague notations in Pace's appointment schedule regarding "Buddy." It looked like Buddy Vega might have stiffed Pace on the final installment of the loot. Pace's half of the take should have been $44K. Assuming Vega stiffed him for 11K, Pace would have netted 33K. Subtract 15K for credit card payments and 5K for pretentious new clothes and pocket money, and he would have 13K left over, the amount hidden in his bathroom. I congratulated myself on my mastery of third-grade math.

I went to work on Buddy Vega and found the wrinkles in his résumé. In 2002 he did a little time in County for aggravated assault. In 2007 he was busted for selling flood-damaged vehicles. He was divorced, living in a little house on Berendo Street, not too far from Celebrity Motors. His previous addresses were in the Hollywood area and Orange County. The most fascinating piece of information: Vega's address in 1999 was Commonwealth Plaza Apartments in Fullerton, in the same Orange County apartment as Oswald Pace's oldest-known residence. Pace and Vega had been good buddies for at least fourteen years.

I called the manager of Commonwealth Plaza Apartments and said I was doing a background check on Pace and Vega. The manager informed me that the manager in 1999 was Mrs. Kilson, but she was now in her nineties and had "lost her marbles." The manager said she could not discuss personal matters regarding current or past tenants, but she would forward my phone number to the property owner, Mr. Sheridan.

Ten minutes later Mr. Sheridan called and said, "I would be happy to bend your ear about Pace and Vega, those rat bastards!"

He told of the roommates being behind on the rent, playing on the sympathy of the saintly apartment manager Mrs. Kilson, and moving out with stolen appliances when she was at her sister's funeral. I listened with genuine sympathy, thanked Mr. Sheridan, and assured him I would do my best to achieve justice.

Pace and Vega were probably the swindlers. Now I needed a positive ID on Vega at the bank where he laundered the loot.

5

elebrity Motors had to settle for the less glamorous end of Sunset Boulevard, out past the bend toward downtown. Nearby businesses provided coin-operated laundry services for the homeless, rooms at a weekly rate for the more fortunate, and bail bonds for the unlucky. Carriage trade patronized the 7-Eleven.

I parked across the street and a quarter block down from the car lot. The smog-tinted sunlight and my binoculars gave me the view I wanted.

The mainstay transaction at Celebrity Motors would be an older, high-mileage BMW, Audi, or Mercedes purchased on high-interest credit by someone who should have bought a Toyota. The vehicles with the flashiest wheels made up the front row. A tile-roofed stucco building, a little larger than a large outhouse, squatted in the middle of everything and functioned as the office. A corroded, corrugated metal shed ran along the back, across the lot's full width. Above all this, dozens of little triangular nylon flags flapped their many colors in the breeze.

A broad-shouldered, thirty-something Hispanic man in a shiny blue suit stepped out of the office. His oversized, hey-look-I'm-a-man mustache sprouted in comic disproportion to his short hair. He shouted instructions at the sales team, which consisted of one gangly white boy in an ill-fitting white shirt and hastily knotted tie. The boy was rearranging cars on the lot and having trouble with it.

I put down the binoculars and called the Celebrity Motors phone number. It rang through a loudspeaker somewhere on the lot. My camera was ready.

The guy in the suit stepped back into the office, and his voice came from my cell phone: "Celebrity Motors. This is Buddy Vega."

I blurted, "Sorry, wrong number."

The suit came out of the office, and I took two photos. Now I had clear images of Buddy Vega, the probable money launderer. My next investigative source would be the Southland National Bank branch in Hawthorne, where I hoped to confirm my suspicion.

On my way to the Hollywood Freeway, I went a couple of blocks out of my way so I could drop down Vendome Street and stop at the long concrete stairway where Laurel and Hardy made their piano delivery in *The Music Box*. An occasional pilgrimage to a holy site is essential to good mental health.

From the freeway, I called Lilith. "This is Jack Salvo. Remember me?"

"Oh yes, I remember. You are six feet tall, or maybe six-one. In pretty good shape . . . for your age. You are good-looking, but not obnoxiously so. You are well dressed in your expensive, subdued clothes, maybe too well dressed. The hotshot L.A. private eye."

"Is that all?"

"No. I was just getting started. You are very intelligent, and you like to use your intelligence to push people around. You think you are a ladies' man, and you think you are tough. I think you're a big softy."

"I'm not a softy. I'm tough."

"So, what does the tough guy need from me?"

"I want you to call the manager at Southland National Bank in Hawthorne and tell him to cooperate with me. I'll be there in twenty minutes."

"Did you find out something?"

"I'm pretty sure Pace did the embezzlement, and his accomplice is a guy named Buddy Vega. Vega runs a used-car lot over here by Silver Lake. I got a photo of him, and if I can get a positive ID at the bank, I will have solved the crime. In fact, you can go ahead and mail me my check now."

"I will call the Southland National Bank manager now. You might get paid later."

"How much later?"

"After I submit my report to management on your performance."

"How do you assess performance?"

"By using various criteria."

"What's the most important criterion?"

"My mood."

"How is your mood now?"

"Melancholy. Let's talk tomorrow."

Twenty minutes later I was going south on Hawthorne Boulevard, past the Fosters Freeze where Brian Wilson got the inspiration for "Fun, Fun, Fun." There weren't any T-Birds or woodies in the lot, just a lowered Honda Civic on which the exhaust was the size of a sewer pipe. Two hard-eyed young guys with tattooed necks leaned against the car, watching the passing traffic, giving the distinct impression they wouldn't mind having fun at someone else's expense.

The Southland National Bank manager was Mr. Malik, a tall, dark-skinned Pakistani man wearing a wrinkle-free tan suit. He said Lilith had called him, and he was ready to cooperate. I set up my iPad on his desk, plugged in my camera, and put together a six-pack of photos: six Hispanic males about the same age and build as Buddy Vega, one of whom was in fact Vega. Mr. Malik brought in the three tellers who had helped the customer identifying as David Lopez. The first teller wasn't sure, but the next two made quick positive IDs of Buddy Vega, aka David Lopez. One of the tellers said he claimed to be a contractor who paid his day laborers in cash.

On the way to my office, I called Darcey Mathis and told her Oswald Pace was almost certainly the embezzler, and his accomplice was a used car lot-owner named Buddy Vega. She listened quietly.

I said, "To top it all off, Vega may have stiffed Pace for some of the loot, maybe a quarter of his share. I can't prove it, so it's not going in my written report."

Darcey laughed and said, "No honor among thieves. By the way, the next meeting of the investigative team has not been scheduled, but I will call you as soon as we set the time. It sounds like you're doing great. I hate to cut you off like this, but I really do have to run. Thanks for the report."

At four o'clock, I was in my office drafting my written report to Culver Aerospace. While sifting through the documents in my evidence file, one sheet stood out: the employment application Oswald Pace had submitted to Culver Aerospace in 2006, when he was working at his previous employer Angeles Foods. He had listed three references. I wondered who might provide a reference for a chiseler like Pace.

The first two were Thomas Johnson and James Diaz, common names that are hard to track without further identifying information. The companies they supposedly worked for were no longer in business. The phone numbers for Johnson and Diaz were out of service. Dead end.

The final reference was listed as the manager of PC support at Angeles Foods. He had an uncommon name, Ismael Whittaker. He was divorced, age forty-four, living in a small garage apartment in Lomita, near Normandie Avenue. In 2000 he was sued in small claims for trashing an earlier apartment and breaking the lease. In 2003 his Lincoln Town Car was repossessed. He was still working at Angeles Foods and did not strike me as management material.

I didn't want to talk to Whittaker directly. He wasn't likely to give me any useful information over the phone, and he might tip off Pace. I didn't want Pace to know I was watching him until I landed on him.

The phone number for Angeles Foods got me a real human operator instead of a robot. Life is full of surprises. I asked the real live human to transfer my call to Shipping and Receiving.

After eight rings, a young, out-of-breath male voice gasped, "Shipping, this is Maurice."

I said, "This is Bob Williams, with the Information Management Institute in Chicago. I'm trying to ship an educational video to a person at Angeles Foods in L.A., but I don't have his mail code. The name is

Ismael Whittaker. Can you look it up? I think he's a manager in the PC support department."

His voice regained its breath. "Let me get on a computer here. Hang on. How do you spell that?"

I spelled it.

He said, "Here it is. Whittaker, Ismael Whittaker. Department 451, Zone C3."

"Do you have his exact title?"

"Nope, sorry. Just name, department, and zone."

"Thanks. I'll put this package in the mail right away."

I called the Angeles Foods operator again and asked for the PC support department. She did not have a specific listing, but she knew where to connect me.

A bored voice answered, "Information Systems. This is Lynette."

I said, "This is Bob Williams in Shipping. Is your department in Zone C3?"

"I didn't know they had a Bob Williams in Shipping."

I put some zest in my voice. "They sure do now."

"Well, we're in Zone C2, but C3 is right up on the next floor."

"I got this package here for a manager named Ismael Whittaker. Is Zone C3 where his office is at?"

"He's not a manager."

"Well, this package says Ismael Whittaker, Manager PC Support Department 451, Zone C3."

"Mr. Whittaker is in PC Support, and you have the right department and zone, but he is not the manager. Tina Crawford is the manager."

"Maybe she's new in the job, and Mr. Whittaker used to be the manager?"

She choked back a laugh. "Not very likely. Mrs. Crawford has been the manager since the department's formation."

I thanked Lynette and said I would make sure the package would go out in the next delivery. My suspicions were confirmed. Ismael Whittaker was a shill, set up to give Oswald Pace a phony reference.

It was almost time to pay Oswald Pace a personal visit and help him with his career planning. It wouldn't hurt to soften him up a little before Culver Aerospace management confronted him. It also wouldn't hurt to stretch the investigation a little and justify my twenty-thousand-dollar fee. This was my favorite embezzlement case of all time. I had a straight path to the embezzler and a client with deep pockets. A piece of cake.

6

S oon after the sun went down, my car and I were stopped in a red
zone across the street from the Brentwood Luau Apartments.
The visitor spaces and street parking were jammed.

I was waiting for a parking space to open up when a blue Nissan
370Z came down the Brentwood Luau driveway. Oswald Pace was
behind the wheel. The Z car turned to the north. My car was pointed
the wrong way. I waited for a gap in traffic and cut a tight U-turn.
There was already a long string of cars behind Pace. He went up to
Sunset and turned right. I followed and worked my way forward until
there were three cars between us. I held back and maintained that
distance, following the curvy boundary between Bel Air to the north
and Westwood to the south.

As we approached the northeast corner of UCLA, I moved up
closer to Pace. He cut off a Toyota and accelerated hard. He made the

traffic light, and I didn't. The light finally turned, the Fates smiled, and the traffic stayed out of my way. I shot down the hill toward Beverly Glen Boulevard. Then the Fates flipped me the finger, and an oncoming LAPD patrol car came to a sudden stop. The driver and his partner snapped their heads to the left as I whizzed past. In my rearview mirror, I could see the patrol car, its lights flashing, trying to turn around in the traffic.

I hit seventy on the next straight, braked hard, and took a quick right onto Charing Cross Road. My car jerked up and down on the broken concrete roadway in front of the Playboy Mansion. My windows were down, but I didn't hear any party noises from Hef's house. I heard a police siren shrieking on Sunset.

The cops hadn't seen me make the turn, but they would soon figure I had dodged them, and they would be coming back this way, trying to guess which way I went. If they caught me, they would probably haul me in.

Comstock Avenue took me to a red light at Wilshire, where a white Cadillac Escalade blocked me for nearly a minute. I sweated in my leather seat, watching my mirrors and the cross traffic.

A pair of distant headlights appeared behind me. The traffic light turned green, the Escalade scooted left, and I crossed Wilshire. Now the headlights were coming up fast. I turned into an apartment neighborhood and into the first alley. A blast from a police siren came from the Wilshire Boulevard intersection I had just crossed. The cop must have caught the red light, and he was clearing the intersection.

I swung my car into the first open garage, stepped into the alley, yanked the door down, and slipped between two apartment buildings. A conveniently placed orange tree gave me a discreet position from which I could see both the alley and the street. An inconveniently placed orange bumped my nose every time I turned my head. The black-and-white sped down the street. I shut my eyes and listened to the sound of the patrol car until it was lost in the background noise.

Quick decision: I could either drive away immediately, or I could blend into the shadows for a few minutes. I chose darkness. The cops' attitude and next move would be hard to guess. My speed demonstration may have been one of several they had seen during their shift, and it was no big deal. On the other hand, the cops might be a pair of hotheads with trembling trigger fingers, and they were now doubling back, crisscrossing the streets. I hadn't run from the police for years. I made a mental note to make this the last time.

A trash bin enclosure gave me a stealthy place to wait. Smelling the garbage made me think of Oswald Pace. Why was he driving toward the Sunset Strip? A nightclub on a work night? Probably not.

Something was in the back of my mind, but not too far back. Celebrity Motors was on Sunset Boulevard, five or six miles beyond the Strip. Pace was in a hurry. Maybe he was trying to collect the final installment of the loot from Vega.

I eased my car down the alley and worked my way south using as many side streets as possible. A quiet winding street with the soothing name Patricia took me almost all the way to the Santa Monica Freeway onramp I needed.

A few minutes after I hit the freeway, I was in front of Celebrity Motors, parked behind Pace's car. The gate was closed and the lights were out. No activity on the lot. The well-lit 7-Eleven was a block away. Other businesses were dark, either closed for the night or out of business. I waited for a break in traffic, checked to make sure nobody was in Pace's car, and climbed over the gate.

From the rear of the pint-sized office building, I saw no movement anywhere on the lot. The multicolored nylon flags hung overhead in the still air, sad and spent, as though they suspected all their flapping during the day had been for nothing. The only sounds were from the random passing cars.

A feeble light whispered at me from under the sliding door on the shed at the back of the lot. The door's hinged hasp swung open. An open padlock hung in the shackle. I muscled the door open about two feet, pulled out my flashlight, and sidled in.

The room smelled mightily of vinyl and other chemical products. It was dark, except for the wall at the far end, on which a low light cast an odd shadow. The shadow was roundish with a point on top. It reminded me of the RKO Pictures logo, a radio tower on top of an earth globe.

I pulled the door almost shut behind me and swung my flashlight around. The concrete floor had been through a few earthquakes, but it was surprisingly clean. Against the back wall was a workbench on which tools and a stack of folded red shop rags had been carefully arranged. Two idle banks of fluorescent lamps hung from the overhead wood framing. I started for the light switch but held back. No need to attract attention.

At the midpoint of the room, an older Audi sedan was angled up to a rolling tool chest. The hood was up, plastic fender covers protecting both sides. I squeezed behind the Audi, aiming the flashlight toward wooden shelves holding automobile interior materials and plastic bins containing spray paint cans, solvents, and adhesives.

I looked again at the illuminated north wall and wondered about the light source. About six feet out from the wall, a row of stacked alloy wheels made an irregular partition four to five feet high. I stepped around it and skidded to a halt.

A compact automatic pistol was on the floor. It looked like a Taurus 9mm. A human hand lay next to it. The base of the index finger had a small laceration; it might have been "slide bite," the result of improperly gripping an automatic pistol and firing it. The hand was attached to a right arm, which was attached to the torso of Oswald Pace.

Pace was on his back, staring angrily into oblivion. He was in the same striped shirt he had worn at the office. His right arm was cocked back like a quarterback ready to throw. A generous volume of blood had pumped onto the floor from a hole in his right temple and spread into a pool.

The illumination came from a utility light on the floor. It reflected off the darkening blood like a hot Malibu sunset and cast a large shadow of Pace's head on the wall. The "radio tower" portion of the shadow was his nose.

I edged around, leaned over, and pointed my flashlight directly at the bullet hole. A barrel imprint and black soot from unburned gunpowder framed the contact wound. A couple of ants meandered around, considering the prospect of an easy meal.

My flashlight beamed on something shiny—Buddy Vega's blue suit. He lay crumpled on his side. I got closer to Vega and aimed my flashlight at a hole in the back of his head. Pieces of gray matter had spewed out and fallen into a pool of blood. Ants had formed a furiously efficient two-way thoroughfare from the baseboard to the smorgasbord.

I took several photos, trying to cover all the angles and details. It looked to me like Pace shot Vega in the back of the head, then shot himself in the right temple. I hurried out the door and realized I had been holding my breath. Air never tasted sweeter.

The drive home was slower and more reflective than usual. Could the embezzlement scheme and the deaths of its conspirators be a coincidence?

A wise police detective once told me, "When it comes to murder, there ain't no fuckin' coincidences."

I figured Pace tried to collect the money owed by Vega, there was a falling out, and things spiraled out of control. Drugs and alcohol were probably involved. That was a plausible explanation, but it was vague and lacking detail. I wasn't thrilled with it.

When I was finally locked safely inside my condo, I punched in the alarm code, leaned back against the door, and ran my hand across the ten-o'clock shadow on my face. When I'd gone out the same door fifteen hours earlier, I was close-shaven, scrubbed, and polished. Now my clothes felt like they were stuck to me with rubber cement.

The clothes went straight into the laundry, and I stepped into the shower. I scrubbed and scrubbed and thought. The cops would find Pace and Vega within a day or two, maybe within hours. Then they would visit Culver Aerospace and announce that Oswald Pace was no longer among the living. My name was sure to come up, and the cops would be especially interested in my discovery of a connection between Pace and Vega. I would need to give a plausible explanation as to how I discovered the connection, without mentioning my sneaking into Pace's apartment or this evening's visit to Celebrity Motors. I also needed to delay that interrogation until I made a few more discoveries.

I got into a fresh warmup suit, poured myself a small bowl of raspberries, and settled in front of the television. I plugged my camera into my iPad and downloaded the photos from the death scene.

The television came to life, and the photos came up on the iPad at the same time.

I scanned through the death-scene images. When the ants appeared for their closeups, I decided I had done enough detective work for one day.

There was a backlog of movies recorded on my satellite receiver. I chose a noir classic starring Robert Mitchum, shoveled in a mouthful of raspberries, and hit the start button. The first image was the RKO Pictures logo: a spinning globe from which a radio tower points upward. The red raspberries rippling across my tongue somehow reminded me of bloody ants.

7

A little before eight the next morning, I was at my office desk taking a last look at the Celebrity Motors photos before deleting them. Then I attacked my backlog of pain-in-the-ass chores. I returned e-mails. I reconciled my checking account. I reviewed my business insurance bill, swore at it, and wrote the check. I adjusted the settings on my Aeron chair and tried to adjust the venetian blind over the front window. The blind was worn out and didn't want to adjust anymore. I made a note to call my contractor.

I started working the phone. There were two cases in particular I wanted to square away. The first was a poor little rich boy who got a frequent urge to cast off the shackles of bourgeois conformity. The last time I retrieved him and delivered him to his parents in Bel Air, I found him in a fetid tent near downtown L.A. His new Maserati was somehow missing. The boy's father had left a message overnight. I returned the call, and Dad said Junior had not actually gone AWOL yet, but he was starting to get that look in his eye. Dad said he would inform me when the time came.

The next task was a favor for an attorney I knew from college. An amorous ex-client had been stalking her. I do personal protection work on occasion, but my best friend Gabriel Van Buren is a bodyguard's bodyguard. Gabe and I worked together at Western Investigative Services in our younger days. Now he's the owner. I called him, explained the problem, and gave the perv's name and address. Gabe said he would take care of it personally. He has a special talent for persuading miscreants to improve their behavior. Either that or they end up like the projectiles in a dwarf-tossing contest.

At eight-twenty Darcey Mathis called me. "Hi, Jackson, hate to do this to you, and I know it's short notice, but can you attend a meeting this morning at ten?"

"No problem."

"I'm getting pressure from above. You won't need to have a written report, but they will want to know what you've turned up so far. From what you told me yesterday, it sounds like you're making good progress."

"You were right about the embezzler having a checkered past. Pace has baggage, and so does his accomplice. I'll have the details when I see you."

"Great. I'll have your temporary badge waiting for you in the lobby. Can you drop by my office, maybe ten minutes before the meeting?"

"I'll see you at nine fifty."

Right on time, I was at Darcey's office door. She was standing over her desk, fishing for something in her gray leather shoulder bag.

She waved me in and pointed to a chair. Her blue floral-print dress held her with much less grip than the previous day's stiff business suit.

She said, "Damn! Every time I organize my purse, it lasts about ten minutes." She pulled out a handful of things, including a cell phone in a red-and-white polka-dot case. She kept the phone and dropped the other items back into the purse. One item jumped out at me: a black and gold embossed matchbook from a ritzy Italian restaurant named Vicenza.

Three years earlier, I went to Vicenza on a date during which I got the complete life story of a petulant soap opera actress, a three-hundred-dollar tab, and indigestion. I give the place a sneer every time I drive past.

Darcey sat down and gave me a big warm smile. "Please have a seat. Now, in the meeting today, I'm going to ask you to provide a summary of your findings for the group. Based on what you told me yesterday, I don't think you'll have any problem. So, what kind of dirt did you dig up on Pace?"

"Insurance scams, small claims suits for not paying his bills. He also put a fake reference in his employment application to Culver Aerospace in 2006."

"That's good. That's all good. It gives us more leverage on him. Tell me about the false reference."

"He listed a character named Ismael Whittaker as a reference at his previous employer Angeles Foods. Pace falsely claimed Whittaker was a manager. It turns out he was just another worker bee, set up to give Pace a glowing review."

"Doesn't surprise me, especially coming from Pace. It's a common ruse." She sat up straight, crossed her hands on the desk, and put some sizzle into her smile. "Now there's something else that's got me burning with curiosity."

"What would that be?"

"How does one go from being a philosopher to a private detective?"

"It's a long story."

"I'm sure it is. I can't imagine the transition. I took a philosophy class in college. It was a tough class, but I really liked it."

"Maybe when this case is finished, you'd like to hear about Ludwig Wittgenstein's theory of language." Pickup lines are one of my specialties.

"Can I hear about it in summary form?"

"It's hard to summarize Wittgenstein. One tends to expand on him."

She glanced at her watch. "The meeting's in four minutes. Wittgenstein will have to wait."

We walked into the conference room and took our seats. The same people from the previous meeting were already there, except Barney Xavier the CEO and Gene Thorne the auditor. Lilith sat straight across from me.

Darcey started the meeting and announced that I would report the status of my investigation. I gave a sanitized overview of my fact-finding efforts and how I concluded Oswald Pace was the embezzler and Buddy Vega was his money-laundering accomplice. I conveniently forgot to mention that Pace and Vega were now resting in peace, their heads ventilated with bullet holes.

Then I recounted Vega's convictions for fraud and assault. When I told of Pace's fake reference, questionable insurance claims, and eviction from his apartment, the tall brunette from PR slapped her forehead. "That sort of thing will kill us with the shareholders. They're going to ask why we hired a bum like him in the first place. I don't know why . . ."

Gene Thorne barged into the room, followed closely by Barney Xavier. Xavier loudly slammed the door. Everyone else, including me, jumped a little bit.

The new arrivals landed on chairs, and Xavier said to Thorne, "Tell 'em."

Thorne slapped a manila folder on the table like it was a royal flush. "We were going over our financial records from earlier years with some new audit software we just got, and we discovered that in 2006 we had another embezzlement." He pulled a canceled check from the folder and waved it back and forth. "Two hundred ninety thousand, four hundred dollars. This check went to a company called Bandini Construction, only there was no such company.""

Hoffman puffed up and said, "How could that much money possibly go unnoticed?"

Thorne said, "Back then, there was seventy million dollars in construction going on around here. There were many different contractors and many problems with the construction projects. We were involved in several lawsuits. It was a very chaotic time."

Barney Xavier's voice came out dry and rough. "And someone found a way to take advantage of the chaos."

Thorne looked around at the group. "They had a pretty good angle. We were sending regular progress payments in that exact same amount, two hundred ninety thousand and change, to two different contractors. One was Bandini Inc. The other was Bandini Supplies. The embezzler figured the bogus check with the name *Bandini Construction* might slip through without being noticed right away, and that's what happened."

Barney Xavier muttered softly through clenched teeth: "That's just beautiful . . . fuckin' beautiful." He turned to me. "What do you think about this, Salvo? You think it might be the work of the same person?"

I pointed at the check Thorne was holding. "This smells like a different embezzler. In the fake janitorial case, the checks were twenty to twenty-five thousand dollars, under the limit for managerial approval, as though the crooks were trying to fly under the radar, not get greedy, keep the scam going. There's a totally different mindset behind this one. A heist in the vicinity of three hundred thousand dollars would be a one-shot deal. I'll bet the embezzler was shocked that the loss wasn't discovered almost immediately."

Xavier said, "*I'm* shocked that it was undiscovered for six years. I don't know why anybody else wouldn't be shocked."

Thorne waved the check again. "There's another difference. In this 2006 embezzlement, there's no record of a disbursement, no invoice. It's like they got directly into the accounts payable program to cut the check."

Lilith caught my eye for an instant and turned to Thorne. "What bank did they use to cash the check?"

"Western Rim Bank, Wilshire and La Brea." He looked at the check. "November 2nd, 2006."

Darcey said, "Unbelievable. We solve one embezzlement, and another one lands in our lap instantly. It's amazing." She sunk her upper teeth into her lower lip and frowned.

Xavier turned to Hoffman and pointed in my direction. "Has our philosopher made any progress on the other matter?"

Hoffman shrugged. "He seems to have solved the case overnight. He says he identified the crooked employee who made the illegal transaction and the outside accomplice who handled the checks."

Xavier looked at me. "I'll want to hear the details on all that, but in the meantime, do you want a shot at this new case?"

"I sure would. As a philosopher, I may have to spend a few days defining the word *case* before I really start moving, but I'll get results for you."

Xavier twisted his jaw into a sort of tired smirk and stood up. As he went out the door, he said to Hoffman, "Keep me informed."

Darcey said, "Let's keep moving on the Oswald Pace matter and get that out of the way. Then we need to decide on our course of action on this new issue."

She led the discussion for devising a plan for interviewing Pace and putting the squeeze on him. Legal would draft the questions. An attorney from Legal, two managers from HR, and Del Hoffman would conduct the interview. Two security guards would be stationed outside the interview room in case the interviewee flipped out. It was a good plan, except Pace was, or would soon be, in the morgue wearing a sheet and a toe tag.

The meeting broke up, and Lilith and I went to her office.

I shut the door behind us. "Thanks for feeding me the bank information."

"I didn't know Mr. Xavier was going to give you the assignment so fast. I am very anxious to see what the hotshot private detective will do next."

"First, the hotshot detective will identify the person laundering the money at the Wilshire and La Brea branch of Western Rim Bank.

Next, he will go through that person's associates until he finds a Culver Aerospace employee." I gave Lilith my Grand Inquisitor look. "By the way, were you working at Culver Aerospace in 2006?"

"I was a naive, innocent girl living in a dorm at UC Irvine. I worked hard at my studies and got nearly straight A's."

"It sounds like you're off the hook."

"You are not going to interrogate me any further? You are already eliminating me as a suspect? What kind of detective work is that?"

"Maybe I'll waterboard you later. In the meantime, let's see which of our four suspects were working at Culver Aerospace in 2006."

"I can tell you right now that Mrs. Ito and Joy Bodie were here. We need to look up Derrick and Oswald."

I pulled their work histories out of my briefcase and glanced at them. "Pace started two or three months after the check to Bandini Construction was cashed. Jenkinson came on board a year later."

Lilith said, "I do not think either Mrs. Ito or Joy Bodie would have the programming skills to manipulate the accounts payable system if it happened the way Gene said."

"Sounds like we have a new embezzler. We'd better get moving."

Lilith called Gene Thorne and asked for front and back copies of the check he had been waving around. A minute or two later, they arrived on her computer, and she printed two copies each for me.

I said, "The people at the bank branch aren't going to remember much from seven years ago. Let's contact their corporate security office and see if they'll play ball."

"They will play ball. We are one of that bank's biggest customers."

Lilith looked up the name of Western Rim Bank's corporate security director. "I know this woman. I met her at a conference in

Anaheim. She gives presentations at national conferences, and she has written a book. Her name is Wendy Storm."

"Sounds like a stripper."

"A perfect woman for you. Would you like me to arrange a date?"

"The sooner the better."

Lilith called Wendy Storm and made the arrangements. She ended the call and said, "You have a date with Miss Storm in forty minutes." She put a heavy emphasis on the word *Miss*. "I suggest you be punctual. She has a reputation for having a very strong personality."

Forty minutes later I was on the thirty-eighth floor of a Downtown L.A. office tower.

8

Wendy Storm met me at the reception desk of the Western Rim Bank Corporate Office. She was about fifty, almost my height, wearing a tight skirt and sweater. Twenty pounds and twenty years earlier, she would have stopped traffic. She looked me up and down like she was grading a side of beef.

She led me to her office, and I gave her an account of the most recent embezzlement at Culver Aerospace.

She spoke in a husky, amiable voice. "For starters, I need to see the check, front and back."

I produced the documents. Her large hands blurred over her computer keyboard, never making a mistake. I listened and took notes.

She said, "On May 17th, 2006, a woman using the name 'Susan Miller' opened an account at our Wilshire–La Brea branch, depositing a thousand dollars in cash. From June through October, she moved money through the account in amounts ranging from four thousand to eight thousand dollars, apparently to make it look like normal business activity. On November 2nd she deposited the embezzled $290,400 Culver Aerospace check. She knew Culver Aerospace would issue the bogus check from our bank, so by having her account with Western Rim Bank, there was no delay for a bank-to-bank clearance. Susan Miller, or whoever the hell she was, wasn't all that dumb. On November 15th, she wired almost the entire balance to a Cayman Islands account."

"How many days total was she in the bank?"

She ran her finger down her computer display and counted to herself. "From May 17th to November 15th, she conducted some sort of transaction on eight different days."

"What are the chances you have archived surveillance video during those days?"

"Going back that far would be beyond the normal retention period for surveillance video. We have a records department that reviews our archives annually and destroys records that are too old."

"Do you have contact information for this Susan Miller?"

Wendy tapped out a few keystrokes. "Here's her customer information. I can't give you the social without going through some red tape. Doesn't really matter, because the number's almost certainly phony, but here's a home address and a cell."

She brought up a map, and we looked at Susan Miller's stated home address, a transient apartment hotel on Santa Monica Boulevard near Wilton Place. Probably a dead end, but I could check out the flophouse if my other leads fizzled. The cell phone was also a probable lost cause; I noted the number anyway.

I said, "Can we identify the bank tellers who helped Susan Miller?"

"You think one of our people might be complicit?"

"I have no reason to, but let's see who they are."

She typed out a list of the tellers who conducted the transactions for Susan Miller:

May 17	Robert Hernandez
June 14	Carmelina Wallace
July 19	Robert Hernandez
August 16	Hector Yanez
September 20	Hector Yanez
October 18	Sophia Karlov
November 2	Cecile Barrett
November 15	Cecile Barrett

I scanned the list. "We have Cecile Barrett for the initial transaction, the big deposit, and the wire transfer to the Caymans."

Wendy nodded. "I have to admit . . . that is thought-provoking."

"If you had any robberies in 2006, is there any chance you still have surveillance videos related to specific robberies?"

"Let's see . . . we had some robberies back about then. Shit, we always have robberies. There might be something down in the archives."

We had to use two elevators, one to the lobby, then a service elevator into the lowest depths. My ears hadn't bothered me on the ascent, but on the downward run, I had to swallow hard and force a yawn to equalize the pressure.

During the descent, Wendy looked me up and down again with no pretense of discretion. "You're pretty well built. You work out?"

"Two or three times a week. How about you?"

"Two or three times a week. We seem to be in the same rhythm."

I was trying to think of a way to change the subject when the elevator door opened, and we stepped into a cavernous concrete tomb. Rows of wire shelving were arranged like library stacks, holding myriad labeled cardboard storage boxes. The rows went off to vanishing points in the dimness. I followed Wendy into one of the corners. The odor of decomposing paper and cleaning agents would gag a wharf rat, but it didn't gag me.

She found a box labeled 2006 WILSHIRE–LA BREA, thumped it onto a metal table, rummaged around, and pulled out three plastic DVD storage boxes. "Looks like we had three robberies at Wilshire–La Brea that year."

That made me scratch my head. "Lotta robberies for one branch in one year. Didn't L.A. bank jobs peak in the nineties?"

"In general, they did peak then. Doesn't mean we don't still have 'em." She flipped through the DVDs. "We watch video of the actual robbery and also of the days prior to the robbery, to see if we can catch the assholes casing the joint."

She compared the list of tellers' names and dates with the dates on the DVDs. "Here we go. We have a video for July 19th. That's one of the days the woman that called herself Susan Miller was in the bank."

I looked at the printed list and saw that Robert Hernandez was the teller on that date. "Let's hold on to that one for now and see if we can find one where Cecile Barrett is the teller."

Wendy found a robbery on November 6th, and that led to the disk for November 2nd, the day the embezzlement check was deposited.

Back in her office, Wendy inserted the November 2nd disk into her computer. From multiple camera positions, we saw all the bank customers: waiting in line, at the counters, at the customer desks, and at the doors. She printed several pages of time-and date-stamped images taken from 11 to 11:20 a.m., capturing at least three shots of every customer and every teller.

At this point, I was confident the photos included the outside accomplice in the embezzlement. The next step would be for me to interview bank personnel who might be able to point out Cecile Barrett and Susan Miller. Wendy called ahead to the branch, told the manager what I wanted and that I would be arriving quite soon. The manager promised full cooperation.

9

Forty minutes later, I was in Western Rim Bank's Wilshire-La Brea branch. The branch manager had worked at this location for only three years, but he said two of the current tellers had worked here during the embezzlement-related transactions. He introduced me to Olivia and Marge, and I spread Wendy Storm's photos on a table and told them what I was looking for.

They had no trouble pointing out the teller Cecile Barrett. In the photos, she dealt with three customers. Cecile's 11:02 customer was an elderly man on crutches. It was unlikely he was Susan Miller, so he was out. The 11:07 customer was a thin female wearing a long, slinky dress and wide-rimmed glasses. Her dark hair was in a long flip, curled inward. The height markers on the bank's doorframes put her at five-ten. I couldn't tell if she was sixteen or sixty. The 11:16 customer was a charming, elderly gossip who had lived near the bank since the La Brea Tar Pits were still slurping down mastodons. Olivia and Marge had looked forward to waiting on her because she always had a lurid tale to tell about someone in the neighborhood.

We went back to the second customer. One of the shots gave us her profile. Olivia looked at it closely and said, "Boy, I haven't thought about this for a long time. The woman you say is Susan Miller is some actress, I'm pretty sure. I think I saw her in the bank once or twice, and I think I saw her on a TV show. I can't remember which show. So many actors and actresses in L.A., and there's so many shows, you can't tell who goes with which."

I said, "Do you recall her name?"

"No. She was never at my window."

Marge squinted at the photo and moved it to different angles. "I don't recognize this woman, but you know, Cecile used to be an actress too. She told us she didn't have much of an acting career, but she was in some movie where she was in a gang of girl criminals."

Olivia said, "Oh yeah. I saw that movie on TV. It was so funny to see Cecile using bad language and shooting people. I just sat there and laughed. She did manage to keep her clothes mostly on, which is a real accomplishment these days. Cecile was a really nice girl."

I asked, "Does anyone know what happened to her?"

Marge said, "Sure. She quit and got married. Actually, she got married and went part-time, then she quit when she got pregnant. She married some college professor at USC. He lived around here, and he used to always come into the bank, and pretty soon he would always make sure he went to Cecile's window. Next thing you know, they're engaged."

I thanked everyone for their cooperation and said I would give them maximum brownie points when I called my report into the Western Rim Bank corporate office.

Back in my car, I turned on my iPad and did a quick background on Cecile Barrett. She grew up in Lemon Heights, one of the swankier inland Orange County districts. Her father had owned a prominent Newport Beach insurance agency. Cecile attended Rancho Santiago College for two years. After that, she moved to West Hollywood and tried to make it as an actress. She shacked up with a small-time director and appeared in one of his movies, a low-budget opus called *Girl Attack*. In a publicity photo, a tear ran down her cheek, but she smiled bravely. She wore a tight, torn T-shirt and held a revolver flat against her chest, which was nowhere near flat. She was attractive in the sense that she had even features, but there was no special quality that radiated outward.

Now she was Cecile Clark. Her husband was Rex Clark, a USC professor. Their house was in an attractive historical neighborhood called Carthay Circle, a five-minute drive from where I was parked.

10

The Clark house was a Spanish Colonial Revival built with the usual white stucco walls and red tile roof. A street sign prohibited parking at the curb without a neighborhood permit, so I backed into the driveway.

A curved walkway directed me to the covered front porch. I admired the terra cotta tile under my feet and pushed the doorbell. A few seconds later, the speakeasy in the door swung open. Cecile Clark's face appeared behind the grill, the same face from *Girl Attack*, ten years older.

I eased my business card through the grill. "Mrs. Clark, my name is Jackson Salvo. I'm a private investigator, and I'm trying to find one of your old customers from the Western Rim Bank on Wilshire."

The voice of a small girl came from inside the house. "Mommy, look at me. Look at me!"

I said, "That sounds important. You'd better watch."

Cecile took my card and turned away. "Very good, Beatrice! Now I have to talk to this man." She read my card quickly. "Sorry. I haven't worked at the bank for five years. I don't remember much about the customers, except for the one I married."

The profile shot of the second bank customer went from my coat pocket to where it could be seen through the grill. "Does this woman look familiar?"

Her eyes widened, then lost focus. "No, I'm afraid I can't help you. Sorry." She nodded her head when she said no.

"She was using the name Susan Miller when you helped her with a transaction. Does that name ring a bell?"

"No. I'm afraid not. I'm afraid I'm not going to be able to help much. Have you been to the bank?"

"Ten minutes ago. Olivia and Marge couldn't identify the customer from the photo, so I thought I'd give you a try."

"Oh, I remember Olivia and Marge. I haven't seen them for a long time. I really should drop by and say hello. Mr. Salvo, I hate to be rude, but I'm taking my daughter to her dance class in a couple of minutes."

From her reaction to the photo, I was fairly sure she knew the bank customer, but I didn't think I could gain anything by being more aggressive at that moment.

I moved back from the door and tried to look harmless. "I'm pretty sure the woman in the photo was a TV actress. I can probably identify her through people I know at Screen Actors Guild, but I'm going to have to burn some favors. If I didn't have to go through all that, it would be a lot easier."

She smiled, but only in the lower part of her face. "I'm sorry I can't help you." The speakeasy shut silently.

Beatrice shrieked, "Mommy, look at me!" Cecile responded, but I couldn't make out what she said.

I was in my car again, checking for phone and e-mail messages, buckling up and starting the engine. Movement in the rearview mirror caught my eye. The garage door at the Clark residence was going up. Cecile stepped into view, watching me as she waited for the door. Beatrice, who was four or five, held on tight and pressed her face into Mommy's jeans.

This was one of those moments when my work makes me feel ill. Maybe I should swagger up to Mrs. Clark and threaten to tell Professor Clark that his wife is a crook. Maybe I should tell Beatrice I'm going to send Mommy to the joint unless Mommy spills the beans. Maybe I should have been a PI a few years earlier, when infidelity was grounds for divorce in California. I could have earned a living by hiding in hotel room closets, waiting for X-rated photo opportunities, wearing a perverted grin.

I drove down to Olympic Boulevard and turned right. Olympic would take me almost directly to my office.

A phone call came from a number I didn't recognize. It was Lilith. She said, "Did you hear the news about Oswald?"

"No." I hadn't heard any news that day, so it wasn't exactly a lie.

"He is dead!"

I made myself sound surprised. "How did that happen?"

"The police say he shot that crooked friend of his—the one you told us about, the one with the used car lot. And then he shot himself. Everyone around here is in shock, including me."

"Is this your cell number?"

"Yes, and it would be better if you call me on this number, not on my office phone."

"Do they monitor employees' phone calls at Culver?"

"Not routinely, but you never know who might be curious. And I have a habit of saying what I think."

"I hadn't noticed."

Another call came in. The caller ID said OUT OF AREA.

I said, "I've got another call. It may be important."

Lilith said, "Phone me later," and I switched to the other call.

"Mr. Salvo, this is Cecile Clark. If you will tell me what is going on, I might be able to help you."

I said, "Hang on for a second," pulled into a small parking lot, and grabbed a notepad and pen.

Over the phone, I could hear piano music in the background. Cecile was at her daughter's dance class.

I said, "Okay, I can talk now. I'm working for a large corporation that was the victim of an embezzlement back in 2006. I am fairly sure the woman in the photo I showed you was an accomplice."

"Are you working with the police?"

"They are not involved, and I doubt they will be."

"If money was stolen, why wouldn't the police be involved?"

"They won't care about a seven-year-old embezzlement. They have bigger fish to fry. And there's the statute of limitations, which may or may not be in effect. Most important, neither the company nor the bank wants any negative publicity."

"So why are you pursuing this?"

"The company wants to know which one of their employees committed the embezzlement. They want to know who they can trust."

"What will the company do when they find out who did it?"

"If the employee still works there, they will probably let them voluntarily terminate, to avoid the publicity. If the person has already left the company, they will probably do nothing. I'm not guaranteeing anything, just giving my opinion."

There was a long pause. I waited.

Finally, Cecile said, "I may know the woman in the photo you showed me. I wouldn't want to get her into any trouble. There was a point in my life when I needed a little boost, and she was very kind to me."

"Who is she?"

"I'm not quite ready for that yet."

"How kind was it for her to involve you in a crime? She could have gotten you fired—or worse."

"All I did was make sure the transactions went smoothly, in accordance with bank policy. I did nothing illegal. I've never even told my husband about any of this."

"I'm not going out of my way to tell him, but I can't promise he won't find out, depending on how this case unravels."

Another long pause. I hoped she was making the calculation that I would learn the identity of the bank customer one way or another, and she would be better off if she were cooperative. The only sound coming over my phone was a piano playing "Dance of the Sugar Plum Fairy." I waited.

Cecile decided to talk. "Okay . . . her name is . . . Sierra McCoy. She was on a TV show called *Heartbreakers*. I met her in acting school.

I was fresh out of Orange County, over my head in Hollywood, and some of the girls in my acting workshop were giving me a rough time. They were from places like Malibu and Brentwood, and I was from Orange County, which to them wasn't much different than the Ozarks. Sierra was the absolute queen of the workshop, and I was nobody, but she went out of her way to treat me decently. She didn't have to. She did it because that's just the way she is. We did a scene together for Director's Night. The guest director liked my work, and that led to my only film role."

"*Girl Attack*?"

"How did you know about that?"

"It's on the Internet."

"Just like everything else, I guess. In a few years, my daughter will be showing her friends the scene where I shoot everyone at a wedding. That was the high point of my acting career."

"It's L.A. Your daughter will be proud, and her friends will be envious."

She laughed nervously. "I suppose so."

"How did Sierra McCoy connect with you for the bank transactions?"

"I saw her at a party. Hadn't seen her for two or three years. She asked how things were going, and I gave her the unvarnished truth. My father had just died, and it was devastating. I was very close to him. My bitch mother practically disowned me, and I had to work at the bank and cut college down to part-time.

"Three or four months after that, Sierra dropped by the bank and said 'Let's have lunch.' So, we went to lunch, and she told me she had some business dealings related to promoting television shows, and hopefully she would get a big check out of the deal. She hoped it would be three hundred thousand dollars. I think the actual check was for a little under that. She said she would make it worth my while if I would see that everything went smoothly at the bank. For her, I would have done it for nothing. So anyway, she opened an account, and the big check came, and she deposited it. Later, I wired the funds for her. That was it. I did nothing illegal."

I said, "Since she was using the name Susan Miller, didn't you think she might be involved in something shady?"

Cecile spoke with a faint tremor in her voice. "I didn't know if it was a stage name or a business name or what the deal was. I never asked Sierra for any details relating to her business. I felt like I owed her something after the way she stood up for me at La Peer Studio. So anyway, two weeks later she calls me and says, 'Let's have lunch again.' She took me to an expensive sushi place and gave me an envelope with five-thousand dollars in cash, all in hundreds. I was shocked. I needed money badly at that point in my life, and it was a pleasant shock. And that was the last time I ever saw her."

"Do you know where she is now?"

"No. I tried to call her about a month after we had lunch, and the number was disconnected, no referral. I tried to track her down, but I have no idea where she might be."

"Was La Peer Studio the name of the acting workshop?"

"Yes. It was over on La Peer, by Melrose Avenue."

"Who ran it?"

"A woman named Maya Fontaine. She had small roles in a few movies in the seventies and eighties. She was quite a character." More nervous laughter. "Mr. Salvo, is there anything I can do to calm the situation? I might be able to get the five thousand dollars for you within a week or two. Would that help?"

I didn't like the idea of Cecile sneaking around behind her husband's back, trying to scrape up five thousand dollars, with Beatrice clinging to her leg. I said, "There wouldn't be anyone to give it to, and I'm not going to pocket your money."

The conversation ended with my assuring Cecile that I would try to complete my investigation without involving her any further.

I eased back into the traffic, called Wendy Storm, and told her the people at the bank were very helpful, but they could not identify the money launderer.

At my office, I researched Sierra McCoy. She had enjoyed a minor acting career, the high point of which was the television show *Heartbreakers*. I found nothing in the way of addresses or phones for her. Her acting coach Maya Fontaine, owned a house in West Hollywood. I might contact her later.

I called my man at SAG/AFTRA and learned Sierra McCoy had been represented by the Sullivan Agency in Hollywood, and she hadn't had much acting work since *Heartbreakers*. I had to teach my philosophy class in less than two hours, so the Sullivan Agency would have to wait.

11

During postgrad I had been on track for earning a PhD in philosophy. I ended up with a master's degree, some progress toward a PhD, and getting kicked out of graduate school. Now I teach one night a week at Coast College. It doesn't pay much, but I enjoy watching the little light bulbs over my students' heads. It's a lot more gratifying than chasing chiselers and stumbling over stiffs.

It was the second weekly meeting of Introduction to Philosophy 101. My class was starting to take shape. A pair of math majors had the edge in raw intellectual power, a redheaded boy from Boston and a local Hispanic girl. They were attracted to each other and too shy to close the deal. I bet myself nature would take its usual course in the near future. I also had one of the school's more prominent football players, a center linebacker who was inclined to attack philosophical questions and try to grind out the truth. Like many of my male friends, he was smarter than he looked.

Socrates and Plato were on the menu tonight. Socrates is one of my favorites. He had an immense genius for slicing through logical weakness and getting to the central issue. He fought heroically in battle. He didn't drink very much, but when he did, he could drink anybody under the table. Socrates's execution by hemlock, on trumped-up charges, is one of the more stylish deaths in world history.

In the discussion of Socrates's trial and execution, some students argued that Socrates committed suicide because he chose to drink the hemlock, even though he had the choice of going into exile instead.

An Asian kid, who looked like he was about fifteen, raised his hand. "Socrates could have just hauled ass, and nobody would have hunted him down. He didn't have to kill himself. His friends . . . even his enemies . . . they were all telling him, 'Don't do it.' Man, that's suicide."

A curvy bleached blonde whom I had privately characterized as "Surfer Girl" responded. "Socrates was willing to accept execution in defense of his beliefs, so I honestly think that if we call it suicide, after all he accomplished, we're ripping him off." Out of the mouths of babes.

I tried to close things out peacefully. "You could argue it either way, but I think Socrates would say it was an execution rather than suicide because it was done in accordance with the law. Now, I grant you that if Socrates had handed the hemlock bowl back to the executioner and said, 'Excuse me, can you hold this for a minute? I have to go out and put money in my parking meter,' and walked out of jail and kept going, the executioner would have looked the other way. That's beside the point. Rule of law was central to Socrates's political philosophy. He chose to live and die by his philosophy." I paused and looked around. I didn't hear any complaints or see any pained expressions. "The law for this class says we break at eight-twenty."

As the students filed out, I imagined Socrates peering down into a bowl of hemlock. That would qualify as a profound, historic moment. I tried to conjure up the image of Oswald Pace blowing his brains out. I couldn't do it. I couldn't even picture Pace with a gun in his hand.

At the break, students always flock to the vending machines. I usually join them, and we discuss profundities such as the Coast College football schedule or the *National Enquirer*'s latest scandal. I walked over to a quiet place behind the math building and called Lilith.

"This is Jack Salvo. Sorry I had to cut you off this afternoon."

"No problem. So how did you do with Wendy Storm the stripper? Were you able to get a date with her?"

"I'm working on it."

"What did you find out from her?"

"I think I got a photo of the money launderer in the 2006 embezzlement."

"Who is it?"

"I'm not one-hundred-percent sure yet."

"How mysterious."

"Lilith, do you think Oswald Pace would really have the guts to shoot himself?"

"I was surprised when I heard what he did. I think he must have been on drugs or something. In fact, other people at the office were saying the same thing."

"What did Darcey say?"

"I didn't talk to her. Del Hoffman said it was a great big tragedy, blah, blah, blah. He really said nothing, which is what he usually says. Where are you now?"

"I'm sitting on a bench behind the math building."

"Oh, your class. I forgot that you are also a philosopher."

"I have to be back in my classroom in a couple of minutes. Tell me more about Oswald Pace."

"It is pretty much what I told you before. He is—I mean was—very conceited. He always bragged his car was fast and he was a great driver. He wore expensive clothes, but not in good taste. He saw himself as God's gift to women. I hate to speak ill of the dead, but to be honest, he was a major-league jerk."

"Did you ever see him get into any kind of conflict with anyone?"

"No. He was not the sort of person to confront someone face-to-face. He would be more of a backstabber."

"Could you imagine him in a fight?"

"No way. He was not small, but he had the physical presence of a hamster. My guess is he was mad at the other guy, and he was drinking or taking drugs, and he just went crazy."

I promised to keep Lilith informed, and we ended the conversation. I sat and stared at the blank concrete side of the math building. It was clear that Pace committed the embezzlement and Vega laundered the money. Vega probably stiffed Pace on part of the take, but I didn't see how that would lead to gunfire and suicide. Pace was the sort of weasel who would shrug off the loss and start thinking of a new scam.

Two minutes later, I was standing behind the lectern, giving my take on Plato's Allegory of the Cave, in which chained prisoners are facing a wall in a cave. They can see nothing of the external world but shadows of things outside that are cast on the wall by a fire. In response to the shadows, the prisoners draw false conclusions about the outside world. That reminded me of my nighttime visit to Celebrity Motors and my interpreting the shadow of Oswald Pace's head as the RKO Pictures logo. I wondered what other false conclusions I had come to recently. Then I flashed on the ants and the slide bite on Pace's hand. An idea wandered through my brain, but I couldn't capture it. I wrote "ants/slide bite" on the margin of my lecture notes.

The class discussion moved on to Plato's political philosophy.

An apple-cheeked girl named Kimberly asked, "If Plato says he wants to kill deformed babies, then why do we spend our time studying him?"

I replied, "If we don't study Plato, we can't fully understand Greek philosophy."

She said, "But in *The Republic*, he actually advocates killing defenseless babies just because they might not be born perfect. He wanted to just leave them out in the cold and let them die! And here we are taking his philosophy seriously. How could these ideas have anything but a negative effect on us?"

"Students have read Plato for centuries, and I am aware of none who, as a result of their studies, have committed murder. He also says people should have sex only for the purpose of procreation and only under close supervision. I don't think many people are going to agree with that, either."

Polite laughter rippled through the room.

With perfect comedy timing, Kimberly said, "My mother would agree with that."

The class roared.

I wondered how Plato handled it when the student got the best laugh.

In the parking lot, I sat in my car and looked at the "ants/slide bite" note. During the drive home, I thought things over. The slide bite on Pace's hand wasn't in the right place. The cut should have been on the web of his hand, not his index finger. Pace's wrist would have been cocked at a severe angle for the slide to catch him on the finger. Maybe he had some help. Maybe somebody was pushing on his hand.

Then there were the ants. Pace arrived at Celebrity Motors no more than twenty minutes before me. Twenty-five at the outside. During those minutes, he would have had to gain control over Vega, argue about the money, maneuver him into the back of the mechanic's shed, shoot him, and work up the nerve to shoot himself. Pace would have had time for all that, but the ants on Vega might not have had enough time to fall into their perfectly organized feeding pattern. When Pace arrived on the scene, Vega might have already been shot by someone else, and Pace was the next victim.

At home, I was anxious to get a better look at Sierra McCoy. I got settled in front of my computer and found a ten-year-old *Heartbreakers* episode. The television show's premise was that each week three highly educated, impossibly attractive, partially dressed young women would achieve justice for some other woman who had been victimized by a man. Sierra McCoy wasn't one of the main characters, but she appeared in many of the episodes in the role of Tammy, a martial arts instructor the girls use when they need extra muscle.

Sierra was a tall drink of water with a long aristocratic nose, dark eyes, and pitch-black hair. In the climactic scene, she sprinted like a cheetah, vaulted a fence cleanly using just one hand, ran down the evil-man-of-the-week, threw a flying kick, and landed on her feet. She did it in one continuous take, no stunt double needed.

For more than a century, the Hollywood meat grinder has processed many attractive, talented actresses. Some of the leftovers go back where they came from and live normal lives. Some stay in L.A. and live normal lives. Some stay in L.A. and become crooks.

12

At nine the next morning, I arrived at the western end of Hollywood, where it blends into the Strip. The Sullivan Agency resided in a 1920s, two-story Queen Anne house that had been converted to commercial use.

I pushed through the front door and found myself in a small room furnished with a gloss-black reception desk, two transparent plastic chairs, and not much else. Indirect lighting came from somewhere.

Eyes that had seen everything, two coats of paint, and fathomless cleavage greeted me from across the desk. The receptionist was dressed in black.

I handed her my card and asked to speak to Mr. Sullivan.

She looked at the card. "Are you an actor?"

"No, but I do a hell of a John Wayne. Would you like to hear it?"

"I've heard it before."

She ignored me and made two phone calls unrelated to my visit. I shifted my weight back and forth from one foot to the other. Eventually, she picked up my business card and tapped her stiletto heels out the rear door.

She returned in less than a minute and motioned me through a side door. In the waiting room I found two unoccupied black velour sofas with exceptionally thin legs and three aspiring actresses with exceptional legs. The girls were seated in identical ultramodern leather chairs upholstered in a quirky red-and-black pattern. Giant circles composed the chairs' sides. Matching ottomans were shaped like big tongues spilling down to the floor saying, "ahhh." I landed on the spindle-legged sofa with the best view. I landed gently so I wouldn't have to pay for it.

Most L.A. girls aren't as good-looking as they pretend. In this case, pretension hit the ball out of the park.

The frail redhead with the soaring cheekbones held a copy of *Yale Review* in front of her big blue eyes, but her pupils didn't move as they would if she were actually reading. Her electric-blue dress and a cautious touch of red in her accessories put everything to its most incendiary advantage.

The flaxen blonde had a body that could stop the Royal Observatory clock. She wore a little black dress approximately one atom thick and stared into space while displaying a delicate, hopeful smile. Maybe Rudolph Valentino would burst into the room, sling her over his shoulder, and carry her out to his Isotta Franchini Town Car.

The youngest of the trio, to put it philosophically, was the platonic ideal for Hollywood jailbait. Thin and muscular, she wore a flimsy pink tank top and low-cut jeans. A remote trace of makeup sang the praises of her pretty teenage face. A trace more would have ruined everything.

The receptionist-in-black came into the room and announced, "Ms. Lund." The blonde rose as delicately as the mist over Monet's *Water Lilies* and followed the receptionist out of the room.

I leaned toward the redhead and said, "Excuse me. Do you know where I can find a copy of *Yale Review* around here?"

She lowered the magazine, slowly cranked her head around, and gave me a look that could have shot down an incoming missile. Her eyes went back to her literary magazine. She spoke in a harsh whisper. "Why don't you try to find it up your ass?"

The jailbait girl threw a disapproving scowl at the redhead and said, "They got *Yale Review* at the newsstand on Las Palmas. My art teacher used to buy it there, he said. I hear it's gotta lotta good shit in it."

I wondered if the art teacher phrased it that way.

The sparkling conversation came to an end, and I found myself in the office of Brice Sullivan. The furnishings adhered to a severe Art Moderne style. Cool blues and grays flared in cold reflective metal, as warm and inviting as slabs in the morgue.

Wide-oval eyeglasses festooned Sullivan's confident, triangular face. Gray streaks in his wavy dark hair implied maturity while heavily lidded eyes implied worldly-wise weariness. His smile had the sincerity of an overpriced undertaker.

He motioned for me to sit, and I did.

He spoke in a strong baritone. "A real live private eye. Tell me about yourself." He held my business card lightly between his thumbs and index fingers, watching and waiting, as though he expected me to sing and dance for him.

"This is not about me. I'm trying to locate Sierra McCoy."

He nodded knowingly. "Sierra McCoy. Quite a girl. Strong personality. Hell of a strong body. Why are you looking for her?"

"I'm looking for a missing person, and I think Sierra might be able to point me in the right direction." That wasn't exactly a lie since Sierra was the missing person.

He gestured at the two shiny metal art deco file cabinets behind his desk. "I don't just give out private information on my clients. I don't know you. I don't know that you really are a private investigator. All I see is this card. Prove to me that you are in fact a licensed private investigator, and I'll see what I can do." He glanced at his watch. "You have sixty seconds."

It would have been fun to just haul off and smack the arrogant bastard. I unclenched my right fist and looked around the room. "The interior design in this place is an L.A. classic. I'd call it Victorian Streamline."

"You're complaining about the decorations? You only have forty-five seconds left."

I stood up and started walking a slow half-circle that would end at Sullivan's side of the desk. I continued to look around. "You have to admit, the art deco furnishings clash with all the intricate moldings and decorations built into the house."

Sullivan leaned back in his chair. "Thirty seconds."

I continued my slow arc.

He swiveled toward me. "You're pissing your time away. And mine."

I arrived at the position I wanted, near the inside corner of his desk. I spoke in a soft monotone. "Brice, I have a message for you.

From someone who has contracted my services. From someone who has a very important message they want you to receive in a very personal way."

Baritone ascended to tenor. "Who?"

"In my line of work, I don't reveal my clients."

He cleared his throat hastily. "Who in the hell are you?"

I pulled thin leather gloves from my coat pockets and snapped them on.

Sullivan stared in horror at the gloves and grabbed his knees. "Melanie. Melanie. H-her husband sent you."

I let my silence do the talking.

Sullivan spat out his words. "That bitch. She came onto me! She said they were separated. She used me to get acting work! I didn't do anything. Hell, I was practically molested. I was a victim!"

I inched forward and took my voice down to a near whisper. "Do you have a final message for my client?"

His voice shot further up the scale, somewhere around castrato. "What the fuck do you mean, final? There must be some way to work this out!"

My tone mellowed. "There might be a way to work it out."

"What does he want?"

I turned around and opened the file drawer for the M's. The Sierra McCoy folder beckoned. A few seconds later I was looking at her last-known residence address, which was in Westwood.

Sullivan spoke cautiously. "What are you doing?"

I put the folder back in place, gently closed the drawer, pocketed the gloves, and stepped back around to the front of the desk.

I stood up straight, my chin slightly elevated, like a Boy Scout receiving a merit badge. "Don't you think I'm a natural actor, Mr. Sullivan? If you sign me, you'll never regret it!"

He didn't respond for a long time, during which his face regained most of its color, in a blotchy pattern. I held my ground and maintained an eager, hopeful countenance.

Sullivan's snarl reminded me of an angry Chihuahua. "I will crucify you for this little stunt. You don't fuck with me like this and get away with it. I will take action. I will take action at the highest levels."

I grinned. "What are you gonna do? Break into a falsetto?"

13

The address I got for Sierra McCoy was about two blocks east of Westwood Village. After seven years, I didn't expect to find her there, but that's where I could pick up the trail.

On the way to Westwood, I called Lilith.

She said, "Well, what have you accomplished today?"

"Quite a lot. I ran into three beautiful actresses at a talent agency. They started fighting when they were all trying to molest me at the same time. Then I saw the agent, and he wanted to sign me as a client because he thinks I could be the next Clint Eastwood. I didn't like the tone of his voice, so I threatened to beat him up. Then I broke into his files and got the address of a suspect."

"How much of that is true?"

"Maybe half."

"I'm afraid to ask which half."

"Any news around the office?"

"Actually, it is very quiet. I haven't seen Darcey or Del today. Things are starting to calm down around here after what happened yesterday."

"Are the cops still coming around?"

"I don't think so. I haven't seen them today."

"Did you hear whether my name came up?"

"I just know what I told you yesterday, nothing else. And now I must go to a meeting. Sorry to rush off, but we can talk later."

Lilith went to her meeting, and I arrived at Sierra McCoy's last-known residence.

The Mediterranean apartment building and three towering Canary Island Date Palms stood solidly planted at the corner of the block. Red bougainvillea vines climbed the gleaming white stucco and kept the redbrick trim from feeling lonely. Cast bronze lettering spelled WESTWOOD HILLS over the courtyard entrance. Solid wood doors hung on ornate hinges, everything thick and heavy. Copper roof gutters and drains had turned to a green-gray patina. If you ignored the satellite dishes, you could convince yourself it was 1925, and Douglas Fairbanks and Mary Pickford would be strolling through at any moment.

According to the apartment directory, the building had twelve units, none of them occupied by Sierra McCoy. California law requires an on-site manager for apartment buildings with sixteen or more units, so I wasn't sure what I would find. Eventually, I found the manager's doorbell and pushed it.

A window curtain moved. The top half of the door swung part-way open. Someone had done a good job of installing the Dutch door without killing the Mediterranean style.

A tall woman in her sixties appeared. Maybe a well-preserved seventy. She had some of the highest cheekbones I have ever seen. Her dark, gray-streaked hair swept back in a short, flattering style.

She took her time looking me up and down. "And what may I do for you?" I handed her my card. "My name is Jackson Salvo. I am a private investigator, and I would like to confirm that a young woman named Sierra McCoy used to live here."

She looked at the card. "I'm sorry, but I really don't want to comment on the tenants. I don't know you, do I?"

"I feel like I know you. Weren't you in those beach movies with Frankie and Annette?"

"That's absolutely wrong, but I have to admit it's a rather good line."

"I'll bet you've heard quite a few good lines."

"If all the lines I've heard were arranged end-to-end, the word count would exceed *Gone with the Wind*. Now what do you want?"

"I just need some basic information, such as the dates she lived here, and did she pay the rent, and did she cause any trouble."

She gave me a million-dollar smile. "Bullshit. Now, what do you really want?"

"I want to be invited in for a cup of coffee and learn everything I can about Sierra McCoy, including her finances, sex life, and hat size."

"Why do you need the information?"

"I'm investigating a case of embezzlement, and I think Sierra McCoy might be able to steer me to the embezzler."

She looked me up and down again. "How do you want your coffee?"

"Black, please."

"That's how I take mine. My name is Constance Bellamy." She offered her hand and ushered me into her living room. "I'll find the file on Sierra McCoy for you. Make yourself comfortable."

She disappeared into the central hallway, and I looked around. The furniture was modern and fresh-looking. The hardwood floors appeared recently refinished. The rugs were handwoven. A canvas print of Gustav Klimt's *The Kiss* hung near the dining room entrance. Constance came back carrying a legal-size hanging folder and said, "The coffee should only take two or three minutes."

I said, "I like Klimt. I have one in my office."

She said, "I'm very partial to his gold hues," and disappeared into the kitchen.

Something caught my eye on the far dining room wall. I navigated through the furniture and scrutinized three framed magazine advertisements. They all featured a very young Constance Bellamy. She was go-to-hell good looking. The first photo was a studio shot in which she draped herself along the side of a black Cadillac. In the second, she wore a sable coat and stood solemnly in an endless field of snow. In the third, she waved cheerfully from a long stretch of grass, the Eiffel Tower in the background.

I was trying to determine whether the Cadillac was a 1966 or a '67 when the aroma of coffee hit me. A minute later Constance and I were seated with china cups in hand. The folder she had been carrying was on the sofa, between us. It was labeled SIERRA McCOY.

Constance said, "I wasn't the manager when Sierra lived here, just a resident, but I heard all the details from Mrs. Bartholomew, the woman who preceded me as manager. She's passed away now. Mrs. Bartholomew was charming but terribly old-fashioned. She used to always say, 'That Sierra, she's a party girl, she is. A real high-stepper.'" She smiled at the memory.

I said, "Do you know why Sierra vacated?"

"I recall that Mrs. Bartholomew was pressuring her to leave. She may have had financial problems after her TV show was canceled. I can't remember the name of her show, only that it was awful."

"*Heartbreakers.*"

"Oh, yes. I must have repressed that memory. The show was absolutely unwatchable. Well anyway, these apartments are very expensive, probably the nicest vintage apartments in Westwood. After Sierra's show was canceled, she sold her red Porsche, apparently as a cost-cutting measure. About two or three months after that, she moved out."

I asked for a coffee refill and got it. I also got the rest of the story. The men at the Westwood Terrace apartments loved Sierra. The women hated her, especially when she would wander around the apartment grounds wearing very little clothing. She had a conspicuously active social life. When boyfriends stayed overnight, the trysts were embarrassingly audible. Mrs. Bartholomew couldn't wait to get rid of her.

Constance set her cup soundlessly on its saucer. "I'm not a prude by any stretch of the imagination, but I would certainly have to say that Miss McCoy was lacking in the modesty department and in the discretion department, as well."

I said, "This has all been very helpful, and I appreciate your taking the time, but what I could really use is her forwarding address."

She opened the file folder and pulled out the lease for Sierra McCoy. "Sierra moved in July 1st, 2001." She dug through more papers. "I can't seem to find her quit notice. That's where the forwarding address would be." She thumbed through the documents again, more carefully this time. She found a note card with a butterfly pattern on the front. She opened it and said, "Here it is. Sierra moved out on September 15th, 2004. Her forwarding address was 9112 Raven Way, Los Angeles, 90069. That would be in the Hollywood Hills."

I took notes and thanked her, and she walked me to the door. I took one step outside and turned around. "Constance, you make me want to run out and buy a Cadillac. Thanks again."

14

During the drive to 9112 Raven Way, the traffic came to a long halt at two different intersections. I used the time to research my destination. It was a single-family home in the "Bird Streets," a prestigious section of the Hollywood Hills. A fifty-two-year-old man named Preston Newbury owned the house. Mr. Newbury held the title to that property and to three apartment buildings near Downtown Los Angeles. In past years, Mr. Newbury had been cited for hundreds of health, fire, and building code violations in his apartments. In 2007, he was sentenced to live in one of his vermin-infested rentals for a month while wearing an electronic monitoring device.

After breaking free of the traffic, I drove up North Doheny Drive and found Mr. Newbury's house. It was an angular, modern two-story painted in three shades of gray. A minimal little strip of grass separated the front porch from the curb. A separate guesthouse rested on top of the carport, which sheltered a big black Lexus sedan and a beige VW Beetle convertible.

I parked beyond the carport, called a DMV contact, and learned that the Lexus belonged to Newbury. The VW belonged to a twenty-six-year-old woman named Mimi Lacordaire, who also used 9112 Raven Way as her home address. She was probably renting the space over the carport. The neighborhood was not zoned for apartments, but the Hollywood Hills teem with illegal rental arrangements, many of which are combined with more personal arrangements. Maybe McCoy and Lacordaire were in a series of women who wangled free rent out of Preston Newbury the slumlord.

I closed my car door quietly and walked toward the house. Female telephone chatter, mixed with classical music, drifted down from a louvered window over the carport. The words were too faint to be understood. The music sounded like an orchestral version of a Chopin piano work, but I wouldn't stake my life on it.

Small concrete stepping-stones led to the shallow front porch. I hit the doorbell. The door opened, and a lazy, saggy face appeared. He was five foot ten, gray ponytail, tie-dyed T-shirt hanging out over his potbelly. He wore a massive gold Rolex, skimpy gym shorts, and no shoes.

He displayed two rows of rotting teeth through which he said, "Yeah, what do you want?"

A putrid odor blew into my face. I gave him my card and leaned back. "I'm looking for a young lady named Sierra McCoy. I believe she moved to this address in September of 2004. Are you Mr. Newbury?"

He hissed, "Get lost." I got another whiff of the teeth.

He pushed on the door. I pushed back. "All I want is a little information. Then I get lost."

He pushed harder. "You're gonna get lost now."

I pushed back harder. "Can you give me her forwarding address at least?"

"I wouldn't give you all the shit you could eat."

I adjusted my right foot and shoulder against the door and got relatively comfortable. "Mimi Lacordaire rents the guesthouse over the carport, and Sierra McCoy used to live there. Can you confirm that for me?"

"Get your ass off this property. You're trespassing. I'm gonna call the police."

I wasn't sure about the rental arrangement over the carport, but I couldn't lose anything by bluffing. "Okay, Preston. You call the police. I'll call my friend at the L.A. Housing Department. You can explain how you're illegally renting an apartment out of a single-family house. And you can explain to the IRS how you're collecting rent and not declaring the income."

He eased the door back a few inches.

I said, "I only need two things. One, who were her friends while she lived here? Two, where did she go from here?"

He looked down at his bare feet, looked back at me, and said, "She moved to some place over on Lime Terrace. I'll have to get the address."

He walked back through the foyer and waved me in. I followed at a distance, leaving the door ajar. He went into the galley-style kitchen, which was separated from the living room by a counter. He picked through a kitchen drawer, rustling papers. I surveyed the living room.

The stereo system was worth well over a hundred thousand dollars. Krell electronics, gigantic MartinLogan speakers, and a turntable from outer space. Hundreds of CDs and vinyl albums were on racks and shelves. There were dozens of framed posters and photos of rock performers, many of them signed. A single recliner chair was in the middle of the room, facing the stereo. Except for two bar stools, there was no other seating or reclining available. Newbury probably didn't get a lot of dates. Certainly not with Sierra McCoy.

I turned back toward Newbury, who had come out of the kitchen. In his left hand, he held a small book with a smiley face on the cover. In his right, he held a snub-nosed revolver, a cheap little Saturday night special.

He said, "You should consider the consequences before you barge into someone's home and threaten them. I could shoot you right now and claim self-defense."

"You'd never get away with it. I'm unarmed. There's no evidence of a break-in. No evidence of a struggle."

"You forced your way in, and I ran for my gun and shot you when you came at me."

"You try to claim self-defense, the Hollywood detectives will bust your story within minutes. You'll never keep all the details straight. When they sentence you, you're not going to get house arrest, like you did for your flophouse apartments. They're going to haul you off to a place for violent offenders, like Corcoran State Prison, and the first thing they'll do is make you go to the prison dentist. You're afraid of the dentist, aren't you?"

Newbury flashed a hateful little sneer.

I said, "Your teeth are so far gone, they'll have to strap you down and dig them out. After the painful recovery, you get choppers. However, the choppers will be convenient because you can take 'em out when you're sucking cock at Corcoran."

He growled, "You know, you are a real world-class asshole. You ought to get some kind of prize for it."

"I wish you wouldn't talk like that. I have trouble handling compliments."

He contemplated his alternatives and slowly lowered the revolver. "I give you the address, and I tell you what I know about her friends, and you go away. That the deal?"

"Don't lie to me, you'll never see me again."

He opened the smiley face book one-handed and thumbed through it. "The address is 8861 Lime Terrace, apartment four. It's up the hill from the Whisky."

"I can find it. What about her friends?"

"Sierra had a string of rich guys she dated. They would stay overnight sometimes. I never knew their names. One guy had a Bentley; one guy had a Lamborghini; another had a Porsche Turbo. After Sierra was here about six months, she got a slightly used Porsche, a red 911."

"You have any idea where she got the money for the Porsche?"

The words were flowing out of Newbury faster and smoother. "I never asked about her personal business. I figured she got money from the boyfriends, and she was in a TV show a few years ago, so she might have got residuals. Anyway, after she lived here around a year and a half, two guys showed up at the same time and they got in a fight, sluggin' it out right in the middle of the street. Neighbors called the cops. Afterward, Sierra called me and apologized and said she was planning to move anyway. She might have had round heels, but she was polite, kept her place neat and clean, always paid the rent. That's all I know."

"She moved out in March 2006?"

"Uh . . . April, because I went to a Dodger game the day she moved out, and the season just started. Had to be April. Had to be early April."

"Have you seen her since she moved out?"

"Around town a couple of times. Now she has a red Mercedes sedan. I saw her in it at the Beverly Center at Christmas. That's the last time I saw her."

"I appreciate the information."

Newbury looked down at the gun in his hand and seemed surprised to see it. He walked around the kitchen corner, into the hallway. Disappearing into the shadow, he said over his shoulder, "Don't let the door hit you in the ass on the way out."

15

I drove back down Doheny, parked at a meter next to Gil Turner's liquor store, and turned on my iPad. A real estate website informed me 8861 Lime Terrace was a four-unit rental property purchased for $1.6 million in 2010. The owner was Victoria Resources Inc., a corporation for which I could find little information. Two minutes later I was driving back up into the hills.

Clark Street climbs into some of the more surreal reaches of the Hollywood Hills. The streets snake around in strange ways, much like the residents. Tightly packed apartments and houses line the ridges and elbow each other for the best view. The architecture, if you want to be generous and call it that, is a jumble of old and new, gaudy and austere, whimsical and pompous. I wound my way through all this and parked near the driveway serving 8861 Lime Terrace.

Four bungalows were tiered up the hillside. At first glance, they were Spanish. At second glance, they were a blend of Spanish and Tudor. The stucco was painted a warm tan that glowed nicely in the sun. Small lawns and individual carports fronted each residence.

I walked up the concrete stairway to where it leveled off for unit number one. An older, clean-looking Mercedes sedan was in the carport. That bungalow's front door was open behind the screen door. If anyone was inside, they could see me, but I couldn't see them. I kept moving.

The carport for unit two was empty. A FedEx package leaned against the front door. Nobody home.

At unit three a trash bin full of construction debris stood in the middle of the lawn. The front door was off its hinges and missing. A red Coca-Cola can was perched on top of an aluminum stepladder just inside the doorway.

In the carport, a young Hispanic guy stood over the missing front door, which was across a pair of plastic sawhorses. He worked on the door with a sanding sponge, using smooth, delicate strokes. He didn't look up when I walked by.

The highest bungalow in the string was Sierra McCoy's forwarding address. The carport was empty. An oversized, glossy fashion magazine lay on the porch, directly under the mail slot. The magazine was addressed to an Adriana Levering. The electric meter was in a wooden cabinet on the uphill side of the structure. A paper tag wired to the meter listed Department of Water and Power customers going back thirty years. Ms. Levering had lived in this rental unit since July 2008. The name of the customer prior to Levering was erased from the tag. The erased customer's residence in unit four went from May 2006 to June 2008, which was consistent with Sierra McCoy's departure from Preston Newbury's illegal granny unit. I walked slowly down the steps, scratching my head and wondering how I could find her current address.

A bushy-haired little guy appeared further down the steps. He wore a Hawaiian shirt, jeans, lightly tinted glasses, and a toothy smile. We came face-to-face at the third level. He said, "Hello there. Would you like to see apartment number three? It wasn't going to be ready for two weeks . . . but at the rate we're going, we might finish it sooner than that."

"I'm in no rush. You the manager?"

"Not officially, but I help the owner out a little."

"What's it renting for?"

"Three thousand. It's a two-bedroom, bath and a half. Pretty good view from the living room. It's a good deal for this area . . . especially with the view."

"How good is the owner on repairs and maintenance?"

"Once she knows you're okay, she's great. She lets you call the handyman direct for little things like stopped-up drains and stuck windows. If you need a licensed electrician or you have serious plumbing issues, you go through her. You mess with her, like you don't pay the rent or something, Sierra knows how to take care of business. You want to see the place?"

Sierra McCoy was now the owner? I managed to keep the surprise out of my voice. "Sure. Let's take a look."

He said his name was Steve. I said I was Bill Edwards, recently divorced and a manager at Allstate Insurance downtown.

When we squeezed past the ladder inside the doorway, I caught a whiff of booze off Steve. I looked at my watch, thinking it was a little early in the day to be drinking.

Steve also looked at my watch. "Are you in much of a hurry?"

"Not terribly. If I see a place I like, I can call my office and cancel a meeting."

I paced off room dimensions, checked windows and water pressure, and poked around the closets. From the living room window, there was a decent view of the Los Angeles basin.

I said, "I like the place. I'd like to talk to the owner."

Steve walked me down to my car, wrote down my disposable cell phone number, and promised to have Sierra call me. As I drove away, Steve's lightly tinted glasses and annoying smile shrunk in my mirror.

I went down to the Strip and parked behind a restaurant named Coucher Du Soleil. It's one of those sidewalk cafés where the tourists hope to spot celebrities, and the local posers hope to be mistaken for celebrities. I eat there once or twice a year, to maintain a connection with my misspent youth.

I took a sidewalk table, ordered halibut, fired up my iPad, and continued researching Sierra McCoy. Every now and then I looked up and observed the human condition at Coucher Du Soleil. The customers were either well-dressed or overdressed. The noise level was reasonable, the laughter never raising to a howl or horselaugh. That was okay with me because I have no tolerance for loud restaurants. During my wait for the food, fragments of conversations floated around:

. . . I simply must be out of here in five minutes. Charles is going to be on Days of Our Lives *at one, and—dumb me—I forgot to set the DVR . . . I sure as hell wasn't gonna be the one to inform Taylor Swift she hit a*

wrong note . . . I'm crashing at my girlfriend's place until the screenplay sells. That way I can keep the Porsche for at least six more months . . . I know people who know people who definitely have money for the project . . . My good friend Jay Leno said . . .

Twenty minutes after the food was served, my plate was clean, I hadn't heard anyone discuss anything of substance, and I hadn't learned much more about Sierra McCoy or the company called Victoria Resources Inc.

A call came in on my disposable phone. Caller ID said OUT OF AREA.

I said hello.

A girlish voice said, "This is Sierra McCoy. Is this Mr. Edwards?"

"Yes. I'm interested in the apartment on Lime Terrace."

"Steve said you looked like a solid citizen. Can you drop by my house, so we can discuss it? I live off North Doheny."

"I'm just finishing lunch. I could be there in fifteen or twenty minutes."

"The address is 1611 Flamingo Way. Just let yourself in the front door. I'm floating in the pool. I hope you don't mind the informality."

"Informality is my middle name."

A melodious little laugh fondled my eardrum. We exchanged insipidities and ended the call.

16

Sierra McCoy's ranch-style house was on a lot between the road and the drop-off to the canyon below. It was the last address on Flamingo Way, no neighbors in sight. The pale pastel-yellow single-story had wide eaves, large windows, and used brick trim. A narrow rectangle of grass trimmed with white roses ran across the front. I had expected something more overblown.

I idled past the house and open garage, which was occupied by a red E-Class Mercedes sedan. The alloy wheels sparkled, even on the inner surfaces. An attractive woman rarely takes care of such details. Such drudgery would be for the husband, the boyfriend, or the ever-hopeful chump. I wondered where he might be.

I circled around at the end of Flamingo Way, drove past the house again, parked, and stood on the edge of the bluff. The view fanned out all the way from downtown to the sea. I had been waiting for one of those perfect late-summer L.A. days—a cool clean ocean breeze and a hot sun. The stagnant haze told me to keep waiting.

Sierra's front door opened into a shallow foyer. Living room to the left, dining area straight ahead. To the right, a central hallway. The far wall was mostly glass, giving the same view as outside.

On the way to the back door, I veered through the living room. Based on Sierra's fast-lane credentials, I would not have been shocked by an edgy, avant- garde decor, maybe Warhol in neon. Instead, there were carefully coordinated Victorian furnishings: carved wooden sofas and chairs with floral upholstery, William Morris carpet, fabric lamp-shades with beaded fringes, and doilies under the lamps. Paintings of ethereal femmes fatales in mythological settings framed a large, flat-screen television on the east wall. The artist's name is Waterhouse, who I always confuse with Waterford.

The dining area led to the kitchen. A kitchen door led to the pool in a low section behind the garage. Flagstone steps went down to the deck.

Sierra McCoy had aged ten years since *Heartbreakers*, which would put her in her mid-thirties. Even in the depreciation of direct sunlight, she could get away with turning her odometer back to the twenties. Reclining in a clear inflatable float at the center of the pool, she wore a white string bikini a little north of scandalous, eyecups, and a coat of zinc oxide on her aristocratic nose. A white towel protected her hair. The white nose could have had a comic effect. It didn't. Her blue toenails matched the glimmering water. A glistening of oil covered her long legs and much more. I regretted not having stroked the oil on her myself.

Sierra didn't speak, even though I had made enough noise to announce my arrival.

I broke the ice. "I like your William Morris carpet, but I'm not sure it matches the drapes."

The voice of a petulant teenager said, "You're not the interior decorator, and you're not looking to rent my apartment. Which one of my ex-boyfriends hired you?"

"I've never met any of your boyfriends. I was wondering if Susan Miller is one of your girlfriends."

There was a pause, and her voice matured. "I don't believe I'm acquainted with anyone by that name."

"Western Rim Bank remembers a customer named Susan Miller. She made a big cash transfer to the Caymans in November 2006. She also looked like a character on *Heartbreakers*."

"You wouldn't believe how often people come up to me and call me by the name of some other actress."

"No, I probably wouldn't believe it."

"Would you have a badge I can see?"

"No."

"Good. I don't like cops. Why don't you make us a couple of drinks?"

"Are you sure you want to have a drink with someone you've never seen?"

"Steve is very perceptive. You're about six-one, well put together, short hair. Sort of like a cop, but with a street racer BMW, Prada shoes, Panerai wristwatch, and no hair sticking out of your nose. Steve would make a good private eye. You should hire him."

"You should hire me to find out who pulled the scam at Culver Aerospace. Maybe I could help you prove your innocence."

"I don't know anything about the aerospace industry, and I don't care to know. It bores me. Grey Goose rocks, please. You can have whatever you can find."

Sierra's immaculate, well-equipped kitchen had plenty of booze and ice. I found two highball glasses and made Sierra's drink a double. For myself, I made orange juice on the rocks. While I was at it, I noted the number of the corded telephone on the kitchen counter.

Back at the pool, I set my drink on a small glass-top table and Sierra's in a floating drink holder. I said, "You have to paddle toward me."

She paddled gracefully.

I placed the floating drink where her hand would fall to it and said, "There you go."

Long, elegant fingers and long, flawless white nails wrapped around the icy highball glass. I gently pushed the float toward the middle of the pool and sat on a deck chair.

She took a long pull on the vodka. "Okay, what do you want?"

"Who was the insider at Culver Aerospace in the embezzlement scam?"

"I never heard of Culver Aerospace. What are you getting out of this?"

"An hourly rate plus expenses."

"What does this aerospace company want after all this time? That was seven years ago."

"I don't think they know what they want. All they know for sure is they don't like bad publicity."

A figure appeared at the top of the steps. Around six-foot-four, chiseled features, lanky and muscular. He was some sort of exotic blend, maybe half African American and half Asian. He shone in the sun like a bronze statue. He wore mirrored aviator sunglasses, black T-shirt, black cargo shorts, and gray New Balance shoes exactly like a pair I own, except his were about size sixteen. He stood perfectly still.

I stood up. "Ms. McCoy, the guy that cleans your Mercedes is here."

The new arrival snapped his shades into a belt-mounted case. His greedy little eyes sized me up. He spoke slowly and precisely. "Do you need the floor mopped, Sierra?"

"Not quite yet, Byron. I have a few questions for Mr. Jackson Salvo. He's a private investigator. He inquired about one of my rental units using a false name."

Byron said, "Oh, how unfortunate. What we have here is a lying sack of shit."

I responded to the affront. "Aren't you the chairman of the English Department at Loyola?" For some reason, he didn't think that was funny.

I said, mostly to Sierra, "Let me guess. Steve, the rummy in apartment number one, got my license plate, and you have a contact who can run the plate."

She said, "Steve may drink a little too much, but he can spot a phony a mile away."

"In this part of town, he can get a lot of practice."

She removed the eyecups and rested them on her flat stomach. She spoke calmly. "You're the one who gave us the phony name." She paddled to the far side of the pool and, with a quick silky grace, climbed the ladder. She set the eyecups on a chair, removed the towel from her head, wiped the white off her nose, and shook her luxuriant black mane.

I should have been watching Byron, who had drifted halfway down the steps. He said, "Okay, fuckface. Why are you here? Start talking."

"I'd like Sierra to turn herself in. It will make her a better person."

"She's a fine person just the way she is. And you don't insult her like that and get away with it, motherfucker."

"Byron, your diction is excellent, but you really need to work on your vocabulary."

He smiled, but not with any appreciation of my wit. He came off the steps with no sense of weight. I didn't like the way he moved. My neck tightened, and I consciously relaxed it.

I leaned forward and said, "Can I get you a drink?"

Byron advanced slowly and silently toward me, almost like an evening shadow just before the sun vanishes. When he was at the distance I wanted, I flicked my left hand upward. His eyes followed the distraction. My right hand tossed the orange juice into his face. He shut his eyes and shook his head, making a harsh coughing noise. He reached out with both hands and staggered toward me, spitting and snorting. I tossed my highball glass into the pool and backpedaled.

Then he came fast. I grabbed his left wrist with both hands and yanked him toward me, to maintain his momentum and my control. Still backpedaling, I swung him around toward the pool. He knew where he was headed and fought it, scrabbling on the deck for traction. He hit the water on his back.

I pivoted off-balance in the hope of taking my first running step toward the exit. Too slow. Sierra banged the right side of my face with the bottom of her clenched fist. She got her weight into it. While seeing little white stars, I backed into her and gave her an elbow to the stomach. She said, "Oof," and doubled over.

Byron pulled himself halfway out of the pool. He looked refreshed, as though the water had washed the citric acid out of his eyes. He was starting to say something when I kicked his face. He fell back in, came up for air, grabbed the pool gutter, and let the blood run out of his nose. Now he was happy to just hang on.

Sierra walked away breathing shallow and fast. She picked up an aluminum pool pole, spun around, and approached me with the pole in an on-guard position, as though she had something special in mind for me.

I held the top of the pool ladder, leaned out, and shoved Byron's head underwater with my foot. The water bubbled pink. I said, "Don't you think we should pull him out of the water?"

She looked at Byron's submerged head and flailing hands and tossed the pole aside. We pulled Byron out of the pool and dumped him on the deck. He coughed and sputtered and gagged.

I walked away quickly into and through the house. On the way to the front door, I left my business card leaning against a vase of fresh white roses on the kitchen counter.

A big black BMW SUV, presumably Byron's, was parked on the wrong side of the street, nosed up to my car. I was checking my front bumper for damage and holding the side of my face when Sierra came out of the house.

She walked boldly, almost lustily, toward me. The white bikini had somehow managed to stay on. The white towel was slung over her shoulder. Her jet-black hair floated against the blue-gray haze. Her eyes drilled into mine. I couldn't tell if she wanted to fuck or fight.

She stood about five feet away. "I am not proud of everything I've done. And given your line of work, I'll bet you have a few peccadilloes in your closet. I got off to a rough start in life. I've never whined about getting a raw deal, and I corrected the problems all by myself. I am now stable and secure." Her girlish voice sharpened to a gleaming edge. "I will do everything possible to protect myself. Anything and everything."

The right side of my face hurt when I grinned. I kept on grinning. "I'd hate to run into you in a dark alley."

She gave me the faintest of smiles. "Worse things could happen to you."

"What happened with Culver Aerospace?"

"I'll call you. I promise. Right now, I have to take care of a muscle-bound invalid."

17

I drove down Doheny for the second time that day. This time I drove slower and contemplated Sierra McCoy. There was a lot to contemplate. She was glamorous, cagey, and smart. She could afford to lawyer up. She knew how to throw a punch. I had little doubt she had been part of the embezzlement, but I needed solid evidence.

Ideas for digging up that evidence were starting to buzz around my head when a white Dodge Charger popped into my rearview, about a hundred yards back. I recalled a similar car behind me when I was approaching Lime Terrace, two hours before, but I hadn't given it much thought. As soon as Doheny bent to the right, I took a quick left onto a parallel street that would reconnect with Doheny at a four-way intersection less than a quarter-mile down the road. I stopped a little short of the four-way behind a parked car and slid down in my seat.

The Charger rolled slowly through the stop sign and accelerated down Doheny at a moderate rate. The driver appeared only as a silhouette through his window. A few seconds later, a silver Cadillac sedan came down the hill and braked to a halt. The driver was a square-jawed blond guy who was clearly visible through his open window. He snapped his head right and left as his car gave a throaty roar and launched through the intersection. I waited until the sound of the Caddy faded, drove across the intersection, and took an alternate route down to the Strip.

Sunset Boulevard took me westward to Alpine Drive, and that set me up for the longer, more scenic route home. A peaceful montage of heavyweight houses and flamboyant foliage floated past. There were hedges the size of prison walls; artist-designed mailboxes that would cost the mail carrier a year's salary; and soaring rows of palm trees slender and tall, with the graceful bend the Santa Ana winds give them.

I was tired of serious thinking, so I tried to give it a rest. With me, that always gets the opposite result. I mulled over the embezzlements at Culver Aerospace, the dead bodies at Celebrity Motors, the athletic bodies of Sierra and Byron, the Silver Cadillac, and the white Dodge Charger that might have been following me, and how everything might be connected. The result of all this contemplation was nothing. No brilliant inferences, no epiphanies, no insights, no nothing.

Aristotle came to mind, maybe because he was the subject of my next class. Did my kicking Byron in the face meet Aristotle's standard for the highest good? If I had Aristotle in the car with me, I could have explained everything, and he probably would have agreed, maybe even bought me a drink at the Bel Air Hotel.

I snaked through lower Bel Air, worked my way around the hill to Sepulveda Boulevard, and parked at a gas station minimarket.

According to the vanity mirror in my sun visor, my right cheekbone was starting to swell. I took a latex glove from my supply bag in the trunk and went into the market.

The wiry young guy behind the counter noticed my face, but he didn't stare. I poured myself a small cup of black coffee and filled the glove with ice from the spout by the soft drink dispensers. I tied off the glove, wrapped it in paper napkins, and approached the counter, holding the ice pack to my face.

The clerk said, "How big was the other guy?"

"Five-ten, hundred and twenty pounds of solid muscle, legs all the way up to her ass."

He grunted and smiled.

I set the coffee on the counter and reached for my money.

He held his hand up flat. "On the house. There's some situations, us guys gotta stick together."

Every now and then you run into someone who restores your faith in humanity.

Back in my car, I was trying to buckle up one-handed while holding the ice pack to my face. A phone call came in, and I gave up on the seat belt.

Darcey Mathis said, "Hello, Jack. How are you doing?"

I would have preferred Lilith's voice, but what the hell, it was warm and female.

I said, "I heard the news about Pace."

"My God, it was a shock. It's on the news now, and everyone at the office knows about it."

"How are they taking it?"

"Everyone was surprised and shocked, of course, but to be honest, there wasn't much affection for him around here."

"At least this solves your Oswald Pace problem."

"Yes, but I didn't want him to *die*. I just wanted him to go away. Let's not talk about it anymore. It's . . . it's . . . disturbing."

I said, "I have a new subject."

"And it is?"

"Now you have to pay me."

"Your check is almost in the mail, and now *I* have a new subject. I'm taking you up on your offer."

"What offer?"

"Now we can get together, and you can tell me about Lippmanstein's theory of linguistics.

"That was Wittgenstein's theory of language. You want to go to the tractor pulls in Tehachapi on Saturday?"

"What a silly boy."

"Strip clubs in San Pedro?"

All I heard was silence.

I said, "Del Sol Grill in Westwood and a movie?"

"Now you're speaking my language. How about Saturday, seven o'clock, dinner at seven-thirty? I'll check the movie listings."

She gave me her home address and cell phone number, and we ended the call. Darcey had caught me off-balance. Wednesday morning in her office, when I offered to explain Wittgenstein to her, I was just wising off. Maybe Darcey had a cerebral side that was never nurtured, and she craved intellectual stimulation. Maybe she wanted to see if it's true what they say about private dicks. What women are thinking usually eludes me, and I find out the hard way. I popped two Advils and drove one-handed, alternately taking slugs of coffee and holding the ice pack to my face.

At my office, I picked up the mail from the floor beneath the mail slot. As I was sailing the final piece of junk mail into the recycle bin, a black Ford Crown Victoria pulled to the curb in front. The car had small hubcaps on black rims, a spotlight, and a trunk-mounted antenna. The shaved head who got out paid no attention to the expired parking meter. His brown sport coat bulged over his right hip and clashed with his gray slacks. That he might be a police detective was a remote possibility.

He came in, flashed his badge, said hello Mr. Salvo, introduced himself as Detective Siqueiros from LAPD Rampart Division, and handed me his business card. He didn't seem to notice the ice pack I was holding to my face. I offered the sofa. He pulled one of the wooden chairs diagonally across from me, took a seat, and let his coat fall back behind the Beretta on his belt.

He said, "I've been investigating the deaths of Oswald Pace and Buddy Vega. The management at Culver Aerospace told me you were investigating an embezzlement in their company, and Pace and Vega were suspects. Pace worked for Culver, but they never heard of Vega. How did you arrive at the connection between those two characters?"

"Culver Aerospace gave me four suspects." I produced the four folders Darcey had given me and spread them on the desk. "I got contact information, work history, badge photographs, and employment applications." None of this would be new to Siqueiros, but I wanted to be perceived as cooperative.

He ignored the folders. "Yeah, but how did you arrive at the connection between Pace and Vega?"

"Pace caught my attention early."

"Based on what?"

"What I learned about him at Culver Aerospace, his background check, and based on I didn't like his looks. I worked the phone and talked to the owner of an apartment he lived in back in 1999 in Fullerton. He said Pace and a roommate named Buddy Vega ran out on the rent and stole appliances when they left. Then I ran a background check on Vega. He was dirty in a petty sort of way, as I'm sure you've already discovered. I took two photos of him at his car lot, over on the east end of Sunset Boulevard. I put his photo in a six-pack and got a positive ID on him at the bank where the embezzlement money was laundered."

Siqueiros leaned forward. "So, you were actually at Celebrity Motors at the same time Vega was there? What day was that?"

"Tuesday afternoon. When I took the photos, I stayed in my car and used a long lens. Then I went straight to the Southland National Bank in Hawthorne and got the ID on him."

"Did you speak to Vega or have any contact with him?"

"No. Other than a fake wrong-number phone call I made when I was down the street from his car lot, I never spoke to him."

"Did you ever encounter Pace or speak with him?"

"I saw him in the Culver Aerospace cafeteria, from a distance. He never noticed me."

Siqueiros had me go over everything again and lay out the timeline of my investigation. I left out the part about my entering Pace's apartment and finding thirteen thousand in cash, and I left out my finding the stiffs at Celebrity Motors.

He asked for the names and phone numbers of the Fullerton apartment owner and the Southland National Bank manager in Hawthorne. I gathered the information and gave it to him. He asked to see the photos I took of Vega on Tuesday afternoon. I showed them, looked at the detective's e-mail address on his business card, and sent him the photos while he waited. He asked me where I was Tuesday night. I told him I was home watching reruns of NFL preseason games. I was prepared to discuss the games that had been on, but he didn't press for details.

He stood and moved the chair back exactly where he found it. "You think of anything else, call me, okay?"

I nodded.

At the door, he pulled it partly open and looked back at me. "How'd you get the face?"

"A girl hit me."

He gave me a grouchy, skeptical gaze, just short of anger—the sort of gaze at which police detectives excel. Then he smiled and shrugged. "Same thing happened to me once or twice."

He went out the door, and I sat drumming my fingers on my desk, watching him swing into his Crown Vic. I wondered if Siqueiros thought I was leveling with him. I was relieved he didn't ask about my suspicion that Vega cheated Pace on the money they stole from Culver Aerospace. Darcey must have not mentioned it.

The police were on their investigative path, and I needed to stay on mine. Before the detective's car was out of sight, I was considering the alternatives for learning more about Sierra McCoy. The least attractive option would take me back to Cecile Clark, who had been at the same party with Sierra McCoy. She would know the names of other partygoers, some of whom would know Sierra. I could track them down, but that would be lots of legwork, and I wasn't anxious to land on the Clark family again. If all my other leads fizzled out, I might call Cecile.

Victoria Resources, the corporate name Sierra was using, was probably just a tax angle. I could have spent more time researching it, but there probably wasn't much to gain since I had already found Sierra.

The most promising option was Maya Fontaine, Sierra's old acting coach. According to Cecile, Sierra was the star student at the La Peer Studio. The teacher would remember everything about her best pupil.

It took just a few minutes to get Maya Fontaine's life story. She had enjoyed a successful acting career from 1978 to 1987, starting with a minor part in *Jacqueline the Ripper*. The leggy brunette with the long neck and go-to-hell smile worked her way up to supporting roles in a few decent films and received favorable reviews. During her acting career, she was married and divorced three times in rapid succession. She formed the La Peer Studio acting workshop in 1988 and had run it since that time. She currently resided in a house near Beverly and Melrose.

If I had been in a more enterprising mood, I would have gone straight to Maya's house and started working on her. I said to hell with that, phoned a deli, and ordered a salmon burger to go. I was anxious to pick up the food, drive toward the setting sun and my comfortable home, and watch TV. That turned out to be the exact sequence of events.

18

At eleven-ten the next morning, I was standing across the street from Maya Fontaine's residence. Her small, neatly trimmed, pastel-blue house looked a lot more sensible than those of her neighbors.

On the west, a Spanish house was painted a murky red-orange that didn't quite match the roof tile. The wood trim was painted a bilious green. I shifted my grimace to the east side and observed a flat-roofed, chocolate-brown bungalow. A convoluted, egg yolk–yellow wooden framework wrapped around the front porch. At least four wind chimes hung from the monstrosity. Don't get me started on wind chimes.

Pushing Maya's doorbell resulted in nothing, so I walked up the driveway and onto a concrete patio that covered the backyard. The window on the side of the closed, freestanding garage displayed a shiny white Audi coupe inside. The back-neighbor's trees arched over the fence, shading a redwood table and two matching side benches. A tall row of ficus trees walled off the neighbor opposite the garage. The setting wasn't elegant, but it was private, quiet, and inviting. Pastoral on a budget. Maybe the acting coach would turn out to be cooperative and chatty. Maybe she would serve lunch at the redwood table and tell me all about Sierra McCoy.

A rasping noise came from somewhere. I stepped around a coiled garden hose and stood close to a back window. The unmistakable sound of snoring came through the screen and curtain. I was at the window only a few seconds, but I was already starting to fry in the direct sunlight and reflected light off the house. I went over to the shaded back steps.

Through the back-door screen I could see the service porch and the kitchen beyond. I said hello a couple of times. The only response I got was more snoring. I spoke louder. More snoring. I slipped the lock and walked in.

The dining room was furnished with a dark cherry table, matching chairs, and a tall china cabinet. The walls were heavy with framed photographs, mostly of Maya's acting career and her acting students at La Peer Studio. I scanned the photos quickly until I found Sierra McCoy. Sierra had looked a little severe in person, but she took a hell of a photo. She had that quality that reaches out from the picture frame and grabs you by the gonads.

Cecile Clark was there too, posing between two handsome young men. One of the men was an actor I had seen, but whose name I did not know. I tried to remember where I had seen him, but the snoring from the bedroom reminded me to stick to business.

A beige leather sectional sofa dominated the living room. There was a tall bookcase full of highbrow and middlebrow fiction, and nonfiction books on film, theater, and other arts. Almost every book was hardbound. Framed prints were on the walls. Every print was signed and numbered. No television. Everything was terribly civilized.

The home office was down the hallway, first door on the right. A stack of bills and an old-fashioned rotary card file sat on a leather-top desk. I hadn't seen a Rolodex for a long time. I spun it to the M's and found Sierra McCoy's phone number, the same number as Sierra's kitchen telephone. I wondered if Sierra and Maya were still in touch. The next door led to a lavender-scented, sparkling-clean, yellow-and-gray tiled bathroom.

Finally, the bedroom. Maya Fontaine sprawled diagonally across a black platform bed, a rose-colored sheet up to her neck. Considering she was in her sixties and snoring with her mouth hanging open like a dead fish, she looked pretty good. Considering the nightstand held a vodka bottle, shot glass, disposable cigarette lighter, and a half-smoked reefer in an ancient-looking Paramount Pictures ashtray, she looked radiant.

Something pushed me back to the dining room. Maybe a little birdie whispering in my ear. I went through the photos again, this time more systematically. Halfway around the room, I came to a sudden halt. Two female acting students were clowning for the camera. Sierra McCoy stuck out her tongue and pulled her ears out wide. The other girl had a lit cigarette stuck in her ear and a slack-jawed, dopey look on her face. The other girl looked a lot like Darcey Mathis. I put my nose close to the photo. The other girl was in fact Darcey Mathis. I turned slowly and looked at my reflection in the china cabinet's glass side. A slack-jawed dope returned my gaze.

The little gears in my head started turning. In 2006 Darcey Mathis pulled the "Bandini Construction" embezzlement at Culver Aerospace, in which she generated a bogus check for almost three hundred thousand dollars. Sierra McCoy laundered the money through Western Rim Bank. It was a smartly designed swindle that should have been detected within days or weeks.

In later years, Oswald Pace pulled a series of smaller, but somewhat similar embezzlements. Pace did not expect his scams to be discovered, but the audit department ferreted them out. Darcey was afraid that a thorough investigation of the more recent embezzlements might lead back to her. That's why she urged me to dig up all the dirt in Pace's background. If Pace had a shady past, Culver Aerospace management would be less inclined to prosecute and more inclined to end the investigation by letting Pace voluntarily terminate. That would greatly reduce the possibility of news headlines such as CULVER AEROSPACE EMBEZZLER HAD SLIPPERY HISTORY—STOCKHOLDERS LIVID. It wasn't a bad strategy on Darcey's part, but it failed.

Soft groans came from the bedroom. I photographed the Darcey/Sierra picture and let myself out the back door. I drove up to Santa Monica Boulevard and found Bertoni, an Italian restaurant. While my food cooked, I settled into a corner table with my briefcase and dove into Darcey Mathis's background.

She grew up in Davenport, Iowa. Her adult residential history started at an apartment in Bloomington, Illinois when she was attending Illinois State. She moved to a Hollywood apartment in 1999, bounced around other apartments, and ended up at her current address, a duplex near Pico and Beverly Glen. Her latest address was the same one she had given me for our upcoming date Saturday night. Her time spent at La Peer Studio appeared to have resulted in no acting work. She had worked at Culver Aerospace for ten years and earned her MBA during that time.

Her mother was a graphic artist living in Palatine, a Chicago suburb. Father deceased. I couldn't find any brothers, sisters, or other relatives. No lawsuits or criminal convictions. No marriages or bankruptcies. She was driving a white BMW 328i sedan.

The waitress dropped off the tab. I reviewed it, calculated the tip, and decided the scampi and scallops were okay for the money. That reminded me, not so fondly, of my date at the Italian restaurant Vicenza, where I took the chatty soap opera actress three years before.

Then I flashed on the Vicenza matchbook I had seen in Darcey's office the previous morning when she was organizing her purse. I wondered why she would patronize a place like Vicenza. Aerospace executives don't hang out in trendy West Hollywood restaurants. Too much culture clash. Vicenza was less than a mile away. I couldn't lose too much by driving down there and nosing around. On the way to the restaurant, I went to a FedEx Office, found a color photo of Darcey on the Culver Aerospace website, and printed a hard copy.

At twelve-thirty-five I cruised past Vicenza, parked a half-block away, and walked back. The head valet was a short, solid-looking Hispanic man, about thirty. He took a gratuity from a doddery, white-haired man who was wearing a white suit and driving a Rolls Royce Drophead Coupé. The old guy was also in possession of a hard-faced younger woman who looked like she would kick you in the family jewels with her Hermès shoe if you suggested she ride in anything less than a Rolls.

The couple vanished, and I approached the valet. I gave him my business card and showed him the photo of Darcey and a fifty-dollar bill. "I was wondering if you've seen this woman."

He signaled one of his boys to take the Rolls around back and squinted at the photo. "I seen her before. Good lookin' broad."

"Who was she with?"

"I seen her two or three times with the same guy. An old guy." He held his hands vertically, framing his face. "This guy had a really big beard and a big mustache. Drove the best lookin' old Jag XK-E convertible you ever seen. Perfect black paint and a tan top. Car looked like new. That old fucker must have a lotta money, 'cause next to her, he didn't look so good."

"How old was he?"

"Fifty, sixty."

"Anything else about him you remember?"

"Not much. I see a lot of people come and go here."

I handed over the discreetly folded fifty and thanked him.

He said, "Thanks. I see him again, I'll see what I can find out. I'll call you if I get anything." He tucked my business card and cash into his shirt pocket, gave me a little salute, and ran off to meet a customer.

Back in my car, I phoned my old friend Franz, the owner of an independent Porsche/Audi garage. I told him I wanted the names of Jaguar garages capable of a high-quality restoration on a 1960s E-Type Jag.

Franz said, "Why do you want to drive a piece of shit like that?"

"It's not for me. I'm trying to locate someone who has a vintage Jag."

"Oh, that's different. Okay, I can think of two places offhand, maybe three."

He consulted his address book and found four candidates. They were in Santa Monica, Costa Mesa, North Hollywood, and Pasadena.

I called Santa Monica first. A mechanic at Lloyd's of Santa Monica told me they did not have the resources for full restoration projects, but he knew where to send me. He gave me the same Costa Mesa and North Hollywood shops Franz had named. North Hollywood was forty miles closer than Costa Mesa, so I headed for the San Fernando Valley and hoped for the best.

Less than a half-hour later, I pulled into Vincent and Ryde Jaguar Specialists on Lankershim Boulevard. A tall blond man in a blue coverall came out of the office, looked at my car, and said in a crisp British accent, "I don't suppose you want that thing serviced here."

"I don't expect you to defile your profession by working on a German car." I handed him my card and showed my PI license. "My name's Jack Salvo. I'm looking for a man who owns a nicely restored, Jaguar E-Type convertible. Black with a tan top. The guy's in his fifties or sixties, and he might have a wide, full beard."

That froze him for a moment. "Let's go into the office."

In his office, he looked closely at my business card and entered a few keystrokes into his computer. He studied his screen and nodded slowly. "Mr. Salvo, my name is John Ryde. I don't normally give out information on my clients, but the character you're talking about is one of the most disagreeable bastards I have ever encountered. He came in earlier this year. I remember it quite well. His 1965 E-Type was beautifully restored from a cosmetic perspective, but someone had bolloxed up the electrical, which isn't hard to do on an early Jaguar." Mr. Ryde pronounced it *Jag-you-are*. "He was incensed that we couldn't diagnose the problem overnight. A really arrogant, unreasonable bastard. In fact,

I shouldn't use that word, because it's disrespectful to all the children of questionable parentage."

He reached into a file cabinet, fished around for a few seconds, and pulled out a work order. He set the yellow sheet on the edge of his desk and said, "Now, if you'll excuse me, I have to see if the engine oil is still draining out of a certain Land Rover." He walked briskly out the door.

I photographed the document. The car was a 1965 Jag E-Type. The name was Lowell Faraday. It gave a telephone number and a West Hollywood PO box. Printed in the license plate field was TEMP. There was no VIN number, no further information.

In the shop area I thanked Mr. Ryde and asked if Faraday had left any other contact information, such as a home address or another phone number.

He said, "Let's see . . . no, that was the only information he left, what you see on the work order, but he did say—I should say he boasted—that he lived up in the hills. He didn't say where in the hills."

I thanked Mr. Ryde, drove around the corner, parked in the shade, and kept the engine and AC running. It was ninety-two in the Valley.

I was anxious to research Lowell Faraday. It wasn't a common name, so I had high hopes. Soon my hopes were dashed. Someone named Lowell Faraday had a PhD in psychology from Georgetown University. Someone named Lowell Faraday attended a security convention in Arlington, Virginia several years ago. No residence, employment, or legal information. The phone number was not in service and could have been assigned to a disposable cell phone. I could work on the post-office box, but I had no guarantee the box was still in his name.

I called Gabriel Van Buren at Western Investigative Services and told him about Faraday and the absence of any information on him. Gabe has a colossal network of informants and PI buddies. He said he would send a message out to his elite mailing list and see what he could dig up.

I headed back over the hill. As I was passing by the Laurel Canyon Country Store, an e-mail came in from Gabe. There was nowhere to pull over, so I dropped down below Sunset, found a side street, and parked.

Gabe hadn't found any immediate contact information on Lowell Faraday, who appeared to be hiding behind corporations, some of them offshore. But there was one intriguing piece of information. About eight years before, Faraday, or someone with the same name and description, hired a PI firm in Long Beach to find his long-lost father, Michael Faraday. The investigators were unable to find Faraday Senior. In my line of work, we get frequent requests like Faraday Junior's, but we usually find the missing person.

Faraday had given a few clues to the Long Beach PI. Michael Faraday abandoned his wife Josephine and son Lowell in 1969 when they were all living in a rented house on Ryerson Avenue in Downey. Prior to skipping town, Faraday Senior had worked as a bartender at the Ebb Tide in Downey and the Executive Lounge in a nearby unnamed city. Mom held an administrative job at the North American Rockwell plant in Downey.

Faraday Junior had given a photo of his father to the Long Beach PI. The faded color photo was of a young man in a white shirt and tie, leaning against a red 1961 Chevrolet Impala. He wore the standard young male smile of the era: a slightly aggressive but good-natured smirk projecting the supreme confidence that his car was faster than your car, our missiles were better than their missiles, and youth would never fade.

If I wanted to follow up on these leads, that would mean driving to Downey and doing some legwork. The Downey information was probably older than the PO box number I had for Faraday, so my next angle would be the West Hollywood post office branch on San Vicente Boulevard.

I went to an art supply store and bought a poster depicting a 1950s C-Type Jaguar in an English hill-climb event. I also got a thirty-inch mailing tube. I addressed the package to Faraday's PO box and printed jaguar heritage as the return address. At five twenty-two, which was eight minutes before closing time, I walked into the West Hollywood post office. After handing the tube across the counter and paying the freight, I sat across the street in my car and waited until they locked the doors.

19

The next morning at eight o'clock sharp, I was again parked in the lot across from the post office. On the passenger seat, sitting in a Styrofoam box, was my half-eaten gourmet breakfast from Stanley's Coffee Shop. Scrambled eggs and hash browns. I kept one eye on the post office, accessed the subscription databases on my iPad, and failed to learn anything new on Sierra McCoy or Lowell Faraday. I gave up on my research and entertained myself by listening to a jazz station and football talk shows.

At ten-forty, a full-bearded man wheeled a tan Jaguar XJ sedan into the post office parking structure. I noted the plate. A minute later the guy walked into the post office. He was fifty or a little older, taller than average. Not fat, but soft-looking, even from across the street. Dark slacks, shiny shoes, long-sleeve white shirt. A little overdressed for Saturday morning errands in West Hollywood.

He came out six minutes later carrying the mailing tube. Before he went back into the parking structure, he stood on the sidewalk and did a slow 360. I slid down in my seat, thinking how lucky I was that his other car was also a Jaguar. That increased the chance he would accept the Jaguar poster as an advertising gimmick from someone he had done business with.

A minute or two later, he drove out of the parking structure and went up San Vicente Boulevard. I followed with two cars between us. The Jag caught the green light at Sunset and turned left. I got the red.

When I got moving again, the Jag had gained two blocks on me. I made up half the distance before a slow-moving van and a double-decker tourist bus maneuvered in front of me, side-by-side. A sheriff's car had come up behind me, so I couldn't pull a stunt-driving display to get around the sluggards in front. In the distance, Faraday peeled off onto a side road along the lower edge of Trousdale Estates, the most northerly neighborhood in the city of Beverly Hills. I got stuck at another red light. The Jag was gone. I wondered how I blew that one. I could only pull the oversize-package-at-the-post-office routine once. At least I got a quick look at the character known as Lowell Faraday.

I sat at the curb muttering to myself and called a DMV contact who could run the Jaguar's plate. The Jag's registered owner was one of the same corporate names Gabriel Van Buren had found for Lowell Faraday. I could pursue the corporate angles, but it would take time and money. I turned to the information Gabe had dug up on Faraday's father and found no current phone listings for Dad's previous employers, the Ebb Tide and the Executive Lounge. The old Faraday residence address on Ryerson Avenue in Downey also came up blank. An Internet map showed a large apartment building covering the site of the Faraday house and probably two or three other old houses that had been demolished. It was only eleven o'clock, and I didn't have to be anywhere until my date with Darcey at seven. Plenty of time for a trip down the freeway.

When you want to go from L.A. to Downey, you take the southbound Santa Ana Freeway and turn right fifteen miles before Disneyland. I dropped off the freeway at Paramount Boulevard and worked my way through the neatly trimmed suburbs of Downey, a burg that goes out of its way to preserve flagrant normalcy. The city is too bland for me, but there's something refreshing about the place. I went out of my way to cruise past the world's oldest surviving McDonald's restaurant at Lakewood and Florence, where the employees wear authentic 1950s McDonald's uniforms.

I parked at the Downey City Library and found the reference department. Librarians are one of my favorite categories of humanity. Their English is fluent, they are not inclined to recklessly split their infinitives, and some have been known to read books. A woman in her fifties, maybe a low-mileage sixty, with an honest face and a thick middle, was seated behind the reference desk. She wore a high-collared dress of enough material to frock all five Best Actress nominees. The nameplate on the desk said Ms. Patterson.

I said, "Ms. Patterson, I'm looking for a *National Enquirer* article on methodological skepticism."

She had a cool, dry delivery. "You might have better luck with Descartes's *Discourse on the Method*. Can I help you with anything else?"

That's what I like about librarians.

I said, "Do you have Downey telephone directories and city directories from 1967 to 1971?"

She swiveled around, pulled three books from a low shelf, and said, "We have phone books for 1968 and '70. We have a city directory dated 1970 to '71. The volumes are pretty old, so please handle them carefully."

Another customer edged up to the desk, so I thanked Ms. Patterson and took the directories to the nearest table. I found Michael Faraday at the Ryerson address in 1968 and his wife Josephine Faraday at the same address in later years. All the directories showed the Ebb Tide as a tavern on Imperial Highway in Downey. No listing for the Executive Lounge.

I returned the books to Ms. Patterson. She carefully placed them back in their assigned shelf spaces and said, "Are you looking for anything else?"

I gave her my Clark Gable leer. "Are you familiar with the bars around here?"

She fiddled with the top button of her dress, as though she were worried it might be undone, and consequently she would be compelled to scream. "I don't go to bars."

"I'll bet I could talk you into it."

"What kind of work do you do?"

"I'm a philosophy professor."

"Are you certain you're not an attorney's investigator?"

"I'm absolutely certain."

"I don't remember a philosopher who arrived at absolute certainty so quickly."

"Descartes made pretty good time with *cogito ergo sum*."

Her deadpan response: "I'll bet you make pretty good time yourself."

"I'm trying to find someone who worked at the Ebb Tide in Downey and at another bar called the Executive Lounge, which was in a nearby city. I don't know which city, just that it was probably nearby. He worked in those places more than forty years ago. Neither bar is still in business, but I thought if I could find an existing bar in this area that goes back forty years, a bartender or an older patron might remember the Executive Lounge."

"You're an attorney's investigator."

I gave her my card. "I work for myself."

She read the card quickly and said, "I don't recall a bar named the Executive Lounge. The Ebb Tide was down on Imperial Highway, east of Lakewood Boulevard. It was torn down back in the nineties. Hang on for a second." She turned to her computer and typed out the names of four bars: Zoom Zoom Room, Lifted Spirits, Dive Inn, and KO Club. She looked up their addresses, typed them into the document, and printed it.

She handed me the sheet. "None of these establishments are in the city of Downey, but they are all nearby. I certainly don't have any firsthand experience at these places, you understand, but I have lived in the area my entire life, and I have heard many, many tales. Most of them are probably true. I believe these taverns have been in business continuously for some time." She looked at my business card again and gave me an unhurried, cool smile. "We get so few philosophers in the Reference Department, drop in again some time."

My next stop was a quiet restaurant attached to a bowling alley. My next task involved a chicken salad sandwich on rye, iced tea, and apple pie. On my iPad, I made up a six-pack of photos that included Michael Faraday. I paid the check and drove out of the city of Downey into less decorous terrain.

The Zoom Zoom Room was a dingy brown box topped with a shingled mansard roof. It sat behind an eroded parking lot half-full of older cars and trucks. The sign on the roof announced dancing girls and depicted an impossibly buxom female silhouetted against a jet airliner. The symbolism escaped me.

I left my car at the edge of the parking lot, positioning it for a quick getaway, and walked toward the bar. "Shotgun" by Junior Walker pounded through the open door. Inside, the stench of beer and sweat fought the cigarette smoke to a draw. I took a stool near the middle of the bar. The all-male crowd cheered a tall, top-heavy blonde clad in a few square inches of fabric. She staggered around the stage and heaved herself into a series of gyrations unrelated to the music.

The patrons leered knowingly at the dancer, shared the leers among themselves, and tried to assume virile postures implying their intimacy with her. The music ended, and she stood and received applause. She collected her gratuities and sashayed through the curtain to the dressing room behind the stage. A big tipper at the table closest to the dressing room leaned over to see what he could see through the partially pulled curtain.

None of the patrons looked old enough to have known Faraday Senior. The bartender looked to be fifty-something, and he had the detached manner of an owner or manager. It turned out he was the co-owner, and he had never heard of the Executive Lounge.

The next tavern on Ms. Patterson's list was Lifted Spirits, whose redbrick front stood between a graffiti-covered, boarded-up motel and an ugly beauty shop. I parked under a neon sign depicting a tilted martini glass and its sparkling, level contents. Inside, I took a stool near the door and let my eyes adjust to the darkness. The red vinyl on the bar stools wasn't new, but neither was it in need of replacement.

The whole place had a nicely broken-in feel. A pretty young woman behind the bar wore skin-tight black pants, a pink satin halter top, and too much makeup. Her hair was bleached to the point of damage. Her blue, unyielding eyes reflected other kinds of damage. A barrel-shaped guy in the back room kept an eye on me.

Two couples and two individual men sat quietly in booths along the opposite wall. A clean-shaven geezer with a threadbare cowboy shirt and towering white pompadour was alone at the middle of the bar, mumbling into a glass.

I bought a beer and gave the girl a twenty-dollar tip.

She said, "Wow, thanks. Hi. My name is Carol."

I asked, "Is there anyone around here who goes back thirty or forty years?"

She shifted her eyes toward the old guy at the bar and grumbled, "Clarence."

The geezer leaned at her and slurred, "Hey, Carol. When are we gonna go out?" With his elbow, he absently knocked his glass off the bar, shattering it on the floor. He jumped off his stool and shrieked, "What the fuck was that?"

Laughter broke out from the booths. Carol ran off and grabbed a broom, dustpan, and paper towels. The guy in the back room came out and glared. Clarence acknowledged the glare with a twisted frown and shuffled out the door.

I followed him outside and asked, "You been hanging out here a long time?"

"Thirty years. Off and on. Hell, *more* than thirty years."

"You ever hear of a bar called the Executive Lounge?"

Without hesitation, he said, "Some Place. Now they call it Some Place. That's the name of it now." He pointed in the direction opposite Rosecrans Avenue. "Over on Rosecrans. Used to be the Executive Lounge. Got kicked outta there once, my younger days, for punchin' a guy in the nose. He made a crack, and I didn't have no choice but to whack him." Clarence showed a wide grin.

I showed a fifty-dollar bill. "You ever hear of a bartender named Mike Faraday? He worked at the Executive Lounge until 1969 and a place in Downey called the Ebb Tide before that."

He gazed at the cash and spoke slowly. "Mike Faraday . . . hmmm . . . can't say as I remember anyone by that name. I drove past the Ebb Tide a few times, never did any drinkin' there. It ain't even there anymore, I don't think. Think they tore it down." He continued to gaze at the cash.

I pressed the fifty into his hand. "You're an honest man, Clarence. Diogenes would be proud of you."

"Who the fuck is Diogenes?"

"An ancient Greek philosopher. He used to piss on people he didn't like."

"Hell, I wouldn't mind doin' that. I ought to be a damn philosopher." I left Clarence grinning on the sidewalk and took Rosecrans Avenue in a westerly direction, into the grayish afternoon sun. Near Bellflower Boulevard an indigo-blue neon sign appeared in the dirty gray sky. The sign said, SOME PLACE.

Inside, politeness prevailed. Two young guys in cheap suits shared a pitcher of beer and watched the Dodgers and Rockies on the TV over the bar; when the Dodgers stranded the potential game-winner at third, the boys kept their profanity at a low volume. Four sensible-looking young women sat in a booth and drank brightly colored cocktails; the girls would never be glamorous, and it would never bother them. A senior couple nursed their drinks; the gentleman wore a tie.

The bartender was a slight fellow, about fifty, with a thin mustache like the ones popular eighty years ago. I showed him my ID and told him what I wanted. He listened quietly, went to the other side of the room, and made a phone call. Then he came back and politely extracted a hundred dollars from me.

He started drawing a map on a cocktail napkin and said, "This guy Stanley Herrington was a regular customer back before I was here, when Mike Faraday was a bartender, back when they called it the Executive Lounge. Stanley's younger brother was in the same class as Lowell Faraday at Downey High. Stanley says come on over. His brother will be there too. They want a hundred dollars each, but he says they can fill your ear about Mike Faraday and his son, Lowell." He handed me the map. "They're over in Paramount in a trailer park, a mile from here, maybe a mile and a half."

20

idled down the Tahitian Mobile Home Park's thinly paved road-way, obeyed the hand-painted 5 MPH signs, and stopped next to the double-wide mobile home occupying space number forty-one.

Stanley and Gary Herrington stood on a concrete walkway, hoisting their beer cans, leaning back to balance the cantilever effect of their distended stomachs. They wore gigantic baggy shorts that fell below their knees and long, baggy T-shirts. Gray-haired, red-faced, blue-collar workers who had hoisted a few too many.

I got out carrying my briefcase, and we introduced ourselves. They invited me inside and directed me to a chair.

Stanley, the older one, grunted, "How 'bout a beer?"

I said, "Thanks anyway. I have to drive."

"Yeah, the goddam law really goes too far these days. They ain't got nothin' better to do than hassle a guy for havin' a couple drinks and drivin' home. I used to drive shit-faced all the time, never had a problem, just slowed down a little bit. Don't really drink anymore anyway, just beer."

The obligatory small talk took a few minutes. Stanley was divorced and retired after thirty years with the gas company. His ex got the house, and he got a trailer. Gary had worked in a maintenance job for the city of Downey for more than twenty years. He and his girlfriend were shacked up in an apartment on Tweedy Boulevard in South Gate. Stanley wanted to know what kind of gun I used. I told him about my two Smith & Wesson .38s, and my Glock G19, and why I usually prefer revolvers to automatics. Gary wanted to know what kind of girls a private detective could get. I told him I had been wondering the same thing.

Stanley spoke in a more businesslike tone. "I knew Mike Faraday the last year he was around, and Gary went to Downey High with his son Lowell. We can give you the full story."

They waited for the money.

I showed a pair of hundred-dollar bills and said, "Before we get serious, I want to make sure we're talking about the same person." I pulled out my iPad and brought up the photo display I had put together at the bowling alley restaurant.

Stanley said "six-pack," as though he were quite familiar with the police slang for the photo lineup. He stabbed his finger at Mike Faraday. The two hundred dollar-bills grew little wings and flew to the smiling brothers.

Stanley leaned over and looked more closely at the Faraday photo. He broke into an easy smile, chuckled, and leaned back into his chair. "Yeah, I knew Mike. Funniest son-of-a-bitch I ever knew. Makes me laugh just lookin' at his picture. Hell of a nice guy. First time

I went to the Executive Lounge was the second I turned twenty-one. Me and a couple of older friends were waitin' at the door right before midnight. I'll never forget that night. The clock hit twelve, I turned twenty-one, and we went in and got plowed under. Mike Faraday was the bartender. He told us jokes, mostly farmer's daughter jokes, until closing time. Man, he knew a million of 'em, and we laughed our asses off. Well, that was the first time I went there, and after that, I was a regular for almost forty years."

I said, "What happened to Faraday?"

"Just vanished one day in . . . let's see . . . had to be '69, 'cause it was right before I got drafted. Had to be September '69. He just didn't show up for work one day."

"Did you ever see his wife?"

"Never did, and he never talked about her in front of me. Everyone said she wasn't bad looking, but they said she was a bitch on big red wheels."

"Anyone ever see Mike again?"

"No, but some guy . . . must have been around 1985 or '86 . . . this old guy used to hang out at the bar, and I heard him tellin' the bartender he heard Mike was in Florida, and now he was sellin' real estate."

"Do you know the name of the old guy or the bartender?"

"Bartender's been dead a long time. Harry Santos. The old guy's name was Chip or Clint . . . or somethin' like that. Haven't seen him since that time. He was pretty old, drank like a fish and smoked like a chimney. Gotta be dead now."

"You ever see the son, Lowell Faraday?"

"Don't remember him. That's Gary's department. Knew him all through high school."

Gary took a hard swig and ran the back of his hand across his mouth. "Lowell was a weird fucker. Always wore a tie whenever there was half a reason to, kissed all the teachers' asses. Here's one thing that's pretty damn funny. This chick Janny Kincaid worked at the New Avenue movie theater, sellin' popcorn, takin' tickets. One of the cutest girls in school. She used to tell about Lowell comin' in to see this James Bond movie. The movie ran the whole month. She said Lowell come in to see it day after day, same movie. And every time he came out of the movie, he always had this real serious look on his face, like he thought he was James Bond. Janny used to do this imitation of him walkin' through the lobby like he had a stick up his ass, and she did it so funny, you could piss your pants. "

Gary's face lit up. "Another thing was his car, this dark green Plymouth Valiant, 1960 or '61."

Stanley interjected: "One of the butt-ugliest cars ever made."

Gary looked at his brother and nodded his solemn agreement. "Anyway, when Lowell showed up with it, it had some pretty bad dents, so he tried to fix 'em with Bondo and spray paint. Looked like he put the Bondo on with a trowel. Bumpy and wavy, and the paint didn't match. Some guy asked him what color his car was, and he says, 'British racing green.' Well, Janny heard about that, and she said he probably thought in his own head he was drivin' a Aston Martin. Then she started callin' him James Bondo. Then everybody did. Whenever Faraday showed up, the kids would say, 'Bondo . . . *James* Bondo.'"

Gary chuckled to himself, chugged the rest of his beer, leaned halfway out of his chair, and tossed the can into a plastic trash bin. He leaned back and said, "Lowell was always findin' some way to get himself in a tight spot. The first day our senior year, this girl caught him lookin' down her blouse in the library.

Babette Bigelow. Second-biggest tits in the school. Well anyway, Babette tells her boyfriend, and he catches Lowell in the parking lot and pounds on him, so the next day he has this big black eye. And I mean it was a fuckin' shiner. He had a lotta grief in high school, but he brought most of it on himself."

I said, "Did either of you guys ever see Lowell after high school?"

They looked at each other and shook their heads in unison.

I was about to say farewell and thanks when a wide leer suddenly spread across Gary's face. "One more thing! Haven't thought about this for years. Right outta high school, Lowell went to work at Norwalk State Hospital. He was an orderly or in the kitchen or some other shit job. That's the nuthouse over on Bloomfield. Got his ass fired for screwin' around with some retarded inmate girl. They accused Lowell of it, and he just denied everything and quit. Our dad was friends with some of the security over at the hospital, and he heard the whole story. Lowell was lucky the girl didn't get knocked up, and they didn't have DNA back in those days, or his ass woulda been grass."

I thanked the brothers, declined another offer of beer, and headed back toward Santa Monica. My visit to the Tahitian Mobile Home Park had been entertaining in a deviant sort of way, but I didn't think it was going to get me anywhere.

On the way home I went to the car wash and picked up dry cleaning and groceries. While knocking off the errands, I plotted my strategy for the big date with Darcey Mathis.

21

Darcey lived on one of the short blocks that dead-end at the western edge of Fox Studios. She had the eastern half of a nicely preserved two-story Spanish duplex. A narrow walkway separated Darcey's apartment from the studio wall. A driveway ran along the other side to the garages in back.

There's a special moment the first time you arrive at the door of an attractive woman, especially when you're invited. It's in the same category as the first sip of a well-mixed cocktail when you're young and alcohol is new, or the first touching of hands on a date. I knew Darcey was a liar and a thief, and the only reason she invited me was to control me, but I got that passing moment. It didn't last long.

I was reaching for the doorbell when Darcey's voice sounded from the distance. I turned and saw her running diagonally across the street, toward me. Gray running shorts, gray-and-white top, hair tied back.

She skidded to a stop, rested her hands on her knees, and tried to catch her breath. "I was into . . . my run when I realized . . . we said seven o'clock, not eight. I am so sorry . . . I can't believe I screwed up like that. I'm famous for always showing up on time."

I said, "I'm sure we can figure out a Plan B."

She straightened up and produced a pair of house keys from a little pocket. She unlocked the dead bolt and door handle, and we went inside. The Band-Aid on my cheek caught her attention. "Your face. What happened?"

"A girl hit me."

Sierra might have called her and told her about the fight by her swimming pool. No way for me to know.

Darcey smirked politely and let the subject pass. "Well, by the time I get cleaned up, it'll be too late for the Del Sol Grill and a movie, so we could eat at a deli or somewhere and come back and see what's on TV."

"That's my idea of a perfect evening. I like to stay home and watch TV." I looked around the living room. "I like your place. I want to see the rest of it." I also wanted to see the best way to sneak in.

She held her arms out wide. "Help yourself. Look around. I'll follow and provide commentary."

Strolling through the living room, I said, "I like the thick ceiling beams, arched passageways, and the way all the Spanish trim contrasts with the modern furniture." That was an exaggeration, but it helped maintain a genial mood.

Upstairs, I headed straight for the home office. It contained the usual items: bookshelves, desk, and computer. There was one unusual piece, a four-drawer file cabinet secured by a military-style metal locking bar and padlock. I didn't know if it would take thirty seconds or five minutes, but I knew I could pick the lock.

Across the hall from the office, a freestanding full-length mirror stood just inside the bathroom door. It was mounted in an art nouveau frame with a peacock at the top, blending into floral motifs down the sides. I stepped into the bathroom and said, "Nice mirror. Is it vintage?"

"That's what my decorator friend says. I got it for twenty bucks at a yard sale."

I said, "That was grand theft," and ran my hand across the pastel-yellow and black wall tile until I was at the corner of the L-shaped room. There was a glass-enclosed shower/tub combo around the corner.

The bedroom was furnished with a platform bed, dressing table, and armoire. A walk-in closet took the length of the west wall. From a north-facing window, I looked down at a concrete walkway between the apartment and the garages.

I went back to the office and started checking out the titles in the bookcase.

Darcey followed and said, "Okay, I have to shower and get ready. Can you entertain yourself?"

"I need to cancel the dinner reservation, and then I can review your books. I like books."

"I will expect a book report." She marched directly across the hall, closed the bathroom door, and started the shower.

I was standing in the middle of the room, phoning to cancel our reservation, when the bathroom doorknob clicked. I looked up in time to see Darcey's hand pushing the bathroom door partway open. The freestanding mirror briefly displayed her bare ass as she rounded the corner and vanished. But she didn't vanish. The mirrored door on the medicine cabinet hung open at the exact angle needed to provide a double-carom reflection of Darcey in the shower.

The voice from my phone said, "Del Sol Grill."

The voice from the shower said, "So where do we go eat?"

I sputtered the cancelation into the phone, stepped into the hallway, and watched Darcey slowly rotate under the water. I spoke loud enough for her to hear. "We could go to Nate'n Al or Junior's."

"I haven't been to Nate'n Al for a long time. I like that place."

I somehow managed to speak calmly. "Sounds good to me. I'm going to work on my book report."

It wasn't clear whether the peep show was a setup or an accident. I didn't think much was accidental in the world of Darcey Mathis. Before picking the padlock on the file cabinet, I had to make sure Darcey didn't have any tattoos, so I went back to the hall and watched her rotate another 360. In an investigation, tattoos can turn out to be vital clues.

The upper three drawers of the file cabinet had the usual stuff: receipts, taxes, bank and credit card statements, canceled checks, insurance policies. The bottom drawer was more densely packed: instruction manuals for electronic devices, outdated catalogs, and cookbooks. Behind all that was a packaged "burner" cell phone. The sort of phone one might use for clandestine activities. The sort of phone I frequently use. Under the phone was a maroon-colored magnetic tape cartridge, about four inches square. No labels. The sort of data storage used in serious computer systems, as opposed to Darcey's home system, which had no attached tape drive. I photographed the tape on both sides, replaced everything in the drawer, and relocked the cabinet.

The computer was password protected. The desk was locked. The bedroom and closet showed nothing more than the usual female surplus of clothing, grooming items, and bric-a-brac.

The shower stopped, and I remembered my obligation to provide a book report. I took a chair by the bookcase and selected an oversized art book. A comical shriek sounded from deep in the bathroom, then bare feet slapping on the tile. I kept my face behind the book. The bathroom door slammed shut. If Darcey was pretending to be surprised by her indiscretion, she was doing a good job of it.

A minute later she came out wearing a white cotton robe, toweling her hair.

I peered over the top of my book. "What do you want to know about Maxfield Parrish, the Early Renaissance painter?"

"Maxfield Parrish is *not* a Renaissance . . ." She caught herself before she took all the bait, giggled all the way into the bathroom, and closed the door.

Darcey's hair dryer started, and I trotted downstairs. There was a direct line of sight from the front door to neighbors across the street. Not a good entry point for my next visit. The back door, off the service porch, had the usual handle lock and deadbolt. It also had an oversized bolt mounted on the inside. Not a good entry point. I checked out the wood-frame window over the washer and dryer—no line of sight to any neighbors or to the front sidewalk—burglar's delight. Using my Swiss Army Knife, I partially loosened the window's security lock and the window screen's hook-and-eye. I also enlarged a small cut in the screen by a fraction of an inch.

The back door led to the garages. A magnetized GPS tracking device went from my coat pocket to the underside of Darcey's BMW. The transmitter battery would last three days.

A half hour later, Darcey and I were sitting in a booth at Nate'n Al in Beverly Hills with our noses in our menus. She ordered a hot pastrami sandwich. I went with the tuna melt.

Darcey gave me a skeptical look. "Okay, I'm dying to hear how you go from philosophy professor to private detective. What's the real story?"

I told her my tale. At the age of twenty, I transferred from Coast College to Long Beach State as a criminal justice major, with the intention of going into law enforcement. The history class I wanted was closed, so I had to take Critical Reasoning 100. The instructor Dr. Lambert changed my world view and my career path. I changed my major to philosophy and planned to become a college professor.

After Long Beach, I entered the graduate philosophy program at UCLA. During the first two years, I earned a master's degree and made some progress toward a PhD. I especially enjoyed substitute teaching in lower-division courses; the students and I got along famously. During my third year, things started to go sideways. I wanted to write an introductory philosophy textbook, but the faculty wanted me to write arcane articles for obscure journals. Before being kicked out of school, I completed the first draft of the introductory text I had in mind.

Darcey asked, "Did your book get published?"

"It's currently in its second printing."

"Is this a joke?"

"We can go to Barnes & Noble, and I'll buy you a copy. I'll even sign it."

"Please tell me the name of your book." She took a drink of water.

"*Philosophy for Morons.*"

She almost spewed on the table and wiped her mouth with a napkin. "I'll believe your book when I see it."

She then gave me her version of the Darcey Mathis story. She earned a degree in theater arts from Illinois State, then entered their MBA program. Severe boredom set in, so she dropped out of school after a year, moved to L.A., joined an acting workshop, and worked as a cocktail waitress. After a year and a half of going nowhere in Hollywood, she took a job at Culver Aerospace as a programmer trainee. She transferred her school credits from Illinois State to USC, finished her MBA, and her career at Culver took off.

Next, she brought up the Oswald Pace matter and the "newly discovered" 2006 embezzlement. She asked if I had learned anything new.

I said, "I think I found the person who laundered the money in the older embezzlement. An actress named Sierra McCoy. She used to be on a show called *Heartbreakers*. You probably never heard of her. She has a house up in the Hollywood Hills. The case is so old, I don't think law enforcement is going to be motivated to pursue it. And this girl is a tough muffin. I think the case is basically over."

She cut a piece off her sandwich, daintily using her knife and fork, and started to push the pastrami in the direction of her mouth, then changed her mind and set the fork on her plate. "I don't think the company will be inclined to pursue any of this much further, but we will want to get a written report from you, and I'm sure I can get the final approval to raise your fee. Your efforts have gone way beyond the original statement of work."

We finished our sandwiches, ordered cheesecake, and discussed our favorite movies. Then we went to a bookstore and found *Philosophy for Morons* by Jackson K. Salvo. Darcey thumbed through the pages and found the section on Ludwig Wittgenstein. She scanned through and said, "That's interesting. He says most philosophical statements are meaningless."

"That's his early work. He softened his position later."

She closed the book smartly and said, "I'm going to study this diligently, and the next time we get together, you can test me."

A few minutes later we were sitting on the sofa in her living room watching the television, holding crystal glasses half-filled with red wine. We ran through all the channels and concluded there wasn't much on. We ended up watching a sitcom in which histrionic women failed to communicate with bumbling men, a high-speed freeway chase, and UFO abductees' stories.

Darcey was a most agreeable date. She was content with the inexpensive meal. She expressed admiration for my philosophy background. She kept me laughing with her impersonations of UFO abductees who claimed they were sexually abused by aliens. She more-or-less accidentally rubbed her breasts on me a few times.

Around eleven-forty, she looked at her watch. "Tomorrow morning, I have to meet some girlfriends in Redondo Beach. I know I got us started late and screwed up the whole evening. We should reschedule and try it again." A few minutes later, she eased me out the door and gave me a quick kiss on the cheek. "Let's talk during the week about a raincheck."

22

woke up Sunday morning staring at the ceiling, trying to remember which football games were going to be on TV. I pulled on a robe, staggered down the hall, and looked around for the remote control. It was on the dining table, next to my shirt-pocket camera, which held the images of the mysterious tape cassette in Darcey's file cabinet.

I passed on the football schedule and reviewed the photos. The cassette was manufactured by TDK. Printed on the side was LTO Ultrium 5. A little research confirmed my suspicion that LTO-5 cassettes were commonly used in commercial computer systems, almost never in home systems.

I was curious about Darcey's tape. The most direct way to satisfy my curiosity would be to steal it, but I would need to leave a blank tape in its place. I called around and found a store in Culver City that was open on Sunday and had the same mag tape in stock.

At ten-twenty a phone call came in. A tender young voice said, "Jackson, this is Sierra McCoy. I was wondering if we could get together and talk."

"We're talking now."

"I really don't want to discuss personal matters on the phone. If you could be at my place at nine this evening, I think we could get a lot straightened out."

"Can you make it any earlier?"

"I'm sorry, but my day is jammed. I have business appointments in the afternoon and early evening."

"What kind of business are you in?"

"I manage my rental property, and I teach acting."

I doubted that Sierra suffered from an exhausting work schedule, but I wanted the goods on Darcey. I said, "Casual dress, I presume."

"Remember? Informality is your middle name."

"How do I know Byron and his friends won't be waiting for me?"

"You have my word. Will I see you at nine?"

"Nine o'clock sharp."

I hung up and laughed at myself. Maybe I should bring her flowers. After all, she only hit me once.

I hadn't been to the gym since Monday night. That made me feel edgy. An hour later I was pumping iron, feeling much better. After the gym, I drove to the computer store in Culver City and bought three maroon-colored LTO-5 tape cassettes. Eventually, I had the luxury of going home, putting my feet up, and watching football.

At six o'clock, my GPS system showed that Darcey's car had stayed home all day, except for one short trip to the Ralphs grocery store near her home. No visit with the girlfriends in Redondo Beach.

At eight twenty-five I rolled out of my parking garage and waved to the security guard.

23

stood high in the Hollywood Hills, taking in the enchanting spectacle of Los Angeles at night. A dour brown blanket of smog tucked in at the base of the hills and stretched to a blurry horizon. The sea of city lights shimmered through the pollutants like glitter in a wet latrine.

There was no light coming from Sierra's house, nor did the streetlight at the turnaround do much in the way of illumination. There wasn't much to hear, except for a distant car gliding down the canyon and one lonely chirping bird.

No parked cars were in sight, but that was no guarantee that Byron and his friends weren't inside. My Smith & Wesson revolver normally rides in my supply bag in the trunk. For this occasion, the holstered gun went onto my belt. It's hard to get a concealed-carry permit in L.A. I try to use mine judiciously.

I leaned on the doorbell and listened to the chime. No response. I hit it again. No response. The door was locked. On the other side of the house, I found the garage locked. A downhill pathway led me to the swimming pool. My penlight led me past the pool and up the flagstone steps. Channel 11 News was visible and barely audible through the south-facing windows. The television was the only source of light or sound in the house. The back doorknob turned easily, so I eased my way inside and switched on a light. Three kitchen drawers were pulled out. That wasn't right. Sierra wouldn't tolerate a disorderly kitchen. My .38 filled my right hand.

The service porch held nothing of interest. Off the porch was a bathroom that had doors on both sides. I walked through the kitchen and dining area and ended up at the far end of the living room, by the fireplace and television. I muted the sound and worked my way through the Victorian furniture and into the central hallway.

The first door was on the right, leading to the home office. I pointed my penlight at the desktop, on which a pile of documents had been dumped. The desk drawers and file cabinets had been gone through, and a few papers were on the floor.

Across from the office was the hallway door to the bathroom off the service porch. The guest bedroom was farther down the hall, on the right. A bare mattress sat on a box spring and a metal frame. Folded bedding and pillows, sealed in plastic, were stacked on closet shelves. One empty dresser drawer hung open.

The final door would lead to the master bedroom. I went in low, my penlight held high. The light swept across the room and flashed back from a mirror. I stood up straight and tried to flip the light switch with my left elbow. It was a dimmer switch that did not wish to be flipped. I worked the slide control, then everything became quite vivid.

A massive Victorian Gothic four-poster bed dominated the room. The grandiose wooden canopy, elaborate headboard, and intricately carved quatrefoils and arches merged into one startling image. Even more startling was the naked female flat on her back in the tangled, bright white sheets. A white pillowcase was pulled over most of her head. Her thin, muscular legs terminated in blue toenails. She had ceased all motion, including breathing.

I stood motionless, holding my breath. The body needed to be checked for signs of life, but my trigger finger told me to clear the room first. I glided toward the two doors on the far wall.

When I passed the foot of the bed, something caught my eye and yanked my head to the left. A wooden ice pick handle extended from the body's left ear. I froze again and stayed frozen longer than I wanted.

In the walk-in closet, most of Sierra's wardrobe was in garment bags, boxes, drawers, and plastic from the dry-cleaner. Purses had been opened and dropped on the floor. Two drawers hung open, and a few pairs of rolled socks were scattered around.

In the bathroom, cabinet doors and drawers were open. A box of Q-tips, a pink bar of soap, and a pink razor were on the floor. I didn't want to go back to the body on the bed, but I knew I had to.

I pressed two fingers on her carotid artery, at the back of her jawbone. No pulse. She wasn't exactly cold, nor was she warm. No visible abrasions, scratches, or other marks. The ice pick handle angled toward her shoulder, as though the tip of the blade sought the center of her brain.

In the kitchen I found a dish towel embroidered with a schmaltzy dog motif. I used it on the surfaces I had touched: Sierra's neck, light switches, television remote, doorknobs, gate handle, and doorbell.

Back at the car, I stowed my .38 and the dish towel in my supply bag. My plan was to idle down Sierra's street and not be noticed by anyone. Instead of dropping all the way down Doheny, I would cut over past Blue Jay Way and take Sunset Plaza down to the Strip. That would minimize the chance of my being seen by Sierra's neighbors.

I was trying to slide into my car when a Golden Retriever galloped toward me, wagging its tail and demanding to be petted. Next was an older woman in a leopard-print jumpsuit and high heels. She waved an empty dog poop bag at me and bleated, "It's all right. He won't hurt you."

I petted the dog, chatted briefly about nothing, and waited for them to leave. So much for my getaway strategy.

I called Rocky Platt, an LAPD detective I've known for a long time, and told him what happened.

He said, "Just sit tight, Socrates. The cavalry is on the way."

Rocky is one of the more important people in my life, sort of like a cool uncle who lets you get away with a reasonable number of excesses, but you know not to push it too far.

On a hot August night in 1986, two West Los Angeles patrol officers responded to a silent alarm at a drugstore on Pico Boulevard. Rocky, a probationer in his sixth month as an LAPD patrolman, took the front. My father Karl Salvo, a five-year veteran, had the back. Rocky heard a gunshot, ran to the back, and found my father down in the alley. Rocky heard running footsteps down a concrete pathway that connected with the next street. He could have chased the footsteps, but he cut away my father's shirt and pressed his hand on the wound until the paramedics arrived.

LAPD scoured the neighborhood and interviewed the residents, but they got no witnesses. The only physical evidence was the bullet removed from my father's corpse. The investigation concluded Rocky did everything right, but to this day he still hears those running footsteps.

When I was taking law enforcement classes at Long Beach State, I built a file on the case. Rocky snuck me copies of documents from the detectives' murder book. I went back to the scene of the crime and interviewed some of the neighbors. Every year or so, I update my background checks on possible suspects and witnesses. It's no coincidence that my office is near the spot where my father was murdered. When I park behind my office and get out of my car, sometimes I hear those running feet.

Less than ten minutes after I called Rocky, two Hollywood Division detectives arrived in an unmarked car followed by a black-and-white. I stood by the front of my car. My driver's license, private investigator's license, and business card were on the hood.

Detective Williams was in charge. He was a hulking, weathered redhead with an unnerving smirk and severely scuffed shoes. The smirk was more like a continuous dirty look. His partner was Detective Kelly, a middle-aged woman with a sweet voice and a broad smile. I could have taken her for a Sunday school teacher until she frisked me with her eyes. They looked at my licenses and kept the business card.

More police vehicles arrived, including another large, dark sedan and another pair of detectives. The senior of the two was a tall, gray-haired black guy; light on his feet, considering his size. The other was a younger man with a lean, earnest face. He seemed too young to be a detective.

I told the cops what was waiting for them in the bedroom. Williams and the tall detective immediately went to the far side of the garage and took the same path I had taken.

Kelly asked if I had any weapons. I told her my .38 was in the trunk and showed my concealed-carry permit. The younger detective found the revolver and determined it had not been fired recently. He unloaded the gun and put it on the hood of my car, thoughtfully using the kitchen towel I had swiped, to protect the paint. I hoped the cops wouldn't link the towel to Sierra's kitchen. Kelly checked my car's registration and insurance certificate. She noted my car's VIN number, license plate, and gas and odometer readings.

Williams came out the front door, conferred privately with Kelly, and walked back inside, leaving the front door open.

Kelly was the first to question me. I gave her a sanitized summary of the investigations I had performed for Culver Aerospace. I told her Sierra had called me earlier in the day and suggested a nine o'clock meeting at her house. I described my entry to the house, the moderate ransacking, and the corpse. I forgot to mention my wiping my prints and trying to sneak away from the murder scene. She and the younger detective listened without interrupting.

Kelly tossed me a couple of softball questions about my PI business. Abruptly, she shifted gears and said, "Did you kill her?"

"No, I didn't. I had no motive, and I had no opportunity."

"You were here. You had all kinds of opportunity."

"The body was already cool when I got here. A security guard saw me leave my condo a half hour before I arrived here. The coroner will tell you she died before I left home."

"We won't know that until we get the time of death and confirm your alibi."

I gave her the name of the security guard, and she wrote it in her little notebook.

They double-teamed me, asking me to repeat sections of my timeline out of order, trying to bust my story. They thought they were on to something when I told them about my fight with Byron and Sierra. The detectives suggested I might want some payback. They were starting to run out of steam when Rocky Platt appeared.

On first impression, Rocky doesn't come across as a tough guy. He saves it for when he needs it. He smiles easily and has no swagger. He's five-eleven and one-eighty, square face, and an off-center nose, the nose from being kicked by a purse snatcher. In earlier times LAPD could do pretty much whatever they wanted with someone who had assaulted a cop. Rocky had it easy compared to the purse snatcher.

Rocky showed his badge and introduced himself to the Hollywood Division detectives. He turned to me. "So, what happened?"

I gave him a brief version of what I had told the detectives.

Rocky said to Kelly, matter-of-fact, "What he says is what happened. He might have left out something that would hurt his client, but he's not involved in any murder."

Detective Kelly said, "How long have you known Mr. Salvo?"

"Since he was shitting yellow." Rocky saw Williams standing by the front porch and yelled, "Hey, Smiley!"

Williams waved Rocky into the house. Detective Kelly and I stood silent, watching the arriving crime scene vehicles and personnel.

A uniform came out of the house, a small Asian girl whose nameplate said PING. She pointed at me and spoke to Kelly. "Detective Williams wants to see him."

Officer Ping led me into the house and warned me not to touch anything. I followed her, and Kelly followed me. A photographer came out of the master bedroom, and we all turned sideways, so we could pass in the hall.

Williams stood on the near side of the bed, Rocky on the far side. A technician wearing gloves was on his hands and knees in the closet. Someone had pulled the pillowcase up far enough to reveal most of Sierra's face. Her eyes were wide-open, the pupils pointed upward and in different directions. Her mouth was slightly open, almost sensuously. My stomach started to shinny up my esophagus.

Williams said, "Rocky says you're a bright boy, so you got any bright ideas?"

I kept my eyes off Sierra and said, "It obviously looks like a home-invasion robbery, but it might be too tidy. The place isn't torn up. The bathroom doesn't look like it was on the receiving end of a frenzied search for pills. If I had to bet money, I would say robbery, but I would keep an open mind."

Williams said, "What else?"

"An ice pick is traditionally used to kill someone without leaving a noticeable mark. This ice pick is a calling card."

Detective Kelly said, "Yes. We've all noticed that, but do you know who might have wanted to do that?"

"Sierra had a large, musclebound friend named Byron. I'd like to pin it on him."

Williams said, "Is that how you got the face?"

Kelly pointed at the corpse. "The girl did it. The three of them had an altercation on Thursday."

Williams's menacing smile widened to the edge of benevolence. He pointed at my face, swung his finger toward Sierra, and arched his shaggy red eyebrows higher than one would think possible. "You mean the *broad* popped you?"

"Sucker punch."

Rocky said dryly, "Jack always had a rough time with the girls."

Williams said, "How about this Byron character, Salvo?"

"I hope you haul him in and beat the shit out of him, but I don't think he did it. I don't see a lot of anger in this. Byron wouldn't be creative enough to use an icepick."

Kelly said, "Mr. Salvo, that's an interesting psychological analysis, but I'd like more emphasis on hard facts relating to who actually might have shoved the icepick into the woman's head or who might have paid for the murder."

"I got the impression Sierra had a few ex-boyfriends from whom she had extracted money. There must be a certain amount of animosity in that group."

"How do you know that?"

"I don't claim to know anything about Sierra McCoy's murder with any certainty, except that she's dead, but when I confronted her on Friday, she accused me of being an investigator sent by one of her ex-boyfriends."

Williams said, "What else did she do for money?"

"She owns an apartment building down on Lime Terrace, so there's cash flow there. She teaches—or rather she taught—acting, which would generate some income, but it wouldn't be a lot. She probably bought her apartment and this house with the help of her multiple boyfriends. Boyfriends who later became persona non grata."

Officer Ping had been taking notes at a rapid-fire pace. She said, "Excuse me. Persona what?"

Kelly said, "She dumped them."

Ping said, "Oh," and continued taking notes.

Kelly shifted her attention back to me. "Salvo, do you know the names of any of these ex-boyfriends?"

"No, but Byron might know."

Williams said, "And where would we find this Byron character?"

"I don't have any contact information for him, but I would start with whatever gym Sierra belonged to. And there's Steve, at the apartment on Lime Terrace. He's the unofficial manager, in unit number one. Sierra was a tenant before she bought the place. Her previous residence was a garage apartment at a house on Raven Way. The owner is a guy named Preston Newbury. Newbury saw a few different men coming and going when Sierra lived there. On one occasion, two of the men got into a fight, right in the middle of the street. LAPD responded, and it's in Hollywood Division territory, so you guys would have a record of the combatants. You can talk to Newbury and maybe get more names."

Williams said, "When was the fight?"

"Early 2006. Probably February or March.

Williams said, "Shit, that's seven years ago. Let's wait till we get to the station, get all this recorded."

Rocky volunteered to drive me to the Hollywood police station, and Williams didn't object. My car stayed inside the crime scene tape.

Every time I'm a passenger in a car driven by Rocky Platt, I remember the day when Rocky unexpectedly appeared at my elementary school. I was in the third grade, starting to grasp the malicious reality that Dad had been shot down by a criminal. I would soon be obsessed with the desire to become a policeman, catch the shooter, and fill him full of hot lead. Rocky took me out of class and drove me to his apartment. He said my mother was in the hospital.

Rocky took two days' vacation, and I stayed at his apartment. We went to the zoo and saw two movies. We ate a lot of pizza. I played in a Little League baseball game, and Rocky helped with the coaching. Other cops moved me from house to house for two weeks until a foster home was arranged. Rocky was the one who had to tell me Mom followed Dad to heaven. In later years, I learned she had taken an overdose of sleeping pills. It wasn't clear whether it was suicide, but the detectives leaned on the coroner to call it accidental to make sure I would eventually get the life insurance from her teaching job.

We went down the hill and stopped for the red light at Sunset Boulevard. A coroner's van approached from the south. When the light changed and we passed in the intersection, the meat wagon driver looked over and nodded. Rocky looked back and lifted his hand off the steering wheel in a routine, relaxed wave. Another day, another stiff.

At the Hollywood station, it took the cops more than three hours to interview me and record my statement. I told of the investigative path that led me to Sierra McCoy: Culver Aerospace, Western Rim Bank, Sullivan Agency, Westwood Hills Apartments, Preston Newbury, Lime Terrace, Sierra's house. I didn't volunteer anything about my illegal entries into Pace's apartment and Maya Fontaine's house, my discovering the bodies of Vega and Pace, or what I knew about the connection between Darcey and Sierra.

They didn't let me go until a pair of detectives called in and said they had talked to the security guard at my condo building Palisades Towers and confirmed my alibi. Detective Kelly pointed out that my alibi was not airtight. She suggested I could have left my place during the afternoon, used another vehicle to drive to Sierra's house and commit the murder, and sneak back home before eight-thirty, when the security guard saw me leaving. She also suggested the security guard might be covering for me. I knew she didn't believe any of that, but I listened politely and kept my mouth shut for a change.

A uniform drove me back to my car and arranged for me to drive it out of the crime scene perimeter. I pulled myself through my front door a little after four. It took me three tries to get the alarm code right. I dropped my clothes and flopped into bed.

24

At nine thirty the next morning, I was leaning against my kitchen counter, yawning, telling Mr. Coffee to hurry up already.

The phone rang. It was Lilith. "I need to tell you we are having a meeting at one o'clock today in Mr. Hoffman's office, and you are invited. Can you meet me in the lobby right before?"

I cleared my throat vigorously and tried to imagine I was fully awake. "Sure. What's on the agenda?"

"Mr. Hoffman is going to thank you for your services."

"You mean my ass is fired."

"At Culver Aerospace Industries, we say it in a more businesslike and a more delicate way. We tell departing vendors and contractors, 'Thank you, and don't let the door hit you in the butt on the way out.'"

"Some guy told me the same thing last week. He had a gun in his hand."

"Such a thrilling life you lead."

"Do you know why I'm being dismissed?"

"Not for sure, but I would think Darcey is behind it. Even though Darcey works for Del, he is her lapdog."

"Is there something else going on between them?"

"Darcey can get anything she wants from him. After the embezzlement was discovered, he made her the leader of the investigation team. She is not really qualified for that position, because she has very little security background. Also, she got her big promotion from him three years ago. When Del divorced his wife, there were rumors he and Darcey had something going. And by the way, you did not hear any of this from me."

"Hear what?"

"Thank you."

"Is Darcey going to be at the meeting?"

"No, just you, me, and Del Hoffman. Del said she will be at another facility."

I thanked Lilith, and we agreed to meet at the Culver Aerospace main lobby at twelve-fifty.

I deleted my overnight junk e-mail and buzzed through four online newspapers. My brain came back to life, so I started using it. It was reasonable to infer that Darcey was involved in the 2006 embezzlement, but I still had no direct evidence. For starters, I needed to go deeper into her background, and while I was at it, into Del Hoffman's. What I needed most of all was scrambled eggs, lox, and a slice of cantaloupe. After I ate, I got back on my computer and researched Darcey and Del.

The main elements in Darcey's life story checked out okay, except for the disparity between her income and her outgo. Her first serious job was at Culver Aerospace as a programming trainee; that would have produced only a modest paycheck. Previously, she had been a waitress. Somehow, she always had a fairly new car and a nice place to live.

Del Hoffman came to L.A. from Bakersfield, an agricultural city a hundred miles to the north. His education and career looked okay on the surface: Cal State Bakersfield bachelor's degree, Cal State Northridge MBA, a couple of earlier defense industry jobs, and his current stint as a vice president at Culver Aerospace. Married once and divorced, he lived in an expensive Marina del Rey condo and owned a new Cadillac Escalade. I didn't have immediate access to his credit information, but he had the profile of a guy who could get into financial trouble.

None of this helped me chip away at the big question. What was behind the deaths of Sierra McCoy, Oswald Pace, and Buddy Vega? The common thread was Darcey Mathis. If Darcey were involved in the skullduggery, her motives might have been to shut down my investigation and prevent Sierra from talking. But if Darcey were identified as an embezzler, the worst consequence probably would be the loss of her job. Not much motive for murder.

Nor would Darcey have the means. I would be surprised at her having the proficiency and the nerve to bury an ice pick in Sierra McCoy's brain, and I couldn't imagine her having the ability to dispatch Pace and Vega in a fake murder-suicide. Of course, I've been surprised before, and she might have had some help.

A hard fact remained: Darcey was the only common connection to the deaths of Oswald Pace, Buddy Vega, and her old pal Sierra McCoy.

Back to Del Hoffman. Maybe he was involved in the 2006 embezzlement. Maybe he and Darcey were ripping off Culver Aerospace in some new scam. Maybe they needed to remove some human obstacles from their path. Hoffman struck me as mostly mouth, but I wasn't sure what he might do if he thought he could safely grab some quick cash and the affections of Darcey Mathis.

I called Rocky Platt and asked him to check for criminal records on Darcey and Del. We decided to meet at a West L.A. coffee shop for dinner.

I called Gabriel Van Buren and told him I had discovered that Lowell Faraday's father might have been selling real estate in Florida back in the eighties. Gabe said he would e-mail a contact in Miami.

The main event on my day's schedule would be sneaking into Darcey's apartment and switching her mysterious mag tape with a blank. It was already eleven-fifteen, so my best bet would be to visit Darcey's place after my one o'clock Culver Aerospace meeting. I went out the door at twelve-ten.

At twelve-fifty Lilith was waiting outside the Culver Aerospace lobby. She moved up close and ran her finger down my face, next to the bruise that no longer merited a Band-Aid. "I bet you got too fresh with Wendy Storm, and she smacked you."

We arrived at Del Hoffman's office door two minutes later. Hoffman was not at his desk. No one was in the hallway.

I said, "Could you do me a favor and watch my back?"

"Who do you expect to attack you?"

In the office, I pulled out my shirt-pocket camera and captured images of various documents on the desk and walls. Lilith stood half inside the door, keeping an eye on the hallway.

She leaned inward and whispered, "Hoffman." She leaned back into the hall and spoke at full volume. "Hi, Del. We are both here."

Hoffman's footsteps sounded from the hallway. Lilith stepped inside and gave me a dirty look. She whispered, "Are you trying to get me fired? We are not supposed to have cameras in here!"

I plopped onto one of the guest chairs and tried to look innocent. Hoffman breezed into the office, sat on his desk chair, and said, "I'm supposed to be in another meeting right now, so I'm going to have to make this real quick. Culver Aerospace management has decided to end the investigations into the two embezzlements. At this point in time, the company feels we have little to gain from pursuing the matter any further except more bad publicity. Mr. Xavier has assigned me the responsibility of forming a team and investigating ways to improve our audit and security procedures. I owe him a report, including specific recommendations, in thirty days." Hoffman looked directly at me. "Mr. Xavier also told me to send you his thanks for your work. Barney has a gruff exterior, but he's fair, and he gives credit where credit is due. We all appreciate how quickly you got to the bottom of things. We understand that you went above and beyond the call of duty, and you might have even put yourself in danger. Because of your efforts, we're going to up your total paycheck to thirty-five thousand."

I said, "I appreciate your taking care of that. I ran out of here so fast on Wednesday, after the second embezzlement was discovered, I didn't bother to give you a client retainer contract."

Hoffman grinned. "I tried to get you forty thousand, but Mr. Xavier can always find some rationale for trimming expenses. Your check is almost in the mail."

"I have no complaints."

Hoffman folded his hands on the desk and took a more serious tone. "You know, it's tragic the way this thing played out. I guess we'll never know what was going on in Pace's mind. We won't forget these events for a long time." He stood up. "Mr. Salvo, I'd like you to send your written report directly to me." On the way out the door, he said, "I hate to abandon you like this, but I have to run. See you later, Lilith. Thanks again, Jack."

Lilith and I headed for the front lobby. Outside the building, she steered us away from three employees taking a smoke break. She spoke in a low voice. "What do you have on Del Hoffman? Why were you taking photos?"

"I've learned some noteworthy things recently, but they don't fit together neatly. I have no definite conclusions. If I tell you what I know or what I think I know, it might put you in a tight spot. You might feel an obligation to pass the information on to someone else. If you blab and my information turns out to be wrong, it could get you in trouble."

"Hmmm. You suspect Del of doing something wrong, and since Del and Darcey have a special relationship, that means you suspect Darcey of something."

"I neither confirm nor deny that, but I can confirm that you're a smart cookie. Now I need to get on the road and see what else I can learn."

"You are continuing the investigation even though you are no longer being paid?"

"I hate to leave a job unfinished. How about you?"

"I have been given a new assignment."

"You want me to keep in touch? I don't want to get you in trouble."

"It might be fun to get into trouble for a change. I never get in trouble. I'm starting to think it might be a character flaw of mine. Just be sure to call me on my cell, not on the office phone."

In my car, I turned on my iPad and brought up the GPS software. Darcey's car was going north on the San Diego Freeway, approaching the Santa Monica. I raced down Imperial Highway and took the sweeping onramp to the northbound San Diego.

Darcey transitioned to the Santa Monica and drove all the way to the Downtown Interchange. I could have peeled off the freeway and gone straight to her apartment, but curiosity kept me on her trail. My visit to her apartment would have to wait. She continued in an easterly direction, exited the freeway at Santa Anita Avenue, and drove to the north.

I found her car in an industrial section of South El Monte, in front of a plain concrete building identified only by street numbers. The parking lot across the street had the surveillance position I wanted. I backed into a space and checked the time, which was exactly two o'clock.

Sixteen hours earlier I had been standing in the bedroom of the freshly murdered Sierra McCoy, Darcey Mathis's embezzlement accomplice. Five days before that, I was standing over the corpses of Oswald Pace and Buddy Vega, both of whom were involved in a scam I first learned about from Darcey. I didn't know how all those events connected or what Darcey was doing in this featureless little building thirty miles from Culver Aerospace, but I knew she was in the middle of something beyond a run-of-the-mill embezzlement. I waited in my car with a firm set to my jaw and a little black cloud over my head.

A half hour later she came out of the building wearing a loose-fitting pantsuit, walking in a stiff gait, carrying a purse and a briefcase.

I gave her a five-minute head start and followed her back to L.A. She went straight home, and I went to meet Rocky Platt at Stanley's Coffee Shop, conveniently located a block from my office. The joint is clean enough to be healthy and dingy enough to be comfortable. It's Rocky's favorite hangout and one of mine.

Rocky was already there, backed into a corner booth. Cops like to have their backs to the wall when they eat in a restaurant. I slid in across from him.

He gave me his trademark crooked smile. "Hey, it's the fuckin' philosopher." Then he told me what he had learned. Hoffman came up clean, except he was a little behind on alimony. Darcey had a couple of blemishes. She had been suspected of low-level cocaine sales in both Illinois and L.A.

Rocky opened up his shirt-pocket notebook and gave me the details. "In 1999, she was going to Illinois State University in Bloomington. She was working as a cocktail waitress, also selling coke through contacts she made at the bar. Detective I talked to was a Polack named Zabinski. Said she was a cool, crafty customer, nice smile. They hauled her in and offered to let her skate if she would give up her supplier. She denied everything and sat in a holding cell for half a day. Cool, calm, collected. They found three singles and one 8-ball in folded papers in her locker at the bar, but they got no prints on the paper, and the dope was in a small cotton sack, which would have no prints. She claimed someone must have planted them. The overall case was weak, so they had to let her go.

"Funny thing is, a similar thing happened in L.A. a year later. She was working at a bar on Melrose, a place called The Bus Bench. Sheriff's detectives heard coke deals were being made there. An under-cover officer made a deal with her for an ounce. She said she'd meet him outside, but she disappeared and never went back to the bar again. The sheriffs didn't know if someone tipped her, or if she smelled it."

Rocky gave me his mind-reading homicide detective look and said, "So what are you gonna do with this Darcey character?"

"Depends on my luck. I had a date with her Saturday night. She wants to get together again."

Rocky made only two speculative, ribald comments. He must have not been feeling well. On the way out, he tried to pay the tab, but I beat him to it.

At home, I sat in front of the television, my camera and iPad at my side. The Ice Pick Murder was the lead news story. I watched the news reports on three different L.A. stations while reviewing the photos I had taken in Hoffman's office. None of the photos excited me: quick-draw competition, MBA diploma, meeting reminders, Culver Aerospace organization chart. The entries in the to-do list were either routine, such as "review Facilities Plan" or too cryptic to understand, such as "DC Consolidation MSE/SDD." A hand-printed telephone list on the wall showed internal Culver Aerospace extensions, as well as outside numbers for companies that seemed like they would have a normal business relationship with Culver. Everything looked like business as usual.

I said to hell with investigating and settled in for some serious television. Bull riding at a Wyoming rodeo made me feel tougher. A political talk show featured big-name panelists, none of whom could form a clear argument; I tried to count their logical fallacies and ran out of fingers. Finally, I caught the beginning of Bergman's *The Seventh Seal*. I hadn't seen it for years. It's one of those 1950s European art films that beats you over the head with its profundity. Soon after the white-faced guy in the black robe appeared on the beach and said, "I am Death," I said to hell with high art, and I went to bed.

25

Tuesday morning, I reviewed the listings for Bakersfield PIs and found what I was looking for: Duane Butterfield Investigations. He had a brick-and-mortar office, no website. Probably an older, established PI.

On the first ring, a gravelly smoker's voice said, "Butterfield Investigations."

"This is Jack Salvo. I'm a private investigator in Los Angeles. I'm looking for information on an ex-Bakersfield resident."

"What's the name you're lookin' for?"

"Delbert Keith Hoffman."

"Let me write that down. Two N's in Hoffman?"

"Just one."

"Doesn't ring a bell."

"You been in Bakersfield a long time?"

"All my sixty-nine years, except two years college in Fresno. If Hoffman was here for any significant length of time, I can find his trail. What have you got on him?"

"He is forty-five years old, and he graduated from Cal State Bakersfield in 1990. I don't have any Bakersfield address or phone number or other information. What do you take for a retainer?"

"What's your hourly rate, down there in L.A.?"

"Three hundred, full pop. Sometimes I give someone a break. Sometimes I get a bonus."

"Shit. The best I can do in Bakersfield's one-fifty, but the cost of living is a hell of a lot cheaper up here. We can talk about payment later. I might not be able to do anything for you."

Mr. Butterfield and I exchanged contact information, and he promised to let me know as soon as he had something.

A few minutes later I was driving east on Pico, toward Darcey's place. I was anxious to snag the tape cassette and learn what was on it. My GPS showed her car in the Culver Aerospace lot. I called her office to make sure she was there. The secretary put me on hold, came back, and said Ms. Mathis would be in meetings until noon. Five minutes later I was wearing disposable gloves and climbing through Ms. Mathis's service porch window.

First priority was the file cabinet with the military-style locking bar and padlock. I picked the lock and removed the heavy metal bar, just like I had when Darcey was in the shower. Nothing looked different in the upper three file drawers. The bottom drawer had changed a little since Saturday night. There were two prepaid "burner" cell phones instead of one. The LTO-5 tape cassette was now folded into a manila envelope. I switched her tape with one of the blanks I bought on Sunday and relocked the cabinet.

The computer was still password-protected. I could have picked the desk lock, but I wasn't sure I could relock it. I quickly looked through the rest of the apartment and saw nothing of interest. A more detailed search would have risked leaving behind evidence of my visit.

I picked up a to-go lunch at a deli, went to my office, and tried to find someone who could read Darcey's mysterious tape. First, I phoned a propeller-head in Westwood who claims he can decipher any data on any storage medium. His answering system said he was out of town. I made more calls, and nothing panned out. Lilith would know someone who could read the tape, but she would want to know where I got it, and I didn't want to burden her with that knowledge.

I was shoveling down my salad when Darcey's GPS icon moved. From Culver Aerospace, she drove to her apartment and stayed there less than ten minutes. A few minutes later, I was driving east on Sunset. Darcey was coming up through the Beverly Hills flats, headed in my general direction. I cut over to Lexington Road, stopped at the curb, and waited until her GPS icon moved north of Lexington, to make sure I didn't run into her.

She took North Beverly Drive up to a narrow road hugging the hillside above Franklin Canyon. The canyon hosts hiking trails, a nature preserve, and two reservoirs. I stayed well behind her, out of sight. She made a sharp right into the lower canyon and cut back in my direction. I pulled over to the right and waited.

When her car appeared below me, I was standing at the side of the upper road, camera in hand. She turned into the parking lot near the main trailhead and got out wearing yellow shorts and a short-sleeved top. I steadied myself against my car and took a couple of photos while she strapped on a waist pack. Given the distance, the photos wouldn't give much detail. I should have had a longer lens on my camera, so I swapped it for my binoculars.

Darcey started up the winding trail, which ascended gradually. She walked five or six minutes, paused, and slowly rotated, as though she were looking for someone—or maybe anyone. She pulled something from her waist pack and disappeared into a wooded gorge. Within seconds, she was marching back down to her car. Before driving away, she faced one of the wooden posts on the trailhead gate and did something to it I could not discern.

I didn't want to be standing by my car when she drove past, so I shuffled my car back and forth three or four times and turned it around on the narrow road. I dropped down into a residential neighborhood, parked on a side street, and waited until Darcey's white BMW blinked through the gaps in the trees.

I drove back up the hill and parked in the same place. Darcey had left something in the bushes, and someone else was going to come along and pick it up. In espionage circles, it's called a dead drop.

About twenty feet down the hillside, I found a relatively flat rock. I sat and waited and watched. A few hikers and mountain bikers went past the drop point, but no one stopped. I amused myself by watching a soaring red-tailed hawk, absorbing the pungent chaparral aroma, and slapping at gnats.

About twenty minutes later, a silver Cadillac pulled into the same space Darcey's car had occupied. It was a Caddy like the one I saw on North Doheny after my poolside love-in with Sierra McCoy and Byron the muscle-boy. Two men got out and walked up the same trail Darcey had. They were too distant for me to get a good eyeball ID.

They moved with a strength and efficiency that caught my eye. They stopped at the same point Darcey had. One of them backtracked about a hundred feet while the other went ahead a similar distance. They slowed to a stop at the same time, looked all around, and jogged back toward each other. One of the figures disappeared into the gorge Darcey had visited and came out a few seconds later. The pair walked casually back down the trail, hopped in their car, and drove away.

From my seated position on the hillside, I had seen an occasional car passing on the road above. I had not seen the Cadillac, so I concluded they entered the canyon from Mulholland Drive, and they would probably leave by the same northerly route.

I climbed up to my car, drove ahead to the T-intersection from which the target car would have to emerge, and pulled into a foliage-shrouded dirt turnout. The target car appeared and turned right, toward the Mulholland exit. I followed at a discreet distance, hoping to keep a car or two between them and me, so I wouldn't end up on their bumper at the Mulholland traffic signal. On the other hand, I didn't want to lose them.

There was no traffic to hide behind, so I had to maintain a sizable gap. By the time I worked my way up to Mulholland, the Caddy was already part of the eastbound traffic. I followed from four cars behind, and our procession dropped down Coldwater Canyon, toward Beverly Hills.

At the T-intersection with Cherokee Lane, they made a left turn. I grabbed one quick photo. A long string of oncoming traffic delayed my left turn. By the time I was going up Cherokee, the Cadillac might as well have gone into earth orbit. I cruised up the hill, checked crossstreets and driveways, and turned around at the edge of Trousdale Estates, a ritzy hillside neighborhood in the north end of Beverly Hills.

Back at the trailhead in the canyon, I examined the wooden post that had attracted Darcey's attention. A fresh piece of black electrician's tape was stuck to it in a vertical orientation, probably her signal that she had made the drop. That's the way spies do it.

A half hour later, I was at my office desk, reviewing my photos. They provided a little more information than what my eyeballs had already reported. The final shot was an angled rear view of the Cadillac. It was the CTS-V model, the high-powered version. That squared with the boy-racer sound of the Caddy on Doheny after the fight at Sierra's swimming pool. It was a new car—no license plate and the dealer's advertising card in the plate frame. The dealer name was illegible, even when I zoomed in, but the shape of the logo was not entirely lost. I found a similar graphic design on the website of Marina Cadillac.

While I was researching my local Cadillac dealers, two e-mails came in. The first was from Duane Butterfield in Bakersfield:

Mr. Salvo, here's the essential facts I got on Delbert Keith Hoffman.

Grew up on the better side of town. Father owned a trucking business. Del started driving for him summers and part time after he was 18. His family was what you might call fairly well-off rednecks.

Hoffman fell in with the cowboy element in Bakersfield. He liked guns and hunting and shooting. The dumb son of a bitch shot himself in the foot rabbit hunting up by the Kern River back in 1989. Practicing his quick draw is what I heard.

Del wanted to get away from Bakersfield and head for city lights. When he drove trucks for his dad, he always tried to get an LA route, so he could spend a little time down there.

Left for graduate school in LA about 1990. Never lived in Bakersfield again. Parents passed away about 15 years ago. No relatives in the area. No one's heard much of him since.

No criminal activity other than drinking and driving fast and shooting and whoring around, all quite common in this vicinity.

I got this on two phone calls, one short, one medium length. With regards to payment, let's say you owe me one. Maybe you can fix me up with a Hollywood starlet some time, if I ever come down to L.A. again. And if I can figure some way to take 30 years off my age. Better make that 40.

If you need more details I can dig them up, but it will take a few days and it will cost you one-fifty an hour. Regards.

D. Butterfield

I sent a reply to Mr. Butterfield, thanking him. Then I drummed my fingers on the desk and thought things over. Hoffman's goal was to go to the big city, make money, and soak up some of the glamour. He had achieved some of that. I wondered what other goals he might have.

The second e-mail was from Gabriel Van Buren:

Jack—

Michael Faraday changed his name to Fairway and was quite successful in Florida real estate until he was convicted for fraud in 1991. After two years in the can, he lived in the penthouse of an apartment building he bought with his ill-earned gains. You usually can't lose your home in civil court in FL. Never married in FL. Shacked up three or four times. Died two years ago, age 77. Left everything to the latest shack-up, a fifty-something bimbo who married a younger man two weeks after she pocketed the inheritance. Ain't love grand?

–Gabe

I could have paid a Florida PI to interview people who knew Michael Fairway, aka Michael Faraday, and try to find a link to his son, but Faraday Senior had made a calculated effort to sever relations with his family. My time would be better spent plowing through the corporate barriers Lowell Faraday had erected. If that failed, I might revisit the Florida angle.

At home, I put the LTO-5 tape in my safe, ate a snack, and took off for the gym. When I returned home, I checked my GPS for Darcey's movements. The battery in the GPS transmitter had expired.

26

The next morning about eight thirty, I was at the back door of my office. My key went into the lock and turned, but it didn't turn with the usual resistance. I released the key ring noiselessly and stepped back. A wire was flopping loose against the back of my building—the telephone line. I stepped back farther. An oval piece of glass had been cut from the kitchen window. I stepped back farther and pulled my .38 from the trunk of my car. I pushed my back door open and pointed the revolver at nobody.

File folders, loose papers, sealed reams of paper, books, and office supplies were piled in the middle of the floor somewhat neatly. The bottom drawer of each file cabinet was pulled out. The supply cabinet doors hung open. Pens, pencils, staples, rubber bands, and other small items remained on cabinet shelves. Framed wall hangings were stacked on the writing table.

Most of the desk drawers' contents were on the desktop, with some notable exceptions. My father's service revolver, a Smith K-38, sat fully loaded in the top right drawer, on a soft silicone cloth, just like it always does. Two speed loaders and a box of .38 cartridges were next to it. My petty cash fund lay unmolested in the right-center drawer, in a small accordion folder.

In the bathroom, the toilet tank lid had been laid across the seat. In the kitchen, cabinets were open, and the refrigerator had been rolled out from the wall. On the wall between the kitchen and bathroom doors, the power cord to the cellular alarm control box was cut. The backup battery had been removed and set on top of the unit like a little trophy on a mantel.

I paced back and forth like Felix the Cat and tried to recreate the break-in. They must have used a jammer on the cellular alarm system. They cut the window glass, lifted out the cut piece with a suction cup or a looped piece of duct tape, and reached in to unlatch the window. I wasn't sure how they disabled the window alarm sensor. Once inside, they cut the power to the alarm system, and they were home free.

I put my revolver back in the car and called the alarm company. They sounded embarrassed and said someone would be there in a half-hour. I wanted time to clean things up, so I said make it two hours.

I rolled the recycle and trash bins inside and started going through the heap on the floor. Most of the documentation went back into the vertical files; some went into the desk; some went into the recycle bin or shredder. I stacked office supplies in the supply cabinet and desk. I tossed junk, something I needed to do anyway. As I put things back in order, nothing seemed to be missing.

I was organizing the pens and pencils when Detectives Kelly and Williams let themselves in the front. They were from LAPD's

Hollywood Division. My office is in the West L.A. Division, so I was fairly sure their visit wasn't related to the break-in.

Williams gave the recycle bin a soft little kick. "Spring cleaning in August?" Kelly walked up to the kitchen window and looked at the hole in the glass. She went to the alarm control box and looked at the disconnected battery and severed power cable. She said, "Do you have any weapons in here?"

I pointed at my desk. "Loaded thirty-eight in the top right drawer."

"Why don't you get comfortable on the sofa?"

I moved to the sofa, but I had little expectation of comfort.

Williams opened the top-right desk drawer, took out the 1960's vintage four-inch revolver, ejected the bullets into his hand, and set each of the six bullets on end, making a row on the desktop. He put the gun back in the drawer, landed on the Aeron chair, and looked through the other drawers. He fanned through the petty cash and said, "About four hundred dollars." He put the money back where he found it. "They didn't take the money or the .38? What were they looking for?"

I said, "I don't know. I was taking inventory when you got here. Nothing seems to be missing so far. It might have been a disgruntled client or investigative subject trying to get into my files."

Kelly said, "Did you report it to West L.A. yet?"

"Not yet. The alarm company is on the way. I can give the police more detail after the alarm company makes an assessment."

I hadn't intended to report the break-in to LAPD. I didn't need a police report for an insurance claim because the loss was too small. Also, an LAPD response would not be a sympathetic visit in which I would receive a pat on the back and a checklist of burglary prevention tips. I would get hit with a series of sharply pointed questions—somewhat similar to the spears Williams and Kelly were about to throw at me.

Williams got up and placed one of my wooden chairs at the west wall so he could watch me from the side. He tilted back and jammed his gunboats' scuffed heels into the tile floor.

Kelly sat on my desk chair and slapped down her aluminum clipboard. "I'm going to get right to the point. We talked to Detective Siqueiros at Rampart Division. He said you had contact with persons named Buddy Vega and Oswald Pace last week. Then Vega and Pace turn up dead last Wednesday morning in a used car lot. You also spoke to several people in your search for Sierra McCoy. You found her, and you got into an altercation, and then she turns up dead two days later. You are the only person linked to all these deaths, so I'm sure you can understand our curiosity."

I said, "The first and only time I saw Sierra McCoy alive was last Friday afternoon, and I told you all about that Sunday night. I never had any direct contact with Oswald Pace. The only time I was near Vega was last Tuesday afternoon when I went to his car lot and photographed him from across the street. He never saw me."

Kelly said, "When we interviewed you Sunday night, you had heard about the deaths of Vega and Pace, hadn't you?"

"Yes, a Culver Aerospace employee told me."

"And you didn't mention it to us."

"I didn't see a connection, and . . ."

Williams cut me off. "You give us information, and we figure out connections."

I continued. "And I wanted to minimize the involvement of my client."

Williams said, "Your client can go get fucked." He banged the chair down on the floor and pulled himself up straight. "This is a murder case, Jack. Multiple murders. We can haul you in right now. We don't give a shit if you went a little too far afield in your investigations and maybe jumped over a fence and jimmied a door lock. What we need from you is anything and everything you know about these deaths. And we need it now."

"Do I understand you to say you're not going to haul me in for some chickenshit violation?"

"Depends on the definition of chickenshit."

"How about my having been somewhere I shouldn't have been and now having something you need?"

"Depends on how bad we need it."

"You need it."

"Let's have it."

"Did you search Pace's apartment?"

Williams nodded. "I didn't personally, but it was searched."

"Did they find thirteen thousand in cash under the bottom bathroom drawer?"

A cold heavy silence filled the room and answered my question.

I said, "Right rear corner, in the framing. The envelope is about the same color as the wood. I left it like I found it."

Kelly said, "When were you in there?"

"Last Tuesday afternoon, about two hours after I got the case."

Williams said, "What's that supposed to do for us?"

"I'm just giving you information. I'll let you figure the connections."

Four fixed, unblinking eyes told me to keep talking.

I said, "Regarding Sierra McCoy, I told you what I knew Sunday night, and nothing has changed. You must have contacted some of her old boyfriends by now, so you know a hell of a lot more than I do about that angle. I don't even know their names."

They kept staring at me, and I kept sweating and talking. "The only thing more I can tell you about Oswald Pace and Buddy Vega is that the murder-suicide explanation doesn't sit quite level with me. By all accounts, Pace was a weak-willed, hedonistic parasite. I don't think he would have had the guts to pump hot lead into his brain. Maybe if he had been drinking and doping heavily, he might have done it. But if the toxicology report shows no dope or booze, or just small amounts, I would at least think about double murder with a fake suicide." I left out the part about my being at the death scene.

Williams said, "What else?"

"Maybe Vega and Pace were involved with some rough characters, and they rubbed 'em the wrong way. Vega has a history of fraud. Maybe he stole from someone, and there was a retaliation. Pace may have just been in the wrong place at the wrong time."

Williams said, "Too many maybes."

Kelly said, "Fake murder-suicide is too clever and too indirect for a retaliation. It doesn't send the right message. Change of subject. Remember the cute little kitchen towel with the adorable embroidered cocker spaniels? The doggie towel that was stashed in your car with your revolver?"

I knew what was coming.

She continued. "Well, that towel just happened to match the cute doggie towel I found in Sierra McCoy's laundry basket Monday morning. We girls notice cute little things like that. You used the towel to wipe your prints. You intended to leave the murder scene without contacting the police, but when the neighbor with the dog saw you and your shiny new BMW M3, and she spoke with you, you were trapped like a rat, and you called your friend Detective Rocky. At that point, you had no choice but to report the crime."

I tried to look angelic.

Kelly stood up. "I'm going to assume the information you've given us is correct—including the cash hidden in Pace's apartment. Detective Williams and I already talked about Pace's personality profile, and you may be onto something regarding the exact manner of his death, but you still owe us." She smiled like a faith healer holding a full collection plate. "And if you withhold any more evidence, you're going to get your private dick license cut off."

Williams made a pained face.

Kelly walked toward the front door. Williams stood up and walked to my desk, opened the top-right drawer, and looked inside again. "Your dad's Smith and Wesson?"

"He was carrying that revolver when he was shot."

Williams lifted the gun and silicone cloth out of the drawer. He opened the cylinder, wiped all the surfaces, and reloaded. He used the cloth to handle everything. He nestled the gun back into the drawer.

The detectives took off, and I was alone. I looked again at the hole in the kitchen window and called Hugo, the contractor I use on my office and condo. He had me measure the pane while he was on the phone and said he would pick up the glass on the way to my office.

The alarm company arrived at eleven, checked out my system, and jerry-rigged a new telephone line as a favor. We didn't want to wait for the telephone company. Hugo showed up at eleven twenty, and we installed my new kitchen window glass. Then he looked at the worn-out venetian blind on the front window, took measurements, and said he would install a new one next week. We walked over to a restaurant on the next block and ate tacos and argued about the upcoming pro football season.

After lunch, Hugo took off, and I decided to take a break and work on a crossword puzzle. A seven-letter word for "extent" was giving me trouble when a phone call came in.

A musical voice said, "This is Lilith."

I said, "Have you ever considered the advantages of a dignified older man?"

"Every year I sing Christmas carols for old people at retirement homes. Maybe this Christmas you will be there. Now listen. I have something serious."

"I'm listening."

"I need to talk to you about something. Is your philosophy class tonight?"

"I arrive at Coast College at six."

"Don't night classes usually start at seven?"

"My class is from seven to nine-fifty. I have my office hour in the Student Union before class. They don't give me a real office because I only teach one class."

"There will be no time for us to meet before your class."

"How about after?"

"I am usually asleep by eleven-fifteen on a work night. How soon could you be at my place?"

"Where do you live?"

"A little south of the Santa Monica Airport."

"I could be there at ten-fifteen."

She gave me her address. I went back to my crossword and tried to find a four-letter word for *hopeful*.

27

I arrived at the Coast College Student Union early and ordered dinner at five forty-five instead of the usual six.

My turkey burger was almost gobbled when the student I had tagged "Surfer Girl" sat at my table and slid a sheet of paper in front of me. Her name was actually Elvira.

She said, "Hi, Professor Salvo. I've got an outline for my paper, and I was wondering what you think about it."

Her paper was titled "Criticisms of Aristotle's Logic," an advanced topic for a community college student. She had organized the outline into three main sections: (1) quantification, (2) law of the excluded middle, and (3) deduction vs. induction. I read the outline and suggested two minor changes.

She told me about her plan to get a degree in philosophy and then go to law school. A counselor had suggested philosophy would be a good prelaw major, and I agreed.

Elvira went to the food counter and came back with a hamburger, fries, and coke. In the meantime, three other students had arrived. Two of them produced outlines for their proposed term papers. I reviewed the outlines and gave my opinion on each. Then the students started reading one another's outlines and critiquing them. I tossed in an occasional comment, just enough to keep the discussion on track. Little lightbulbs blazed over their brainstorming heads.

I reflected on my long-term impact on my students. Since I started teaching at Coast College, about four hundred young people had taken my classes. Some were just along for the ride; they wouldn't remember how to spell Plato. Some would remember my class as entertaining and somewhat enlightening. A few, such as the kids at my table, would remember Professor Salvo guiding them through the realm of rational thinking and putting a few extra wrinkles in their brains.

About ten before seven, we all headed for the classroom. When the clock said seven, the class was seated, my notes were carefully organized on the lectern, and I was ready for action.

I started the lecture, "Aristotle is the first Western philosopher to develop a comprehensive system of thought. He is considered by many to be the most influential thinker of all time. Consequently, he gets a full class session all to himself. It's the least we can do."

I had to go quickly through his Metaphysics, Categories, Ethics, and Politics; there's only so much you can do in less than three hours. Aristotle's Logic ruled the roost for almost two thousand years, so I spent a little extra time on the subject. The math majors tried to dominate the discussion on logic, but Elvira was ready for them, and that led to a spirited exchange. I liked the way the class was shaping up. I ended the class five minutes early, so I could be sure to arrive at Lilith's place on time.

28

ilith lived in an L-shaped stucco and clapboard apartment near Venice Boulevard and Beethoven Street. Two of the seven units were over the carports in back. The ground-floor units, including hers, were in the section running out toward the street.

At ten-ten I knocked lightly on the door of apartment number three. Lilith cracked it open, peered out, and unlocked the chain. She was barefoot, wearing celery-colored shorts and a gauzy, pale-orange tank top.

Her apartment gave no surprises. It was fresh and clean, modern-on-a-budget, and absent of pretense. Bills, letter opener, calculator, and checkbook were arranged on the dining table as well-ordered as surgical instruments.

She put me on one end of her sofa. A gray cat slinked toward me, jumped up, and sniffed my hand. Lilith sat on the other end. The cat abandoned me and spread out on Lilith. She stroked the cat and said, "This is Yvonne."

There was a brief silence while Lilith studied me. Then she said, "I am going to be direct, and I am going to trust you to not get me fired over what I am about to say. Darcey Mathis has been watching me, and I think she knows I am still interested in the embezzlements. I am not supposed to be working on them anymore."

"You have my vow of secrecy."

She said, "I think there is a chance Darcey was involved in the 2006 embezzlement." She watched me as though she expected me to slap my thigh and cackle hysterically.

I said, "I have come to the same conclusion. You tell me your evidence, I'll tell you mine."

Her eyes widened. "How did the hotshot private eye come to that conclusion?"

"Ladies first."

"Okay. Back in 2006, Darcey was the manager of a group of programmers, and that gave her full access to the accounts payable system. I looked at the change control records on microfilm and found out she submitted changes to the system during the weeks prior to the fraudulent check."

"Is there a way to find the details on the changes she made?"

"Absolutely none. The next year we installed a totally new accounts payable system, so there would be no need to keep a detailed record of programming changes in the old system."

"Is it possible Darcey had a legitimate reason to make the changes? She started out at Culver as a programmer."

"It would be very unusual for a manager to make a change to the company's application software. It is normal for a programmer to make the changes and for the manager to oversee the process. Are you following me?"

"Yes, and you're not talking about making an entry into the system to cut a check, like what a clerk would do. You're talking about changing the actual programming code."

She nodded energetically. "That is what I think she did. I cannot prove it right now, but that is what I think. It definitely fits in with what Gene Thorne said in the meeting. Now you tell me your evidence."

I took Lilith down most of my investigative path: Wendy Storm, Western Rim Bank, Cecile Clark, the Sullivan Agency, Sierra McCoy's Westwood residence, Preston Newbury, and Sierra's house in the Hollywood Hills.

When I mentioned there was a fight at Sierra's house, she said, "*That* is what happened to your face."

"Are you impressed?"

"How big was the other guy?"

"It wasn't exactly the *guy*."

She let me off with a thin smile, and I continued my tale. When I told her Darcey Mathis and Sierra McCoy were in the same acting workshop, she said, "That means we can turn them in. You have the connection between Darcey and Sierra McCoy, and it was back at the time of the embezzlement they pulled."

"Not quite yet. We don't have any direct evidence that Darcey did anything wrong."

I told her about Sierra's murder, leaving out my discovering the body.

Lilith's mouth formed a capital O. "The TV actress in the Hollywood Hills! The Ice Pick Murder! I saw it on the news." She looked away and tuned me out for a few seconds while her brain percolated. She came back and said, "Oswald is dead. And the TV actress is dead, and she was Darcey's accomplice in a crime that was similar to Oswald's crime. Something very bad is going on. Very bad. This is making my head spin."

"Have you ever seen Darcey in the company of an older man with a full beard and wide mustache?"

"No."

"Any other men?"

"I never see her with other men, except for people at work. I would not know about her social life outside of work."

I didn't mention the dead drop in Franklin Canyon or the tape cassette I lifted from Darcey's place, but I decided to tell her about Darcey's trip to the unmarked building in South El Monte on Monday afternoon.

She listened carefully and said, "Tomorrow at work, I can probably find out what she was doing at the El Monte facility. What are you going to do next?"

"Find out who was driving a silver Cadillac I saw Tuesday afternoon."

"How about the license plate?"

"New car. No plates."

"Oh."

"But I'm pretty sure it was purchased at Marina Cadillac."

"How do you know that?"

"I got a fuzzy photo of the car. The paper advertising in the license plate frame had a large M, like the Marina Cadillac advertising."

She made a sour face. "What do you do now? Climb in the window of Marina Cadillac in the middle of the night and search their records?"

"You have the general idea."

"You are not actually going to break into the car dealer, are you?"

"No, but I'm starting to get another idea."

"What kind of idea?"

"Can you go to work late tomorrow?"

She gave me the uniquely female smile that blends reproach and encouragement. "It sounds like you are getting a very big idea. Why would I have to be late for work tomorrow?"

"I thought you might want to be a private detective tomorrow morning. I have an idea on how to identify the owner of the Cadillac, and I could use an assistant. Can you take the morning off?"

"Maybe."

I explained my idea, and she added a few good suggestions. I was out the door at ten-forty.

29

At nine twenty-eight the next morning, Lilith was waiting for me in her Honda Accord Coupe, about a block from Marina Cadillac. I parked behind the Honda, and we both got out.

Her outfit had my full attention: low-cut flared jeans with flourishes on the rear pockets, a skimpy black lace-up top, and black sandals with towering heels. Her hair was out of the ponytail, flowing across her bare shoulders. In the direct sunlight, her hair was darkest brown with auburn highlights. The first time I met her, I thought her hair was black. She swung her multicolored shoulder bag in a full circle and said, "You are the sugar daddy, and I am the bimbo. This is going to be fun."

We parked on the Marina Cadillac lot and entered the showroom. We went straight to a black CTS Coupe and pretended to be engrossed in the window sticker as we observed the office layouts.

A young salesman in a three-piece suit approached us. "Hi. My name's Bruce. Can I help you today?" Bruce was somewhat tentative, as though he were new on the job.

We shook hands and I said, "My name's Jackson, and my girlfriend Lilith needs a car. We think a CTS Coupe would be right for her."

Lilith chirped, "Red, with gray interior," and slapped me on the butt. The slap had a stinging effect—and other effects as well.

Bruce said, "Well, let's see what we have in our inventory." He led us to a sales office, and we all took chairs.

Lilith pulled her chair next to Bruce, so she could see his computer screen. "Can we see all the red ones?"

Bruce said, "We can see all the red CTS Coupes, and we can see all the options on all the red ones. Whatever you want."

Lilith said, "Cool!"

We watched Bruce type BRUCE as his password. Lilith snuck me a quick sneer that said, "What a moron!"

Bruce typed a few more keystrokes. "It looks like we have one red CTS Coupe in stock."

Lilith said, "Gray interior?"

"No. It's Ebony...black. We call our gray interior Light Titanium."

"That's the one I want."

Bruce pecked at the keyboard. "Other dealers in our area have several in red with the interior you want. We can get any one of those on a dealer trade within an hour or two. Get it right here on our lot."

Lilith scooted her chair closer to Bruce. "Does the computer tell you how many people buy red ones instead of other colors?"

Bruce took a good look at her breasts. "Uh . . . well, I can show it to you." Then he demonstrated how he could display recent sales by model, color, and other variables.

That was all the training Lilith needed. She said, "I would like to go outside and see the red one."

The three of us went out to the lot and found the red car. Lilith opened the passenger door, wrapped her arm around me, pointed at the interior, and said, "I think I would definitely like a gray interior better. Gray looks better. It softens everything. I saw one like that at Century City. It looked great."

My hand found her cute little butt and gave it a soft little squeeze. She started to bend away, changed her mind, and rubbed her head on my shoulder.

Bruce said, "Would you like to buy a new Cadillac today?"

I closed the door. "This is the first dealership we've gone to, and I don't think we're going to buy one today. I'd like to get an idea on price, and I have a couple of questions about the options."

Lilith let go of me. "You two can talk about boring stuff. I am going to powder my nose." She walked back toward the showroom.

My job was to distract Bruce and keep him away from his office. Lilith's was to gain access to Bruce's computer.

A few minutes later, I eased my car out of the Marina Cadillac lot. Bruce waved at us. Lilith waved a Cadillac brochure back at him.

She pulled a folded sheet of paper from her purse and studied it. "Somebody named Carl Victor purchased a new silver CTS-V sedan almost two weeks ago. Eighty-one thousand dollars. The only silver CTS-V sold in the last two months. Everybody seems to want black. And Carl Victor's address is a hotel . . . Airport Suites . . . on Century

Boulevard. That's suspicious. Nobody lives in a hotel by the airport on a regular basis." She refolded the printout, placed it in the center console, and said, "Mission accomplished!" She sat silently, her hands in her lap.

I parked near Lilith's car, and we got out and stood on the sidewalk. Something made me look up at the sky. It was the perfect late-summer day I had been waiting for. The Pacific Ocean delivered a clean breeze. The sun blazed through the cool air. There was another source of heat; I wanted to grab her and hold her against me hard.

She said, "Why are you looking up at the sky? What are you thinking about?"

"I love these late-summer days. Hot sun, cool wind."

A fist jabbed my chest. Hot Asian eyes froze me. She spoke slowly and softly. "Why are you talking about the fucking weather?"

We melted into each other. Our lips fused. Some guy hooted at us from a passing car. We finally unclenched, held on loosely, and looked into each other's eyes. She pulled me toward my car, and I floated along with her. We didn't speak on the way to my place, but much was communicated by the way she held my hand.

Inside my condo, I almost forgot to enter the alarm code. I pushed the buttons with my right hand while Lilith tugged on my left. She pushed me down the hallway, yanked off my sport coat, and dumped it on the floor.

In the bedroom, she pushed me toward the bed, set her purse on the dresser, and resumed pushing me. "What you have to remember is I am a naive country girl, and I am unaware of the ways of the big city." As she spoke, she unbuttoned my shirt, unhooked my belt, unfastened and unzipped my slacks, and put a shoulder into me like she was throwing a block. That knocked me backward onto the bed. She had my shoes and slacks off in a few seconds.

A few seconds more, and all her clothes were off, and she was straddling me. I tried to stretch over to the bedside table and open the drawer. She beat me to it, pulled out a strip of Trojans, and held it up high like a trophy fish. She ripped one off, tossed the remainder into the drawer, and slapped the single package into my hand. She bounced off the bed and said, "Excuse me, I will be right back." She went into the bathroom, swinging her multicolored purse.

I got the rest of my clothes off and went down the hall to the other bathroom. When I returned, she had pulled the bedding down and was reclining on her side. I flashed on a Modigliani painting of a reclining nude and contemplated art history for about a tenth of a second.

Sometime later, we lay entwined in the sheets and each other, breathing hard. The open window was all sky. Ocean air flowed in, quenching the excess heat that had built up in the room.

Lilith pointed and said, "I see what you mean about the perfect summer day. Your window is a perfect azure-blue rectangle."

Neither of us wanted to let go, so we just stayed horizontal and breathed.

She said, "So how did you make the change from philosopher to detective?"

I told her about my part-time work as a bodyguard and investigator during my college years and my aborted scholastic career.

"Did the other teachers know you were working as a private investigator?"

I nodded. "There was also an unfortunate news item in which I was mentioned by name."

"Was it very bad?"

I displayed the six-inch scar on my outer left forearm. "You should have seen the other guy."

"What happened to him?"

"He died."

She gulped. "Did you get in trouble?"

"The police were on my side all the way. So was the DA."

"What happened?"

"I was twenty-four years old, walking to a night class, and I saw some pervert trying to break into a car with three little girls inside. The girls ranged from six to twelve years old. They were in a parked car by the Medical Center. Their mom had gone inside for a couple of minutes and left them in the car. When the perv saw me approaching he ran into the Botanical Garden. When I ran up to the car, the smallest girl looked at me like I was another monster who intended to kill her, and she let out a scream I will never forget. The oldest one could tell I was just a citizen walking down the street. She put her window down a couple of inches and told me the guy tried to get inside the car. I chased the perv and caught him, and he pulled a knife."

I pointed again at the scar on my forearm. "I took one slash on my arm and smashed his head against a wall. It took the detectives less than a day to interview all the witnesses and determine I acted in self-defense. The event didn't play so well in graduate school. I was pegged as a Neanderthal. Some of the students and faculty refused to speak to me."

"Wow! What a story!" She took my arm and gave the scar a close look. "This is not very noticeable. In fact, it is sort of cute, like a Heidelberg scar." She put my arm down and patted it. "Where is your family?"

"No family. My father was a policeman, killed in action when I was six."

"I am so sorry."

"My mother took an overdose of pills when I was eight."

She groaned and said, "How did you survive all that?"

"It wasn't that bad. My first foster home didn't work out. The second one was great, better than most families. My foster parents are retired in Orange County now. I see them frequently. After I was orphaned, some of the cops looked after me. I'm still friends with one guy, a West L.A. detective. Sort of like an uncle."

"You don't have other family?"

"I have distant cousins. I'm not sure where they are."

"You are alone."

I ran my calloused hand across her smooth cheek and took my time. "Not at the moment. What's *your* life story?"

"Well, I already told you how my family immigrated to the U.S., and how we returned to Taiwan for two years, and then we came back here. My father was a very smart farm boy. He got a full-ride scholarship for college. Then he worked as an engineer for a company that makes expensive bicycle parts. Now he is a vice president. My mother has always been happy to be a housewife."

"How hard was it to adjust to high school in Taiwan after being in the US?"

"At first, some of the girls tried to pick on me, because my clothes were different, and they were jealous because I was from California, which is where they really wanted to be. I slugged one of them in the face, and gave her a big black eye, and that ended the bullying. I took all the combat training in school I could get."

"Combat training for girls?"

"They have military classes for students in Taiwan. If mainland China ever invades, everyone will fight." She giggled and drew her finger across my throat. "I learned how to fight with a knife." She put her hands on my throat. "I learned how to strangle." She pointed her finger between my eyes. "I'm a very good pistol shot. One time, I even got to throw a live hand grenade. That was so much fun!"

"I'll keep all that in mind."

She climbed on top and pinned me down, sliding her hot, moist body around in a circular motion. She put her mouth on my ear and spoke in a low, threatening voice: "I am an innocent girl from a rice farm." We laughed all the way to the shower and kept on laughing as we stood under the warm rain.

Lilith had a one-thirty meeting at Culver Aerospace, and I needed to go to the Airport Suites Hotel. When we arrived at her car, the windshield had been decorated with a parking citation. The ticket went from the wiper blade to my pocket. We lingered on the sidewalk for a while and appreciated each other and the perfect late-summer day.

30

I drove south on the San Diego, called the Airport Suites hotel, and learned that the guest named Carl Victor had checked out.

During the cruise down the freeway, I tried to imagine being with Lilith on a permanent basis. The images refused to snap into focus. I tried to imagine a six-year-old, half-Chinese Jackson Junior, and I got more clarity. We ran around a freshly mown lawn and tossed a little football back and forth. He threw sloppy spirals and wounded ducks. He listened eagerly to my coaching advice and immediately improved his mechanics and accuracy. The kid was a quick study. A female figure stood in a doorway, watching. I expected her to be Lilith, but every time I glanced over, she faded into a haze.

A freeway sign said AIRPORT, and my mind returned to business. Nailing Darcey for a seven-year-old embezzlement was starting to seem less important and less likely to happen. If I couldn't learn more about Faraday or the guys driving the silver Cadillac and the white Dodge Charger, I might be at the end of the road.

I made my way into the Airport Suites underground parking structure, where I hoped to bribe an attendant for information on the silver Cadillac. No luck. The system was totally automated.

A new silver Cadillac without plates was on the third level, backed into a corner space. I parked nearby and walked back to it. Nothing inside the car caught my attention. A little more snooping revealed that the car was not the model I was looking for. I drove down farther, parked my car near the dead end at the fourth level, and took the elevator up to the lobby.

It was a newer hotel, clean and fresh, with all the character of a meat-packing plant. A shuttle van stopped at the curb in front and discharged a load of guests and their luggage. They were herded to the front desk, hastily processed, and sent to their rooms. Another van loaded up departing guests and whisked them back to the airport, where they would be packed into their jets like sausage.

I folded a fifty-dollar bill into my shirt pocket and explored the ground floor, looking for a hotel snitch who might provide information on Carl Victor. There was a concierge desk, but no concierge behind it. The "business center" turned out to be a table in a hallway and three pay-by-credit-card computers, none of them in use. The fitness room was empty. The gift shop was run by a man who looked like my ninth-grade gym coach. I suppressed the urge to smack him and went looking for the restaurant. I thought I might get a bite to eat.

Wide, shallow steps tiered down to the restaurant. Too many blustery business types were banging their silverware and chewing with their mouths open. I wasn't very hungry, and I didn't feel like paying double because I was near the airport.

For covert information-gathering on a hotel guest, the best source is usually the bartender, but the ReLAX Lounge didn't open until four. I was climbing back up the steps, thinking about returning to the hotel bar that evening, when I was blocked by a slim, young African American man.

He was a little less than six feet in height, dressed in a dark suit, white shirt, and striped tie. He said, "My name is Jerrold Johnson. I am the manager of hotel security. May I help you in any way?"

I gave him my card and said, "Can we go to your office?"

"Certainly."

He gestured me up the steps and down a short hallway. Some guy in a blazer tailed us. Rough complexion, all belly and shoulders. I snapped him a salute behind Mr. Johnson's back. I got a lazy sneer in return.

Mr. Johnson let me into his office, shut the door, and stood behind his desk. He did not sit, nor did he offer me a seat. I showed him my PI license and told him I was investigating a case of embezzlement, looking for a gentleman named Carl Victor. My subject was driving a new silver Cadillac sedan. He had probably stayed at Airport Suites, and he may have been traveling with another man.

Mr. Johnson listened politely. Then he adjusted the controls of a video monitor on his desk and said, "Are you a guest in the hotel?"

"No."

He rotated the monitor toward me, pointed to a still image of me in the parking structure, and said, "What were you doing there?"

"Looking for a new Cadillac registered to Carl Victor."

He pecked at his keyboard, and the image changed to one of me, penlight in hand, peering into the interior of the Cadillac on parking level three.

He sounded like a traffic cop issuing a citation. "If you're not a guest in the hotel, and you're not meeting a guest or conducting legitimate business, and you're just wandering around the hotel, you are trespassing. You know that, don't you?"

"If the men I'm looking for are as dangerous as I think they are, you don't want them in your hotel."

"Airport Suites does not provide information on our guests to outside parties."

I knew the guy was just doing his job, but sometimes I get steamed. I started out snarling and managed to tone it down as I spoke. "These guys are shit-bags. I don't like shit-bags, and you strike me as the type who doesn't like them very much either. You can have me thrown out of your hotel at any time. Or just snap your fingers and I vanish. It's up to you. Me, I want to nail the shit-bags."

"What did they do?"

"This case started with a small-time embezzlement, and it's starting to snowball into something bigger. I can't make any specific accusations or go to the police or other agencies until I have more direct evidence. And that's what I'm trying to get now."

His eyes narrowed at the mention of other agencies. "What else do you know about them?"

"The guy with the Cadillac has short blond hair. The other guy drove a white Dodge Charger, but I never saw his face. I think they are capable of extreme violence. I don't know that as a fact, but I strongly suspect it."

Jerry looked down at my image on his monitor, then back at the real me. He looked away, as though he were trying to recall which section of the Airport Suites Security Handbook would apply to this situation.

He said, "I probably shouldn't do this. Follow me." We went out of the office, and he waved off the guy with the blazer and the gut.

We went into a room containing maids' carts. He pulled a key ring from a coat pocket, unlocked a storage cabinet, and set a partially filled trash bag on a table.

He said, "This stuff came from their room," and pulled two disposable gloves from a box and put them on. He untied the bag, reached in, and picked through the wadded napkins and Kleenexes and paper cups. He produced a torn piece of paper about an inch square and placed it so I could see it. Eight neatly hand-printed letters were on it:

A VIS

A RID

Jerry explained that the scrap was on the floor behind the toilet, as though someone had torn up and flushed a note, but they dropped one paper fragment.

I wondered if Jerry scrutinized all the hotel guests with so much vigor. I took a three-by-five card and short pen from my jacket and copied the letters in the same size, layout, and style—more or less.

He put the paper fragment back in the bag, retied it, and locked it back in the cabinet. He discarded the gloves and said, "I'll save their DNA, just in case I see them in the news."

Back in his office, he offered me a seat. He said, "Those guys caught my attention right away. The one who called himself Carl Victor was a blond, like you said. The other was dark-haired. They were in their mid-thirties, athletic build, six-feet-tall, maybe a little over that. Carl Victor looked Nordic, and the other one Middle Eastern. I never got a name for the other guy. They only spoke French to each other, but it wasn't their native language. They would sound like a couple of provincial rubes in Paris. They also looked like they knew how to handle themselves when push comes to shove. I'm not sure what they were up to, but they were up to something.

"When they first checked in, they had a white Dodge Charger. Looked like a rental. The second day they showed up in the new silver Cadillac you were looking for, and they also kept the Charger. I think the Caddy was the go-fast version. I don't know the model name."

I said, "CTS-V."

He nodded. "That sounds right. So anyway, I'm sitting at my desk, going through my e-mails, with one eye on my closed-circuit security system." Jerry patted the top of the video monitor on his desk. "I watched them park their new Cadillac all the way at the bottom, four levels down. Instead of taking the elevator, they walked all the way up the stairs.

"Being a curious kind of guy, I went down the hall and into the stairwell and quietly closed the door behind me. I could hear them talking on the way up. They didn't know I was there, and they didn't know I had four years of French in college, and I spent a summer in France. I heard one of them say, 'When we are finished, I will leave the Cadillac in some parking structure, and we will take the Dodge to the airport.'"

I said, "They were going to just dump the new Cadillac?"

"That was the distinct impression I got. I couldn't imagine someone abandoning a new car unless something very crooked and very profitable was going on."

"And you can't call in the police with flimsy evidence like that, even if you know the characters are dirty."

"You got that right. If I called the police on a guest, without iron-clad evidence of a legal violation, I would be out the door with a boot mark on my ass. I need to keep this job, for the time being."

Jerry brought his computer to life and found that Carl Victor had checked into the hotel eleven days previously and had checked out after two nights.

I noted the dates and said, "Have you been working as the house dick for a long time?"

"One month short of two years, and it hasn't been especially fulfilling. I applied to the FBI and passed the phase-one test. Phase two is next month."

I stood up. "Thanks for your help, and good luck at Quantico."

"I sure hope so. I'm getting tired of telling our distinguished drunken guests not to piss in the parking structure. That's what I thought you were doing when I first saw you on the security monitor."

I left the office chuckling to myself. The blazer was waiting for me in the hall. He followed me while I continued chuckling. At the elevator, I gave him my card and told him if he ever needed a job, don't call me.

I cruised up the San Diego Freeway and came to some conclusions, some more conclusive than others. The French guys were tailing me in the Hollywood Hills last Friday. They may have seen my car at Sierra McCoy's house. That made them suspects in her murder.

The guys picking up the package at the dead drop were probably the same pair. Their silver Cadillac got away from me on Cherokee Lane, which branches out to various canyon neighborhoods including the upper regions of Trousdale Estates. When I lost Faraday on Saturday morning, after seeing him at the post office, he was driving along the lower boundary of Trousdale Estates.

This I was fairly sure of: the French guys and Faraday were somehow connected, and there was something rotten in, or very close to, Trousdale.

On Montana Avenue in Santa Monica, there's a small market and deli that frequently stands between me and starvation. I exchanged friendly insults with the owner and ordered lunch to go.

Back at my office, I cleared my desk and writing table. One of the cleared items was Lilith's parking ticket. I wrote the check, stuffed the envelope, and sailed it into the outgoing basket.

On my writing table, I spread out the following: lunch, an L.A. map folded to Trousdale Estates, the three-by-five card on which I had printed "A VIS" and "A RID," and an illuminated magnifying glass. I always look for an excuse to use my vintage Bausch + Lomb magnifier. I like to think Sherlock Holmes would be jealous.

I shifted the map to different angles, moved the card to different positions, and looked for connections. Half a sandwich later, the "A VIS" in Loma Vista jumped at me. Loma Vista Drive is the main drag in Trousdale, running from the upper regions, all the way down the hill. I scanned Loma Vista's cross streets, starting in the lower regions. Near the top of the hill is an intersecting street named Carla Ridge. I grabbed a notepad, looked again at the map, and squinted. I wrinkled my nose too. That always helps. I wrote "Loma Vista" above "Carla Ridge" and drew a line around the relevant portions. It came out like this:

L O M |A V I S| T A
C A R L |A R I D| G E

It all came together. The two French-speaking guys flew in from somewhere, landed at the hotel, and called Faraday. Faraday gave them directions to his house, which was probably near the inter-section of Loma Vista and Carla Ridge. They memorized the direc-tions and destroyed the note, except for the fragment Jerry Johnson found. Tuesday afternoon, when I chased after the silver Cadillac on Coldwater Canyon Road, I gave up and turned back less than a quar-ter-mile from the intersection of Loma Vista and Carla Ridge. Very soon, my car would be at that same intersection.

31

cruised around and checked out the expensive, single-story houses set into the Trousdale hillside. The cognoscenti refer to the architecture as "mid-century modern." I refer to it as too much money for a house that looks like a car wash. Of course, if I were in an income bracket that would put me into a Trousdale home, I might look at it differently. I saw no vintage black Jag, silver Cadillac CTS-V, or white Dodge Charger. No surprise there. The Jag would be kept dust-free in a garage, and the people I was looking for would be keeping a low profile. A private security cop drove by. He didn't seem to notice me.

A white Toyota pickup was parked halfway down Loma Vista. A tall Hispanic man wearing a cowboy hat was loading a power saw and a bright orange extension cord. I stopped behind his truck, handed him my business card, and showed a fifty-dollar bill.

On my iPad, I showed a picture of a dark green 1965 E-Type roadster. "I need an address. The guy I'm looking for drives a Jaguar like this one, only it's black, with a tan top. And he's got a big beard and mustache. He's probably in his fifties."

He spoke without hesitation. "I've seen him. That old Jag's engine sounds great. It has this really deep-throated sound. I've seen him going up and down the hill a few times, but I don't know where he lives."

I offered the fifty. "I appreciate the help."

He hesitated briefly, took the cash, and said, "I might be able to make a couple of calls and find him for you. I know people who work up here. I'll call some people and get back with you for sure, one way or the other."

He gave me a glossy business card that said HERNANDEZ CONTRACTING. We shook hands, and I drove back up the hill.

I was about to call Lilith when she called me and said, "I have learned something you need to know. When can we get together?"

I pulled over to the side. "How about pizza at my place after work?"

Her voice sparkled. "Yes."

"Six o'clock?"

"Yes."

"You pay?"

The sparkle in her voice brightened further. "You might get your half in the face or maybe a more southerly region."

"Don't you believe in women's liberation?"

"I will tell you my views on that subject sometime when I am beating you with a frying pan."

"Like I said, I pay."

We decided to meet at Milesian Pizza in Santa Monica at five forty-five. We negotiated the pizza ingredients, and Lilith volunteered to phone in the order.

As soon as we ended the call, my phone vibrated again. Mr. Hernandez said, "I called a plumber who works Trousdale all the time. Says the guy with the beard and the old Jag lives somewhere on Brewster Drive, up near the top of the hill. Couldn't give me a street number, but he's sure it's on Brewster. It's a short block, so you can probably find the guy pretty fast."

I thanked Mr. Hernandez, drove up the hill, and found that Brewster Drive had sixteen houses and one vacant lot on its gradual curve and cul-de-sac. While looking for the Jag and scrutinizing the houses, I noted the range of street numbers.

I turned around in the cul-de-sac and drove in the opposite direction, inspecting the houses from a different angle. The same rent-a-cop I had seen earlier slipped his car out of a foliage-covered driveway and followed me all the way out of the neighborhood. The nosy bastard would soon be passing my license plate and description to his buddies.

32

During the drive to Milesian Pizza, I drummed my fingers on the steering wheel and considered the options for finding Faraday's residence. I decided to borrow Angela Vasquez, one of Gabriel Van Buren's female operatives. She could go door-to-door on Brewster Street, wearing a maid's uniform, asking about the bearded man with the vintage black Jaguar. I figured she could get Faraday's address in five minutes. Angela could talk her way into the Pentagon. I got Gabe and Angela on the phone and gave them the story. I didn't mention espionage or spying, because I didn't want to burden them with that information, but I made it clear I was dealing with some heavy hitters. We planned to meet at their office the next morning at nine.

I walked into Milesian Pizza right on time. No Lilith. I paid for the food, and a firm, slender arm seized me. Lilith smiled and said, "I hope you're leaving a generous tip."

She followed me down Wilshire Boulevard and Ocean Avenue, and into my parking structure. Inside my condo, I set the food on the kitchen counter and opened the curtains wide. A sizzling orange sphere hung over the blue-gray sea.

Lilith said, "What is nice about this view is that you do not have to travel somewhere to see it. When you come home, it is just there."

I started reheating the pizza. Over my shoulder, I said, "Wander around and check out my place."

She said, "I am looking forward to this. All I saw this morning was your bedroom ceiling. But first, can I help you with the food?"

"This is all under control. You can help with dessert later."

Lilith walked through the living room and dining area, then into the hallway. She came back a minute later and said, "I like the way you mix modern and Stickley furniture, and I like the framed art, especially the orange crate labels. How many books do you have in those bookcases in your office?"

"About eight hundred. There must have been something you didn't like."

"Your TV and stereo have wires and components and speakers all over the place. It doesn't really blend into the décor. Your living room would look better if some of the technology could be hidden."

"I agree. When I upgrade my audio-video system, you can help me move all the heavy components around, and crawl around on the floor and pull wires. Then we would have to clean up the mess."

She leaned across the counter and gave me a big, cheery smile. "No, I can give my opinion, and you can do the work. And then I will change my mind, and you can do the work again. That would be a normal male-female relationship."

I knew better than to swing at that pitch.

We took our trays out to the patio and arranged our chairs. We ate, watched the view, and watched each other. Lilith's natural skin tone hinted at gold. The sun and its ocean reflection teamed up and painted her a brilliant gold.

She spoke first. "Have you had a girlfriend recently?"

"Until early this year."

"So, what happened?"

"Anastasia always wanted to go somewhere, and I always wanted to stay home and watch television or listen to music."

"That is the only reason it did not work out?"

"She disapproved of my profession. She thinks I should be a college professor."

"I think I might agree with her. Don't you think you would be happier if you were a professor?"

"I would have to go back to school for my PhD, but I don't fit into the scholastic world."

"Do you feel like you really fit into the private detective world?"

I thought about that for a moment. "Good question."

"I love the name Anastasia. What does she do?"

"Officially, she's a clinical psychologist. She has an office in Westwood. One of the high-rises on Wilshire."

"Officially?"

"It's not a money-making operation. She works a few hours a week with paid clients, and her friends drop by and they all talk about how they feel. Her father pays the bills. Anastasia likes the title "doctor" in front of her name. She spends most of her time doing charity work and shopping. She is very skilled at both."

"How long were you together?"

"Off and on for seven or eight years."

"How long since you have seen her?"

"About a year."

"Have you ever been married?

"No. How about you?"

"I have never been married, and I have had two boyfriends."

"Does that number include me?"

She leaned over and lightly slapped the side of my face. "No, I have not even started testing you. And you had better be ready for a rigorous testing process."

She finished her pizza, unfolded two paper napkins, carefully wiped her mouth and fingers, and let out an uneasy sigh. "I might as well tell you this. This is not an easy thing to say. I did some investigating today at work. When you saw Darcey in South El Monte, she was at our classified off-site data backup facility. She was supposedly conducting an audit. It is very unusual for a manager in her position to be doing the actual hands-on work in an audit. After all the other things you told me about her, I have to think maybe she is doing something wrong with classified data." She spoke sadly, like it was a death in the family.

I thought about the mag tape in my safe. "Let's say, for the sake of discussion, Darcey stole classified data from Culver Aerospace. Would it be on magnetic tape?"

"Yes, probably on a cassette called an LTO-5, or it might be an LTO-4."

The gold light turned gray. Icy fingers crept up my back and grabbed my neck. I could see the *L.A. Times* headline: SALVO GETS LIFE FOR ESPIONAGE. I held out my thumbs and fingers to form an approximate four-inch square. "Is it about this big, and is the TDK version in a maroon color?"

Lilith looked directly into my eyes. "Why am I starting to worry about what you are going to say next?"

"I snuck into Darcey's apartment Tuesday morning and found a tape like that. I switched it with a blank tape."

"How did you know the tape was in her apartment?"

"I didn't know about the tape specifically, but I suspected she had something hidden in a locked file cabinet. It had one of those locking bars on it."

"Yes. We use locking bars at Culver. I use one on my file cabinet. But how did you know she had the file cabinet? What were you doing at Darcey's house in the first place?"

"Last week, right after I discovered her connection with Sierra McCoy, she called me up and asked for a date."

Lilith's upper lip developed a little curl I had not seen before. "So, of course you had to say yes, because it was your duty as a hotshot L.A. private eye."

"Would you like a blow-by-blow account of the evening?"

"Yes, but you do not have to be *that* graphic."

"That was a boxing metaphor."

"With Darcey as the punching bag?"

"Would you like to hear about it?"

Lilith smiled, but without the angry curl to her lip. "Tell me about your big date, slugger."

"We ate at a deli, went to a bookstore, watched TV at her place, and she kicked me out at midnight." I saw no point in mentioning the shower and the peep show.

"What is on the tape you found at her place?"

"I haven't been able to access a computer system that will read it. You could probably do it at your office."

"I could get in a lot of trouble."

"That's why I didn't tell you about it earlier."

"Do you have any more wonderful surprises?"

"Tuesday afternoon, I followed Darcey to a canyon north of Beverly Hills. She dropped off a small package in the bushes, near a hiking trail. A half-hour later, two men came by and picked up the package."

Lilith's eyes widened and she talked fast. "I went to a conference in Washington D.C., a security conference. There were all kinds of government agents and other experts. They told about cases where spies drop things off at a secret place, and another spy picks it up later. If we think this is about spying, we must call the FBI. Culver Aerospace has a couple of very important classified programs. You saw the Paladin. If the Russians or Communist Chinese got our secrets, it would be very bad. It could change the outcome of a war!"

I said, "Tomorrow I'll deliver the tape to your office, and you can see what's on it. If the data is classified, we have to call the FBI immediately."

Lilith banged a fist into her palm. "I can't believe this is happening. A spy. Right under my nose. If the Paladin program has been compromised, this is going to be very embarrassing for the company and for me."

"You haven't committed any crime. Why do they have to store the data all the way out there in South El Monte?"

"Disaster recovery. If our main computing facility in El Segundo burns up or there is an earthquake, we can always buy more computers, but the data must not be lost, so we store it at an off-site location."

"Won't someone notice the missing tape that Darcey took and blow the whistle?"

"Darcey would be too clever to just steal it. She would probably switch it with a blank tape, like you did at her apartment."

"So that means her only risk of getting caught would be if there were a major disaster at El Segundo, which is unlikely. Right?"

"Probably, but there would still be some danger for her. There are multiple generations of data in off-site storage. Sometimes the computer operations people retrieve data from off-site when they have everyday problems with the computers in El Segundo, but they usually retrieve the newer generations of data. If you were going to steal classified data, the smart thing would be to take the oldest tape, right before they destroy it to make room for a new one. The blank tape she left behind would have been destroyed that night or the next morning, and then nobody would ever know the difference."

We picked up our trays and took them to the kitchen. I closed the windows and curtains and turned on the television. The San Francisco 49ers were playing the Bears in Chicago. The second half had just started.

I looked warily at Lilith and said, "I suppose you hate football."

"I am a huge 49ers fan."

"You like pro football?"

"Yes."

"You mean you actually like to watch football on TV?"

"No, I do not like it. I love it. My first crush was on Jeff Garcia, the 49ers quarterback."

"I used to love watching Garcia get crushed."

"Why?"

"I started hating the 49ers about the same time I stopped believing in the Easter bunny. My father hated the 49ers, and I continued the tradition. I must have been six years old. That's one of the few things I remember about him."

"Who is your favorite team?"

"Normally, it's the Rams. Tonight, it's the Bears."

She pushed me onto the middle of the sofa, rearranged the pillows, eased into place, and swung her legs across me. During the next ninety minutes, we squabbled over the game and wrestled. Every time I said "Frisco" she hit me with a pillow. We had a great time.

Toward the end of the game, Lilith said, "I have to be at work at seven. I should go."

"I think you should stay here. Someone has been watching me for the past few days. Maybe they followed us here."

"Are you sure someone is watching you?"

"I'm pretty sure I've been followed. And I'm absolutely certain someone searched my office Tuesday night."

"What do you think they were looking for?"

"They might have been looking for the tape. The break-in was a pro job, not the usual scum. They might have seen us together. I'm concerned they might be a danger to you."

She stood up. "Tomorrow we will have a better idea of what we are dealing with, when we see what is on that tape."

"I'm talking about tonight. We can go to your place, and you can get your clothes for work tomorrow. You can stay here, I will deliver you to work at seven, and you will have the mysterious tape in your purse."

"If we are together tonight, we will not get any sleep. Tomorrow is Friday, and then we have the weekend."

I could see Lilith was going to be unyielding on the subject. "Okay, but I want to follow you home and check your windows and doors."

"That would be very nice."

We drove in tandem to her apartment. I watched for a tail but didn't spot one. By prearrangement, we circled two different blocks, about a quarter-mile from her place. I didn't pick out any following cars.

When we arrived at Lilith's apartment, I made a security assessment. The front windows had decent latches. The front door had a dead bolt and a chain lock. The back door had a useless handle lock and a cheap, misaligned dead bolt with only a half-inch throw.

I stepped out the back and told Lilith to lock me out. I whipped out my custom Swiss Army Knife, and the door handle lock yielded immediately. The dead bolt took a little more effort. I yanked the door open and gave her my crazed killer face. She helped me wedge a table across the door, trying not to laugh.

I looked at the doors and windows again while Lilith prepped for her next day's work. When I got back to the bedroom, the bedding was turned back and Yvonne the cat was curled on a pillow. White flannel pajamas lay across the foot of the bed. Bedroom slippers were side-by-side on the floor. Purse and keys on the dresser. Her work clothes were on hangers, on a closet door hook.

Before I went out the front door, she clung to me for a while and told me what she was going to do to me the following night. She laughed when I blushed. I left a little before ten, feeling elated and uneasy. I drove two blocks and pulled over. There was no way I was going to leave her alone.

33

My surveillance position was at the curb in front of the Rosewood Apartments, almost straight across from Lilith's building. A white Nissan van sat in front of my car. A red Jeep Cherokee sat behind. The front doors and windows of Lilith's building were partially obscured by tall evergreens that filled the gaps between the porches. There were too many good hiding places in the shrubbery. The only illumination from Lilith's building came from her porch light.

The front would be the obvious entry point since we had barricaded the back. Someone could cut a front window with a glass cutter, reach inside, and work the latches, or they could get through the door by picking the locks and using a cable cutter on the chain.

By ten thirty, the street traffic had thinned out. An occasional pedestrian or two traveled the sidewalks, some with dogs. No one seemed to notice me. About eleven-thirty, a young couple came up the central walkway from the garages at the back of Lilith's building and entered unit number one, at the front. I hoped they would turn on their porch light. They didn't.

At eleven thirty-five, a stern-looking woman sporting a towering beehive hairdo, bathrobe, and fuzzy slippers marched down the walkway from number 102 at the Rosewood Apartments. She opened the front passenger door of the white van and retrieved a large shopping bag. She pounded back up the walkway and into her apartment. If she noticed me, she gave no indication.

About an hour later, a little guy puffing a big cigar strutted out of the same apartment unit. He wore a Lakers jersey down to his knees and medium-rise elevator shoes. He gave me a quick nervous glance, climbed into the red Jeep behind me, revved it, and peeled rubber during his U-turn. He or his girlfriend or anyone else who noticed me might call the cops and report a suspicious man parked in front. A risk I had to take.

Lilith routinely arrived at her office by seven a.m., and she had a fifteen-minute commute. That meant she would probably leave her apartment about six thirty-five or six-forty. Since her back door was blocked, she would go out the front. All I had to do was endure the boredom, wait for her to come out, and follow her to work. I put my car seat farther back and stretched. I turned the radio on low and listened to jazz, news, and talk shows. There ought to be a federal agency to deal with the problem of Surveillance-Induced Boredom Syndrome. Maybe I could go on disability.

A little after four, the red and blue lights of an LAPD patrol car came up behind me. I turned on my interior light, unlocked the doors, put the windows down, and put my hands on the steering wheel at ten and two. A slim but sturdy-looking female cop approached my door.

Her nameplate said BIRCH. She had the hard glaze cops develop after they've come up against hundreds of predators. Her mouth said, "How are you doing, sir?" Her eyes said, *What the fuck are you doing out here at four in the morning, asshole?* She held her flashlight on me, not directly in my face.

"Officer Birch, I'm a licensed private investigator on a case, conducting a surveillance."

"May I see your driver's license, registration, and insurance, please?"

I could see the other cop in my right-side mirror, a young flattop with his right thumb hooked over his pistol. I slowly reached over, kept an eye on Flattop, and pulled the glove box release. It fell open with a *thunk.* Flattop flinched. I lifted out the owner's manual using only my thumb and index finger. I lifted slowly, so no one would mistake the book for a bazooka. I set it on my door ledge and pulled out my registration and insurance certificate. Officer Birch took them and said, "How about the driver's license?"

"I'm not reaching for my pocket until you put your junior partner on a shorter leash."

She looked over the top of the car and said something I didn't quite catch. She looked back at me and said, "Please step out of the car."

I set the owner's manual on the dashboard, slowly got out of the car, and dug out my license. The cops moved me to the sidewalk. I tried to position myself so I could see Lilith's place, but they had me facing the wrong way.

Officer Birch told Flattop to run my license, and he took it back to the patrol car. She looked at my PI license and asked what kind of cases I worked. I gave her an abbreviated history of Salvo Investigative Services and told her I knew a West L.A. detective named Rocky Platt. She was in the Pacific Division, but she had heard of Rocky. She loosened up and asked more questions about my business. If I had to bet money, I would have bet she was thinking about leaving the department and going into private work.

The cops finally cut me loose and drove away. I turned my attention back to Lilith. Her porch light was off. Ten minutes before, the light had been on. Yvonne the cat was waiting to be let in. The cat was supposed to be on the pillow next to Lilith. I got my .38 from the trunk, tucked it into my waistband, and joined the cat. The front door was not locked, the chain not hooked. I followed my .38 inside, and the cat darted in between my legs. The chain had been cut.

I elbowed a wall switch. The living room looked the same as before. Lights were on in the bedroom and kitchen. I left the front door almost shut and sidestepped to the right. Now the kitchen and back porch were visible. The table barricade had been moved away from the back door.

I shut the front door, prowled through the apartment, and found no indication of a struggle and no Lilith. Her bedding was pulled back. Her purse and keys lay on the dresser in the same position as before. The purse contained her wallet and her cash. Her work clothes were still hanging on the closet door. I went out the back, down the narrow walkway to the carport. Her car was in its slot.

On the way back to the bedroom, I stopped in the kitchen and noticed a bulletin board on the wall. There was a circular display of photographs on the square board: Lilith at various ages; another girl, probably her sister; the parents; an elderly woman, probably Grandma; a gray cat and a white poodle; and combinations of all those.

Each photo was held in place with four pushpins. The pins were of different colors, but each photo was mounted with pins of matching colors. In the center of the photo display was a hand-written list of phone numbers: Mom and Dad, Sis, a dentist and two doctors, Honda service department, Clara's Hair and Nails, and five or six Culver Aerospace numbers.

All you had to do was look at the bulletin board and you knew Lilith was a decent, honorable girl. No background check needed. No drug test needed. And how did I fit into this young, well-lived life? All I did was use her as a free investigative resource, screw her, and let her be kidnapped. Maybe I got her killed. Nice going, Salvo.

I stood over Lilith's empty bed, called her cell and office phones, and left hopeless messages. Maybe she was sick and drove herself to the hospital. Maybe she had a special project at work and needed to be at the office early. Maybe she led a double life, and she was dancing at an after-hours club. But her car was here. Maybe she took a cab. But her purse was here. It was time to stop dreaming and start moving. My watch said four thirty-four. Fifteen minutes later I was standing over another bed in another apartment.

34

A Fox Studio light sliced through the gap in Darcey Mathis's bedroom drapes, sketched an irregular white line on the wall, and faintly illuminated the room. Darcey had lost much of her bedding during the warm summer night. The only sounds were her breathing and mine. I turned on a floor lamp, moved the dressing table stool next to the bed, and took a seat. Her breathing became more forceful. She turned onto her side, pushed her face into the pillow, and moaned through most of an octave.

I said, "We have a lot to talk about, so you might as well get up."

"Mmmm."

"You gotta give me some answers, Darcey."

"Mmmm?"

I grabbed her hip and yanked it back and forth.

She lurched up and pulled the sheet to her neck. She was wide-eyed and panicky at first. That gave way to an angry sneer, then a slow fade into acceptance and calculation. She squinted against the light and cleared her throat. "You didn't have to do it like this, Jack. We could have gotten together in a more friendly way."

I said, "Someone abducted Lilith from her apartment this morning."

She sat up higher, holding the sheet a little lower. "Did you call the police?"

I said nothing.

She threw the covers aside, swung out of bed, and rubbed her bare hip on my shoulder as she went past. She pulled a couple of intimate items from the armoire and disappeared into the walk-in closet.

I stood next to the closet door. "Darcey, I know for a fact you're into something crooked, and it smells like espionage. Your best bet is to tell me what you know and tell it fast."

There was a rustling of clothes and no response to my comment. She came out wearing a black and turquoise warm-up suit, carrying a pair of running shoes and socks. She sat on the stool, pulled on the footwear, and started tying the shoes. "This all sounds so histrionic."

I wanted to kick her off the stool and watch her bounce, but I took a more measured approach. I said, "They have abducted Lilith. They might be torturing her right now. If you want her to live, you have to start talking. For starters, I need Lowell Faraday's exact address, and I need it now."

She finished the shoelaces and examined the nail on her left index finger. "I don't have the slightest idea what you're babbling about. Maybe you need a vacation. I know this past week you've had it pretty rough."

"You're going to have a rough time maintaining that Brazilian wax job in federal prison."

She jumped up, facing away from me. "I believe this conversation is finished."

I turned her toward me and barked in her face. "Pace and Vega are dead. Your old pal Sierra McCoy is dead. Lilith may be next. You may be next."

She tried to stand firm, wobbled, and sat hard on the stool. She slowly elevated her chin and spoke carefully, as though she had rehearsed her speech and didn't want to make the tiniest mistake. "I know a man named Lowell Faraday. He used to work for the CIA. Now he's a security consultant. I met him at a conference in Boston. It turned out he also lived in L.A. We went to dinner a couple of times, and he gave me some good advice on how to manage computer security in my department. He asked me for information about our security procedures at Culver, and it seemed innocent at first, but to tell the truth, I was starting to suspect he was up to something. I was thinking about contacting our security people and telling them. I should have done it earlier." She rose, stood up perfectly straight, and looked me directly in the eye. "I can guarantee you I have done nothing wrong." She looked as innocent as Little Bo Peep making a chastity vow.

I said, "I know you went to the data storage facility in South El Monte on Monday. I watched you drop a tape cassette in Franklin Canyon Tuesday afternoon. A half-hour later I watched two of Faraday's boys pick it up." I was guessing they were Faraday's boys, but it was a guess with some sense behind it.

Her words came out shrill and brittle. "Are you sure you haven't been imagining things?"

I jabbed my thumb in the direction of her home office. "I did not imagine the maroon-colored magnetic tape cassette you stashed in your file cabinet. I climbed in your window Tuesday morning and switched it with a blank. Your tape is going back to Culver Aerospace today, so they can confirm that it contains stolen classified information. Then they call the FBI."

Her neck muscles tensed up and let go. Her shoulders sagged, along with her pretense of innocence.

I said, with all the gentleness I could mobilize, which wasn't much, "You stole classified data from Culver Aerospace. You were selling it to Lowell Faraday. He knows by now that the tape you gave him was blank. He thinks you betrayed him. I don't think he's going to take that sitting down."

She looked at her shoes. Her mouth drooped as if she were asleep.

I kept going. "You know what happened to Sierra. Now she can't talk. Pace and his crooked pal were set up in a fake murder/suicide. Your best bet is to call a defense attorney and tell him you want to turn yourself in to the FBI. When you're in custody, you will be safe from Faraday and the dark forces behind him, and you'll get less jail time when you cooperate. If you don't know a good defense attorney, I can give you a name, but first you have to tell me where I can find Faraday."

My phone vibrated, and I grabbed it.

Lilith's voice had aged about a half-century. "Jackson! Listen please and get ready to write."

I said, "Where are you?" and ran into Darcey's office.

Her voice shivered. "I only have a minute. You must listen and write this down."

I hit the light and grabbed a chair, paper, and pen.

Lilith said, "Do you have the tape?"

"Yes."

"You must bring it. Can you write this down?"

"I'm writing."

"There is a park on Mulholland Drive called Wonderland Overlook. Do you know it?"

"Yes."

Her words came out deliberate and jittery, as though she was reading a recipe and there was a gun at her head. "Go to the Wonderland Overlook parking lot at exactly seven a.m. . . . Take the trail to the east forty yards and go to the green wooden post . . . Take the small trail that goes to the right . . . Go twenty yards to the burned tree stump . . . Put the tape on top of the stump . . . Go back the way you came . . . Go straight to your office." The tempo and power of her voice picked up. "They will let me go, and I will call you to pick me up somewhere. If you call the police or bring other people, they will kill me. Please, Jack, I am—"

The call cut off.

My scribbled notes stared at me, taunting me. I stared back, paralyzed. Car tires squealed from the driveway. I ran down the stairs and out the front door. Darcey's car disappeared into the night.

Back upstairs, I got a clean sheet of paper and rewrote Lilith's instructions while the memory was still fresh. I muttered to myself, "Calm down. Review the instructions and devise your plan. Think. Don't fuck this up."

Kidnapping and espionage were now staring me in the face. It might have seemed prudent to hand the problem to the FBI and let them solve it, but there would be no telling how the feds would balance

Lilith's safety against getting their hands on real live spies. And I would be entirely out of the loop, in custody for hours, maybe days. On the other hand, I could go home and get the tape from my office safe and deliver it per Lilith's instructions. But as soon as Lilith's captors got what they wanted, they were likely to dispose of her. I needed to contact the FBI, but it would have to wait.

35

The people who had abducted Lilith knew my car too well, so I drove to a car rental agency, picked up a Chevy, and bribed the rental agent to let me park my BMW in the corner of their lot. He gave me a weird look, but he didn't ask me to explain why I wanted to downgrade my ride. I parked the rental car a half block from my condo, entered my building through a rear entrance, took the service elevator up to my floor, keeping my .38 handy until I was locked inside.

On my home computer I found a satellite view of the Wonderland Overlook and vicinity. The first part of the route Lilith had described stood out plainly, snaking to the east of the overlook parking lot. The second part was narrower, leading to a small clearing. The tree stump she had described wasn't visible, but it had to be there.

There was another route to the clearing, a rough trail from a turnout on Mulholland; that would be a logical path for any ambushers. From a turnout farther back on Mulholland, there was a more difficult path, one involving climbing and bushwhacking; that would be my route.

I opened my office safe and took out the mag tape that presumably was filled with enough rocket science to change world history. That tape went into a mailing envelope addressed to Lilith Lin at Culver Aerospace. I put too many stamps on the envelope, just to be sure.

I took the two remaining blank tapes I had purchased Sunday and locked one into my safe. I folded the other one into a small shopping bag, trimmed the bag with scissors, and wrapped the package tightly in duct tape. Faraday and his helpers were probably in a fiendish mood over the blank tape Darcey had delivered earlier in the week. When they learned this second package also contained no data, they probably weren't going to hold hands and dance around in a circle.

I dressed for the occasion with trail-running shoes, lightweight hiking pants, and a long-sleeve shirt. My waist pack held a small flashlight with a red lens, snub-nose .38 revolver, two five-shot speed loaders, fixed-blade knife, and compact binoculars.

At five-fifteen I dropped the package addressed to Lilith into a mail collection box in front of the post office branch on Wilshire. From there, it took about a half-hour to drive to the point on Mulholland Drive where I planned to start my hike and deliver the bogus package.

I turned off the engine, put the window down, and listened. The dry wind made a throbbing, low-pitched whistle in the power lines. I would have preferred dead quiet. I also would have preferred moonlight. What I got was nearly total darkness.

I left my condo and office key ring in the glove compartment, locked the car, and zipped the rental car key into a pocket. Then I strapped on my waist pack and scurried up the hillside. After four or five minutes of high-intensity climbing, I was at the top of the ridge. I sat in the dirt, caught my breath, and took in the view. A section of the lighted San Fernando Valley floor was visible, as were a few houses on the hillside above the Wonderland Overlook. There was enough light to keep my orientation, but not enough to eyeball a precise route down the ridge.

I made a scientific wild-ass guess as to the location of the clearing and worked my way toward it, sometimes following my red flashlight beam. At one point, the foliage closed in on me. My KA-BAR knife came out of its sheath, sliced a few branches, and I was on my way again.

At six-twelve, the sky was turning from light black to dark gray. At six-sixteen, I tried the binoculars. In a clearing below, a protuberance that could have been a tree stump was visible.

It would have been easy to walk down the bare ridgeline, but my silhouette might have been against the eastern sky. I took a parallel route and crept through the foliage. The well-wrapped computer tape was in my left hand and my .38 snubby in the right. The path flattened out and I entered the clearing. There was a lull in the wind, and suddenly it was quiet. I rotated slowly and saw nothing of interest, except for a charred tree stump. I set the package on the stump. My plan was to retreat a short distance, hide in the chaparral, and wait for Faraday's boys.

I started up the trail and, after advancing a few feet, I stopped. A rattlesnake was stretched out in front of me. It was small, as far as rattlesnakes go, but it would still have a poisonous bite. I bowled four small rocks at it from a respectful distance. The first two missed, and the third kicked dirt in its face. A forked tongue wiggled. The next rock skipped off its back. The rattler raised its head, wiggled its tongue more vigorously, and shook its namesake. It drew a smooth, curvy track in the dust and disappeared into the brush. I was congratulating myself on my outdoor skills when a crunch sounded behind me. Then I was aware of nothing.

36

Some son-of-a-bitch was moving my bed back and forth. Some people have no sense of propriety. I ought to get out of bed and kick his ass. No, wait. It's just a small earthquake. We have 'em all the time. Go back to sleep and catch it on the news later. And why the headache? I don't drink that much. Maybe I was dreaming I had a headache. I needed to sleep it off, but the pillow felt like sandpaper. Actually, I had no pillow. I tried to reach for it anyway. My arms wouldn't move.

Full consciousness returned, and a cold bucket of reality dumped on my head. I was not dreaming my head hurt. My head hurt. I was in the trunk of a moving car, my arms bound to my torso, my legs bound together, my face pressed into the abrasive carpet. I forced myself to take a couple of deep breaths. That made me wonder how long the air would last.

There are things you can do to escape from a car trunk. There's supposed to be a glow-in-the-dark release handle on the underside of the lid. Maybe I could work it with my knees. I didn't see anything but blackness. I tried to feel around with my feet and figure which way I was oriented. There might be tools under the trunk mat. Maybe I could pull a wire out of a brake light and attract a cop's attention.

The car stopped and a garage door opener sounded. The car moved forward and the garage door sounded again. Car doors opened and voices muttered.

The trunk opened. The light slapped my eyes shut. Two men lifted me out and set me on my feet. Fast and efficient. One of them cut the tape off my legs. I never saw the knife. They spoke quickly and quietly in French. I can understand some French, especially if it's a ten-year-old speaking slowly. I understood almost nothing these guys were saying.

It was the pair Jerry Johnson had described. One had blond hair, Nordic features, and white skin, not to be confused with pink skin like mine. I tagged him "The Aryan." The other was darker, maybe Middle Eastern. I tagged him "The Algerian."

They were lean, clean, and clean-shaven. They wore tan linen sport coats that were similar but not identical, dark slacks, and blue shirts. Everything fit well. Their polished, soft-soled shoes were similar to the ones I wear. Their shoelaces were tied flat and even. They wore identical Glock pistols on their belts.

The car I came out of was a silver Cadillac CTS-V. We were in a three-car garage in which the only visible items were two cars, the French-speaking torpedoes, and me. It was a garage that took itself seriously. Generous overhead lighting, wood-paneled walls, built-in cabinets, no open shelving, and nothing on the painted concrete floor.

The Aryan pulled the tape off my mouth and said, "Are you awake?"

I mumbled that I was okay, trying to look and sound more dazed than I really was.

They walked me past a low-slung sports car. It was under a tan flannel cover, but the cover was not pulled all the way over the right rear. Chrome wire wheels shone. Deep black paint mirrored a ceiling light. The termination of a thin, elegantly tapered chrome bumper flowed around the car's rear corner. Mr. Ryde would pronounce it *Jag-you-are*.

They led me into the house. The yawning, pitched-roof living room was empty the way an unoccupied blimp hangar is empty. An extra-large fireplace was cut into a wildly asymmetrical, gray stone wall. The wall to the backyard was all glass behind sheer white drapes.

We took a sharp corner into a shiny kitchen. There were acres of stainless steel, but no bowl of fresh summer fruit, no Mr. Coffee, no refrigerator magnets holding discount coupons, no kitchen towels embroidered with adorable cocker spaniels.

Next was a laundry room that looked and smelled antiseptically clean. A wide sink and two pairs of washers and dryers lined one side. Closed cabinets and empty shelving were on the other.

They pointed me toward a short flight of stairs running down to a door. Three plastic trash bags were next to the door, stuffed and tied. Newspapers and magazines were piled next to the bags. I descended awkwardly, which was the natural thing to do with my arms taped to my torso. I deliberately stumbled and ended up with my nose in the magazines.

I said, "Sorry about that," and sprung to my feet, trying to show how cooperative I was. A magazine address label said 1660 Brewster

Drive. That put us on the east side of the cul-de-sac I had visited the previous day.

The Algerian told me to stand still. He cut the tape from the lower part of my arms, so I could keep some balance when I walked. They directed me through the door and onto a limestone pathway to the backyard. A tall hedge blocked the adjacent house, which might have been within shouting distance. I kept my mouth shut for the time being.

We came to the backyard and crossed a patio made of the same limestone. I looked over a triangular swimming pool, hoping to see a house on the other side of the yard. All I saw was fencing and foliage.

I wasted a few brain impulses wondering how the hell you swim laps in a triangular pool. The fog in my head finally rolled out to sea and left an unclouded vision of reality. In a hostage situation, you usually get no more than one chance to escape. I could either seize that single chance or die a slaughterhouse death, probably with Lilith.

Stone steps went down the hillside through the native vegetation, and so did we. The tall hedge ran along on the right, slowly coming down in height. The steps ended. The scrub brush gave way to a thicket of oleander bushes in white and two shades of pink. I wondered if this might be the kill zone.

The same dry wind from Mulholland was swirling the oleanders, quieted by its passage through the canyons. It would, however, make enough noise to mask the gurgling of a slashed throat. That reflection led to another hostage survival tip: connect emotionally with your captors.

I said, "Have you guys ever been to the American University of Paris? I taught a seminar there once."

The Algerian said, "Shut up."

"I thought you might know about it."

The Aryan said, "We know about it. Now, shut the fuck up."

There. We connected. Now we were pals.

We went through a gate in a chain-link fence, and the descent suddenly got steeper. Six-by-six wooden beams were sunk into the earth at measured intervals. Each footstep recharged my headache. The gradient eased. The oleanders thinned out. A roof appeared, then a two-story house under it.

The houses in Trousdale are mostly single-story. We had to be in the upper reaches of Laurel Canyon, down the hill from 1660 Brewster. The two houses would share a rear property line, but to drive from one address to the other you would have to go up to Mulholland or down to Sunset—and end up driving a distance of four or five miles. A lot had to be at stake to justify investing in such an expensive backup strategy.

We crossed a brick patio and entered the house. A hallway took us into the living room. Two wide windows flanked the front door and showed the Los Angeles flatlands behind a descending ridgeline. The morning sunlight slanted in from the right, which meant I was facing northeast, more or less.

The house appeared to be furnished for a short-term stay. There was a minimal arrangement of cheap furniture that looked new: velvet sofa, small table, and four wooden chairs. Nothing on the walls. One floor lamp. No TV.

I edged forward and looked out a front window, hoping to see a nearby house. The lawn sloped downward, the driveway curving away into the foliage. Other houses had to be down there somewhere.

A new voice said, "You won't see any opportunities for assistance out there, Mr. Salvo. We are quite isolated." The voice came from the right, through the arch to the dining room. The Aryan pushed me in that direction. A serious-looking desktop computer system was on the dining table. One of the system components was an outboard tape drive; I had a sneaking suspicion the device could read an LTO-5 tape cassette.

A man with a full beard and a wide mustache was seated behind the computer—the guy who picked up my package at the West Hollywood Post Office. Lilith sat next to him, her cuffed hands on the tabletop. Her handcuffs were part of a dual restraint system that included a chain running down to leg irons. She wore the same pajamas that had been laid out on her bed, the same slippers. Her hair was all over the place, but she appeared uninjured. When she first saw me, she sat up straight and locked onto my eyes. Hope flashed across her face for a couple of seconds, then she wilted.

The gentleman at the table regarded me with a feeble little sideways smirk. He rhythmically tapped the tabletop with the wooden handle of an ice pick—like the one shoved into Sierra McCoy's brain. He said, "Hello, Mr. Salvo. I am Lowell Faraday." He said it like he was hosting the *Lowell Faraday Show*. He wore a gray cardigan sweater with leather pocket trim and leather elbow patches, and a tattersall plaid shirt. He had manicured nails, a bulbous forehead, and large eyes. His weak chin would have given his head a top-heavy look if it weren't for the hairy camouflage.

The Algerian handed Faraday the package I had delivered to the tree stump. Faraday held it in one hand and shook it up and down as if he were estimating the weight. He looked at it solemnly, as if it contained his destiny.

He said, "Take them upstairs."

They took us upstairs, and now we were in a bedroom, about twenty-by-twenty. The only window was shuttered from the outside.

The only light came from a ceiling fixture. An open door led to a bathroom, another to a walk-in closet. There were no furnishings other than two metal patio chairs. Another set of handcuffs and leg irons hung over the back of one of the chairs. They put Lilith on her chair and relocated one of her leg cuffs to the spindle between the chair's front legs. She could move around the room, but she would have to drag the chair with her.

The Aryan handed the Algerian his pistol and produced a folding knife. The Algerian stepped back and pointed the Glock in my general direction. The knife snapped open. Lilith flinched. At close range, most people fear a knife more than a gun. The Aryan cut the tape off me, made the knife disappear, cuffed me in front, and attached me to my chair the same as Lilith. The duo left the room and locked the door.

I dragged my chair up close to Lilith, cradled her face with my hands, and said, "Did they hurt you?"

"No. I am okay. They did not hit me or anything like that. Those two men put me in the back of a car and took me to that icky old man." She lowered her eyes and spoke bitterly, like she wanted to purge herself of the words. "He rubbed his creepy soft hands all over me—almost everywhere—and showed me that ice pick. He said if I did not tell him where the tape was, he would stick the ice pick in my ear all the way to the handle. I told him you had the tape, but I did not know exactly where you had it. That is why you are here. I am sorry. They made me call you and read that message."

"This is my fault, not yours."

I took off my left shoe and pulled out the orthotic insert. A small, flat, oval-shaped folding knife was taped inside the carbon fiber arch. I loosened the tape, put the shiny, stainless steel knife on the carpet, and started to retie my shoe.

Lilith said, "May I see the knife?"

"Okay, but be careful. It's very sharp."

I handed it to her and finished retying my shoe.

She opened the blade with one hand and gazed at it. "This is small, but it could be very effective." She carefully closed it using both hands and gave it back.

I put it in the right front pocket of my hiking pants, positioning it so the outline was not visible.

I said, "You handled that knife pretty well."

"I told you before, in Taiwan we all take military training."

"We need to talk more about that, but first I want to check out this room."

I dragged my chair behind me and looked for opportunities. The pins could have been worked out of the door hinges, but that takes time and makes noise. The toilet tank lid was heavy enough to bash out the window shutters, but that makes lots of noise, and we would have to drop ten feet with the chairs attached to us. No way. The toilet lid might come in handy as a bludgeon if I could get at one of our captors alone. The closet was empty—not even a wire hanger to fashion into a garrote. The bathroom drawers and shelves were empty. I had a slight hope of finding a bobby pin in the bathroom. When I was in high school, Uncle Rocky showed me how to pick handcuff locks with a bobby pin. While shuffling around the room, I discovered the best way to move was to step sideways, holding the back of the chair and dragging it or lifting it off the floor.

While I inspected the room, I gave Lilith a running monologue on my findings. She stayed silent until there were voices outside the door. She whispered, "They are coming!"

37

They all barged in. Faraday said, "Place his chair facing hers, six feet distant. Use the tape to secure her upper body to the back of the chair."

The French guys put several rounds of gray duct tape around Lilith's torso, arms, and the back of her chair. They weren't exactly gentle, but they didn't rough her up. Then they took positions behind me.

Faraday stood by Lilith and held the top of her head with his left hand. He held his ice pick in his right. He spoke with a pompous serenity. "It would be such a terrible pity to spoil this delightful example of femininity, rather like breaking a Fabergé egg."

He gave me an exaggerated, prolonged version of his sideways smirk. "Mr. Salvo, the tape you provided this morning was supposed to contain the entire database for Culver Aerospace's stealth technologies—all their low observables knowledge, all the engineering data from their research. The tape is blank. What do you have to say for yourself?"

I had intended to play dumb. I was going to tell Faraday the tape I delivered to the Wonderland Overlook was the same one I found in Darcey's place on Tuesday. That could lead to some cute speculation about who did what to which mag tape and when they did it. Try to pin everything on Darcey.

The ice pick in Faraday's hand flashed me back to Sierra McCoy's twisted, dead eyes. I tasted a little of the nausea I had felt in Sierra's bedroom. I said, "I'm going to tell you everything I know. I'm going to just blurt it all out." That wasn't a big fat lie, nor was it the whole truth.

He said, "That would be the intelligent approach. There's really no need for any unpleasantness in correcting this problem." He kept a hand on Lilith's head and the ice pick near her head. "I must tell you, there is absolutely zero tolerance for any misrepresentation or evasiveness on your part. Now, why did you provide a blank tape this morning rather than the original tape Miss Lin requested?"

"I had no guarantee she would be released."

"Where is the original tape—the one you took from Darcey—at this moment?"

"In my home office, in the safe." If I had said it was at the post office, on the way back to Culver Aerospace, it might be *adios* for Lilith and me.

"Exactly where did you get that particular tape?"

"File cabinet in Darcey's house, bottom drawer."

"When?"

"Tuesday, about noon."

"How did you manage to find the tape at Darcey's house?"

"She didn't hide it very well. It was in . . ."

"No. I mean why were you in her house in the first place?"

"She asked me for a date."

Faraday shook his head and bared his teeth. "Such a clever girl. Well, at this point in time those details are not important. Now this is the second time I have received the unpleasant surprise of a blank magnetic tape. How would you propose we correct the situation?" He moved the ice pick closer to Lilith.

I said, "We can correct the situation if we go to my place. The tape is in my home safe."

"No. You will be staying here." He nodded toward the Aryan and the Algerian. "My teammates will be visiting your residence." He took his hand off Lilith's head, reached into a pocket, and dangled the keychain holding my office and condo keys. We found these in your rental car, so we shouldn't have any trouble getting into your residence."

I nodded. "Okay, I can give you my safe combination and the alarm code for my condo, and I can brief you on how to get in and out of my building without being noticed.

Faraday stepped away from Lilith and looked down at her as though she were a bug in a test tube. She was trembling uncontrollably. He glanced at his watch, and the trio abruptly left the room.

Lilith's voice shook. "You did not bring the real tape? How could you do that?"

"If I brought the real one, we would be of no further value to these guys. They would just get rid of us. We know too much."

"Please give them what they want! It is our only chance."

I dragged my chair and got close to her. "We need to buy time. I was supposed to be at my friend Gabriel's office at nine." I glanced at my watch. "That's only twenty minutes from now, and I always show up for meetings early. When I don't show up, Gabe will know something's wrong. When I don't call, and I don't respond to his call, he will know something is very wrong. He knows I was trying to find Faraday's address, and he knows I had it narrowed down to just a few houses. He will definitely come looking for me, and he will bring other people with him.

"But that is the wrong house. How will he know we are down here? They made me walk down a mountain to get here."

"Gabe gets paid to find people. He is very good at it."

"Who is he?"

"My best friend. He owns a private investigation and bodyguard company."

Lilith whispered, "Our only hope."

"No. We have the knife, and we have our hands and our brains."

"Who are those two other men? They are so scary, but they are kind of polite . . . almost like gentlemen, but they are weird. I never saw anyone like them before."

"I think they're ex-French Foreign Legion."

"What makes you think that?"

"In the first place, they speak French to each other, but it's not their native language. From their accents when they speak English, I think the blond is Russian and the other one . . . I don't know."

"You said *French* Foreign Legion."

"There are almost no Frenchmen in the Legion. That's why they call it the *Foreign* Legion. When they get killed in battle, the political fallout is reduced if they don't take French casualties. They learn to speak the language in basic training. And these two guys are dressed very carefully. Not expensive clothes, but they have a tailored look. Everything is clean. Shoestrings are laced flat, perfectly even. In the Legion's code of conduct, it says they are always immaculately dressed. Also, these two guys have teamwork the same way the Green Bay Packers have teamwork."

"What are we going to do?"

"When those two characters are gone, we can get Faraday alone. Then we have to get up close and personal."

"I think he would like to be personal with me, the way he put his hands on me. He should be put up against a wall and shot."

I leaned in closer. "We have another angle. I snuck into Darcey's place early this morning and pulled her out of bed. I told her I knew all about her espionage scheme, and she's definitely going to prison, the only question being how long will she be up the river. I told her the best thing for her would be to turn herself in to the FBI, but first tell me Faraday's address so I could get a head start in rescuing you. She got away from me when I was talking to you on the phone, but there's a chance she came to her senses and turned herself in already. If she went to the FBI or police, we could be rescued any moment now. What we need is time. We need to stall."

Lilith started to say something, but there were noises at the door, and then our three captors were standing over us.

The Aryan held a clipboard and a felt-tip pen. He walked up close and looked down at me. "Tell me, when did you teach at the American University of Paris?"

"I taught a seminar on existentialism. Summer, 1997." Actually, I had only visited the American University of Paris, but this was no time to split hairs.

"What philosophical insight did you provide for your students?"

I was puzzled by the line of questioning, but I went along with it. "I told them Sartre isn't much of a philosopher, and existentialism is more a cultural trend than it is philosophy."

The Aryan said, "That must have gone over poorly with the French intellectuals. When I was in school, I did not see the value of existentialism either. It was weak thinking. What books did you use in your seminar?"

"We stuck mostly to Sartre. *Being and Time, No Exit,* and *Nausea.*"

He gave me a heavy-lidded look and said, "One thing I must say is that if the information you give us about your apartment is bad, or if the tape is not real, things will be very bad for you."

Faraday said, "Mister Salvo, if the tape we obtain from your apartment is not real, things will be especially bad for Miss Lin. I know you must think a lot of her, since you were willing to sit in your car all night and watch her apartment. I'm sure you want her to remain alive . . . and unsullied."

Faraday probably intended to get rid of us as soon as he got the tape and validated the content. I played it semi-dumb and said, "*You* reported me to the police last night." I tried to make it sound like a compliment.

Faraday gave me his standard little smirk. "One uses the most effective resources one can find."

I spent about fifteen minutes briefing them on how to burglarize my home. They took my handcuffs off temporarily, and I drew diagrams of Palisades Towers, and access routes into the building and into my condo. I printed my alarm code and safe combination.

The Algerian cut the tape off Lilith and peeled it away, taking great care to not cut her. Before the trio left the room, Faraday leaned over Lilith and winked at her. "I'll be back a little later to check on you. I think you're going to be okay." He patted her on the knee and left the room.

Suddenly it was quiet. We had about an hour and a half. That's how long it would take the French guys to drive to my condo in rush-hour traffic, sneak in, grab the tape, and return to Laurel Canyon.

I maneuvered my chair to where I could get my hands on her. "Lilith, we can get out of this, but we have to stay focused."

She opened her mouth and tried to speak, but nothing came out. She took a deep breath and grimaced as she held it. Her voice came back. "I still don't see how they can find us down here in this house. Your friend should just call the police."

"He probably called Uncle Rocky already."

"Who is that?"

"He's a West L.A. police detective, not really my uncle. He's a very good friend. Now listen. When those two characters bring that tape back from my place and Faraday discovers it's blank, he is going to be pissed."

Her jaw dropped almost into her lap. "You mean you are giving them *another* blank one? You heard what they said they would do."

"Once Faraday has the real tape and he validates the content, we are dead meat. He will have no further use for us." I paused and tried to let that sink in.

Her eyes lost focus, and she was lost in her own thoughts. Finally, she said, "I am afraid I see what you mean. So where is the original tape?"

"It's in the mail. It probably will arrive on your desk at Culver Aerospace on Monday."

"They will kill us when they find out."

"We need to get out of here before they find out."

She looked at my head. "You stayed up all night in your car to watch out for me, and now you have that bump on your head. It is my fault. I should have stayed at your place."

"It doesn't hurt." That was a lie, but it calmed her.

She said, "Okay, I understand why you did not give them the real tape. Now we have more time. But what are we going to do?"

"Tell me, if you had the chance, could you slice Faraday open and watch the blood gush out, or would you panic and freeze?"

She gripped my arm. "I will do my part. Just tell me what to do. I want out of this place!"

I took the knife from my pocket and handed it to her. "You're more likely than me to be in a position to use this."

"My position will probably be on my back."

She clipped the knife over the waistband of her pajama bottoms, the clip facing out. Her pajama top covered the small weapon.

I said, "When Faraday comes back, don't pat the knife to make sure it's still there. He may be trained to look for things like that."

Lilith pulled the knife from her waistband, opened it one-handed, and stared at it.

I said, "Your handcuffs and the other restraints will make things more difficult for you, but you have the element of surprise. When you're using a knife as a defensive weapon, the best outcome is when your opponent doesn't know you have the knife until you've cut him with it. And you can't just cut him. You have to rip him open. And I have to remind you of something. When you shove a knife into someone, it gets messy. You have to be ready for some disgusting images and noises and smells. And you're likely to get blood on you."

She closed the knife and clipped it back inside her waistband. "I used to hear that all the time in my military training in Taiwan. As long as it is his blood, that will be perfectly acceptable."

I looked her straight in the eye. "When it comes to crunch time, remember this. You don't have to be perfect. You just have to do it. There will be a moment of truth when you have to act. At that moment you can't hesitate. You have to do it."

She looked at me calmly and said nothing. I felt better.

We practiced moving across the room while dragging our chairs with us, drank water out of the bathroom faucet, took turns using the bathroom, did some stretching exercises, and waited.

38

The door opened and Faraday appeared. He spoke directly to Lilith. "Ms. Lin, I hope you are not too uncomfortable.

"I am okay."

Faraday leaned against the doorjamb in a casual posture. He stood there for a long time, savoring his dominance. He took a small automatic pistol from the pocket of his cardigan sweater. A Walther PPK.

I thought, *The beer-guzzling Herrington brothers at the trailer park in Paramount weren't kidding. Faraday thinks he's James Bond.*

I said, "Nice PPK. Is it vintage or one of the U.S. versions?"

"German. Early sixties."

"How can you have such good taste in guns, cars, and mid-century modern architecture, and such bad taste in thievery? This espionage scam is going to put you in federal prison."

"I think not. It's all been planned in some detail. All contingencies have been considered."

"I don't think you considered my getting in the way of your plans."

"How would you know anything about my plans?"

"Inference."

He laughed politely and said, "Inference. The philosophical private eye. The gun-toting logician." He made a derisive noise, somewhere between a laugh and a snort. "Please. Tell me what you have inferred about my plans."

I was in no position to wring his neck and stick the gun up his ass, so I answered the question. "Darcey Mathis was supposed to steal classified information from Culver Aerospace for you. She was just about ready to snag it when the auditors discovered the Oswald Pace embezzlement. She was worried my investigation of the newer embezzlement would lead back to her 2006 scam, and that would end her aerospace career and her access to the classified data you wanted. She should have told you about the problem immediately, but she tried to fix it herself."

Faraday cut me off with a wave of the hand. "You're wrong on that count. Darcey told me about her previous indiscretion when the new embezzlement was discovered. She trusted me to help her solve the problem. But please tell me more. This is fascinating."

I continued. "When the Oswald Pace embezzlement was discovered, Darcey got herself appointed leader of the investigative team and tried to sell the idea that the embezzler, when identified, should be allowed to leave the company voluntarily, and then Culver Aerospace could forget the whole thing. Companies let embezzlers off the hook all the time, to avoid bad publicity. Darcey wanted to make sure that happened, so she told me to dig up all the dirt I could find in the

259

embezzler's background. I'm sure she would have preferred to pick her own investigator, but her upper management chose me, and I uncovered more than she expected."

Faraday stayed silent. I kept talking.

"You tried to fix things. Your torpedoes got rid of Pace and Vega, and they did an artful job of making it look like murder-suicide. You figured the investigation of the Oswald Pace embezzlement would come to an end. Then your boys got rid of Sierra McCoy, so she couldn't rat out Darcey. Pace and Vega made sense. The cops were ready to buy the murder-suicide, but silencing Sierra McCoy was a mistake. It attracted too much attention, including mine."

Faraday shrugged. "I have to agree that there have been some minor complexities, but no deal-busters."

I gave him my first punch line. "My people are sure to find you within a day or so." I didn't say within a few minutes, because I didn't want to spook Faraday into panicking, dispatching Lilith and me prematurely, and running for safety.

"Who are these people of yours?"

"Investigators I work with."

Faraday said, "You work alone, out of a cheap little office on Pico Boulevard."

"I'm part of a network of investigators who routinely share information. One of my people found information on your father Michael Faraday in just a few hours. The Long Beach investigator you went to struck out. My people get results."

That got his attention. He pulled himself up straight and said, "Over the years, I have hired two different private investigators to track down my father, and they both gave me the same answer. My father vanished. Not a trace. You didn't find him. You're simply trying to maneuver your way out of your present situation."

"I have to admit that I would prefer not to be in this situation. The fact remains that your father changed his name to Mike Fairway, and he did rather well for himself in Florida real estate, except for a two-year stretch for fraud."

Faraday was breathing a little harder now. "And how did you manage to discover the undiscoverable?"

"First I found the bar where he worked. It used to be called the Executive Lounge. Now it's called Some Place." I jabbed my thumb in a southerly direction. "It's down on Rosecrans in the city of Bellflower. The bartender connected me with a patron who knew your father before he abruptly left town in September of 1969."

Faraday blinked quickly a couple of times. There was no way I could have known the exact month and year of his father's skipping town unless I had solid information.

I kept going. "When your torpedoes bought the new Cadillac, they failed to remove the paper advertising from the license plate frame. That led us to Marina Cadillac, where we learned the car was sold to a Carl Victor. That led us to the Airport Suites Hotel, where Mr. Victor and the other French guy—or whatever their nationality is—stayed for two nights. An item in their hotel room trash pointed me toward upper Trousdale Estates."

Faraday said, "And how did you manage to access their trash?"

"Hotel security combed their room and found a fragment of a hand-written note behind the toilet. It was supposed to be flushed, but it wasn't. The fragment contained portions of the street names Alta Vista and Carla Ridge. As you know, the intersection of those two streets is near your house."

"And why did hotel security pay so much attention to these particular guests?"

"The hotel dick didn't like their looks. He's also fluent in French, and he overheard some of their conversations."

"This is a rather implausible story."

I gave him another punch line. "I saw Darcey and the French boys at the dead drop in Franklin Canyon Tuesday afternoon. Darcey made the drop and your boys picked up the package."

Faraday froze for a moment, then recovered. "Why didn't you report that to the FBI?"

"At the time, it looked like plain-vanilla industrial espionage."

"And you thought you get could a piece of it. A reward maybe?"

"Maybe, but it doesn't matter now. Look, Faraday. You're going to get caught. Too many people know what I know, and if I disappear it's just a matter of hours before you get the knock on the door, or maybe a flash-bang grenade through the window. If you kill Lilith and me, that could make the difference between the federal pen and the federal needle."

Faraday stood motionless, apparently thinking things over. "I have to hand it to you, Mr. Salvo. Your investigative technique has been very thorough."

"You have no idea how diligent I am."

"Really?" Faraday stretched the word into three syllables.

I put some extra strength in my voice, like a sixteen-year-old shouting in the boys' locker room. "Bondo . . . *James* Bondo."

Faraday's mouth made a tight angled line.

I gave him my best sadistic adolescent leer.

He said, "So the intrepid private eye has been rummaging through my past history."

"Yeah, and what a past it is. Like when you went to the New Avenue Theater in Downey and saw the same James Bond movie day after day. Janny Kinkaid worked there."

The girl's name sent a flash of recognition across Faraday's face. Everyone remembers the cutest girls in high school.

"I hear Janny still does a hilarious imitation of you walking out of the theater like you think you're Sean Connery in a tuxedo. My favorite story is the one where you got your lights punched out for looking down a girl's blouse in the library. No, wait . . . my favorite story is the one where you were screwing a mentally challenged girl at Norwalk State Hospital. Quite the young man about town, weren't you, Lowell?"

Faraday's face was now bright pink, which had the effect of making his facial hair seem even more extravagant than usual. He glowered in my general direction, his pupils changing focus and darting side to side. His face slowly faded to the usual pinkish-gray color.

He took a deep breath and gave me a formal, almost respectful nod. "I want to thank you for reminding me of all that. You've given me inspiration. Now I want you to drag your chair over to the wall heater." He motioned with the pistol. He snapped, "Do it fast."

I dragged my chair over to the gas heater.

Faraday said, "Reach down and take out the bottom panel from the heater."

I popped off the panel and laid it aside. The gas pipe, gas control valve, and various wires were now visible.

Faraday pulled a key ring holding one key from his left sweater pocket and tossed it to me lefthanded. He instructed me to unlock my leg iron from the chair and lock it around the gas pipe. He had me pull on the cuff hard, to show it was locked. I tossed the key back to him. The klutz couldn't catch it lefthanded, with the gun in his right. He picked the key off the floor and put it back into his sweater pocket. He walked out of the room, leaving the door open.

On the way out, he said, "Don't go anywhere. I'll be right back."

Lilith and I looked at each other, said nothing, and sat still.

39

A few seconds later, Faraday returned. He held his ice pick in his left hand, his Walther in his right.

He stood in front of Lilith and said to her, "Do you want to live?"

She nodded.

"Well, Miss Lin, I also want you to live, so let's get started. The first thing I want is for you to remove your clothes . . . to the extent it's possible with all those restraints, and then you will demonstrate your oral skills for me and then . . . who knows what we might figure out." He looked over at me and said, "And you, Mr. Salvo, will watch."

He edged closer to her and said, "Well, go ahead."

Lilith sat as still as the sphinx.

Faraday mumbled something incoherent.

Lilith dropped her chin to her chest.

I said, "Faraday, you ought to go back to Norwalk State Hospital. You'll have better luck with those girls."

He stepped away from Lilith and turned toward me. A spasm fluttered through his jaw and neck. Lilith's hands crept toward the knife on her waistband.

Faraday carefully sighted his pistol and put a 32-caliber hole through the outside edge of my left calf. I've been shot at and missed at close range before, and the blast concussion was deafening. In this case I hardly noticed the sound. I noticed the lightning bolt shooting up my leg and into my back. I howled, grabbed my leg with both hands, and held on tight.

Faraday said, "Just sit back and enjoy the show, Professor Salvo."

He turned back toward Lilith. She was unbuttoning her pajama top. From the way she used only the thumb and first finger of her right hand, it looked to me like the closed knife was in her hand.

Lilith pulled her pajama top apart, keeping her right hand mostly in a fist. Faraday gawked at her breasts, looked away, and gawked again, as though he couldn't decide whether to be embarrassed or lecherous. Lilith put her hands in her lap. She was waiting for a chance to open the knife. I tried to think of another one-liner to throw at Faraday. It's hard to be witty when you're taking bullets.

A shapely leg swung through the door. The leg belonged to Darcey Mathis. She looked through me as though I did not exist. She glided sideways and leaned back against the wall, directly behind Faraday, who had not seen her. She wore a long-sleeved blouse, blue jeans, and a black leather shoulder bag. She pointed a four-inch revolver at Faraday's back.

Lilith got a full view of Darcey's arrival but made no response.

I said, "Faraday, how much money are you getting out of this?"

He reached out with the ice pick and gently widened the gap in Lilith's unbuttoned pajama top. "Somewhere around fifty million."

"How much was Darcey supposed to get?"

"Twenty million reduced to two million."

"How did that happen?"

"She didn't deliver the goods, and she got more than she deserves."

Darcey said, "What do I deserve, Lowell?"

Faraday whirled around, his mouth agape.

She held the gun steady and spoke in a flat, lifeless monotone like nothing I had ever heard from her. "Did Sierra have to die, Lowell?"

Faraday cleared his throat forcefully and said, "I had nothing to do with that."

Darcey's voice started to pick up energy. "It was on the news, Lowell. An ice pick was jammed into Sierra's head. You killed my friend with an ice pick—a fucking ice pick of all things. How gruesome. How vulgar. It's like something from a horror movie. She was the best friend I ever had. And there's another ice pick right there in your hand. We don't see any blocks of ice in the room, do we?"

Faraday took a slow half-step toward Darcey. "We need to discuss this."

She said, "I can't talk anymore. I'm already dead."

For some sinister stretch of time, there was no sound in the room, no movement.

Faraday broke the malignant silence. "Darcey, we shouldn't be standing here pointing pistols at each other. We should be together. This situation is not what it appears to be, and you have me at quite a disadvantage right now . . . but I'm afraid *your* disadvantage is that your gun's safety is on."

I figured he was going to shoot as soon as Darcey looked down at her revolver.

Darcey kept her eyes on Faraday. "Revolvers don't have safeties, you lying bastard."

Lilith jumped to her feet, holding her knife in her cuffed right hand. Her left hand grasped her right hand, strengthening her grip on the small knife's handle. Faraday flinched at the jangling of Lilith's restraint chain. She reached around and stabbed the knife into his gut. Faraday's Walther blasted once before it fell to the floor. He gasped explosively and lurched backward. Still pushing the knife into Faraday, Lilith leaned into him and ripped the blade through his lower abdomen. He shrieked and twisted away.

Darcey's back slowly slid down the wall. Her feet gave way, dumping her on her right side. Faraday's wild shot had caught her directly in the left eye. The fluid in what had been her eyeball dribbled across her face.

Faraday held his wound with both hands, loudly sucked in air, and spun on one foot, sending a spiral of blood onto the carpet and onto Darcey. He tripped on her, grunted soprano, and landed on the floor in a fetal position, holding his guts in.

Lilith ended up on her knees, her left hand flat on the carpet. She held that position, staring at the knife in her bloody right hand.

I said, "Get the key out of his pocket. Do it now!"

She didn't respond.

I growled through clenched teeth. "Get the fucking key!"

We made eye contact, and she snapped out of it. She dropped the knife and crawled toward Faraday, dragging the chair behind her. I took another look at the remnants of Darcey's eye and wished I hadn't.

Lilith pulled the key from Faraday's pocket, unlocked her handcuffs and leg irons, and ran over and freed me. I slid my pant leg up and we looked at the damage. There were entry and exit wounds on the left side of my calf and a little hole in the wall next to the heater. Blood droplets and little pieces of my leg were stuck to the wall. My leg was bleeding, but it wasn't gushing.

I dumped the contents of Darcey's purse on the floor. No car key. The cell phone didn't work—no signal in the canyon. There was a notecard with hand-printed phone numbers and other numbers that made no immediate sense. I shoved the card into my pants pocket.

In the meantime, Lilith had buttoned her pajama top, swung out the cylinder on Darcey's Ruger, and confirmed it was loaded. Lilith kept the Ruger. I took the Walther and checked the magazine. The little knife went folded into my pocket.

I stuck my pistol into my waistband, slid Darcey's phone into a pocket, and limped over to Faraday. He lay curled on the floor, holding his wound with both hands. His intestines glistened through red fingers. A roundish, red, foot-wide stain, wetted the beige carpet. The stench clobbered me. I was thankful for the burnt gunpowder in the air.

Faraday's wide, terrified eyes wanted to pop out of his face. "You win, Salvo. Call an ambulance."

I leaned over him. "Does this house have a hard-wired telephone?"

"No."

Lilith poked me in the back and said, "Those men will come back. We have to go!"

I looked down at Faraday. "Who is your handler?"

He didn't answer. I kicked his hands, which were still trying to hold his guts in. He squealed. My shot leg sent a thunderbolt all the way up through my neck when I shifted my weight for the kick. It was worth it, so I kicked him again. He squealed again.

I said, "I'll stop kicking you when you tell me who your handler is."

He spat out his words. "Syrian Consulate, Newport Beach. Leo . . . his name is Leo."

"That name would be fake. How do I find him?"

Now he could only whisper. "One blue eye . . . one brown . . . don't hit me."

The carpet stain had expanded in size and palette. The stench was also growing.

Lilith pushed me toward the door. "If I stay here, I will throw up."

As we crept through the backyard and up the hillside, the sound of an arriving car came from the front of the house. The French guys had made better time than I thought possible. We climbed the trail toward the Trousdale house, with me as the slow boat in the convoy. I moved slower and slower. Lilith got behind me and pushed. My shot leg felt like it was on fire. I sat on a wooden step and gripped the leg.

I held out the phone. "I'm not sure I can make it to the top. You need to run up there and call 911 and do it fast."

She whispered, "I do not want to leave you here alone."

"You're gonna get us both killed. Go now! Go fast!"

Her bloodstained hand grabbed the phone, and she sprinted up the hill.

I got up and fell into a slow, methodical limp. The gate in the chain-link fence appeared, which raised my spirits and sped me up. My leg gave out, and I half sat and half fell on the ground.

The Aryan's voice said, "Keep your hands away from your body."

I looked straight down the barrel of his Glock.

The Algerian emerged from the oleanders, also aiming his pistol accurately. He said, "Stand up. Throw the gun away. Left hand. Two fingers."

I stood and considered my odds in a gunfight.

The Aryan knew what I was thinking. He said, "We have thirty rounds of forty caliber aimed at you. You have five or six rounds in that mouse gun, which is not even in your hand."

I slowly drew the Walther out of my waistband, using my left thumb and index finger, and tossed it.

The Aryan said, "What did you do to Faraday and that woman?"

"Faraday shot the woman. Lilith gutted Faraday when he tried to get too friendly with her."

The Algerian picked the Walther out of the dirt.

The Aryan said, "Where is the girl now?"

I looked back over my shoulder. "She's up at Faraday's house right now calling 911. Did you know the average Beverly Hills police emergency response time is less than one minute?"

"I'm not going to be in Beverly Hills. Coming up through all those narrow little roads in Laurel Canyon, the Los Angeles police will take ten minutes."

The Aryan eased close to his partner, and they whispered to each other. The Algerian ran back down the hill. The Aryan turned his full attention back to me. I was the clay pigeon, and he was the guy with the gun. He had said it was forty caliber, but the hole in the barrel was starting to look like the Culver Aerospace Wind Tunnel.

I said, "At this point, there's nothing to gain by shooting me. Lilith can identify you. Shooting me does not eliminate that problem for you. The gunshot will make noise and get the police here faster." He kept the gun on me. I was thinking about the little knife in my pocket and calculating my slim chances of using it.

He lowered his pistol. "Two things. First, I do not ordinarily work with degenerates like Faraday, and second, Sartre did not write *Being and Time*. It was Martin Heidegger." He shot me, but only with a sneer. He blended into the oleanders, and I was alone.

He was right. I should have said *Being and Nothingness*. No big deal. I never gave a shit about existentialism anyway.

40

I limped and staggered up the hill. Crawling was starting to seem like an attractive option when the roof of Faraday's house appeared. I tried to reach out and touch it, but I came up short and planted my face in the dirt. The next thing I knew, paramedics were cutting off my left pant leg and sticking a needle in my arm. The next thing I knew, I didn't feel so bad.

The Cedars-Sinai emergency room crew patched up my leg, x-rayed my head, and went out of their way to make me comfortable. They wanted to examine Lilith, but she declined and insisted she was not hurt. A nurse gave her a robe, slippers, and a blanket. Another crew transported me to my private room.

In my room, Lilith got on the hospital telephone and ordered meals. As soon as I got my bed adjusted the way I wanted it, two FBI agents showed up. The lead agent was Gil Balcom, a graying, angular-faced Missourian. A younger female agent from Long Island named Rose Mastrangelo let Balcom do most of the talking. I told the agents I was worn out and that I could give them a half-hour now and talk again tomorrow. They knew I could have the nurse chase them away, so they agreed. Once we started talking and I started eating, I felt better, and the FBI stayed more than two hours.

First, I told them how I mailed the classified tape to Lilith's office. Balcom whipped out his phone and relayed the information to someone. I figured they would intercept the package at the post office where I dropped it or at a mail distribution center. They sure as hell wouldn't wait for it to land in the Culver Aerospace mail room.

Then I gave an account of my investigation, leaving out nothing. I told about the path the classified tape had traveled, Lilith's abduction, and my attempt to rescue her. I gave them my theory on Darcey and Faraday's espionage caper and how it came apart. Lilith added some comments, and we both answered the agents' questions.

Balcom was especially interested in the pair I called "the French guys" and my theory that they might be ex-French Foreign Legion. The agents' favorite part of the interview was when I said, "Faraday talked before he died. He said his handler was from the Syrian Consulate in Newport Beach. Called himself Leo. One blue eye, one brown." The smiling agents didn't ask if I used enhanced methods in questioning Faraday. They probably forgot to ask.

They wanted to talk to Lilith in more detail, so they offered to drive her home. She accepted the offer and said she would call me later.

I was wolfing down another bland hospital meal when Rocky Platt called. He wanted to know if there were any good-looking nurses. I said, "Come on down. My nurse looks like Paris Hilton. Yours looks like Yogi Berra."

Five minutes later, Gabriel Van Buren called and wanted to know if I was okay.

I said, "I'm all patched up, and I go home tomorrow. How long did it take you to figure out I was in trouble?"

"When you didn't show up for the nine o'clock meeting, I phoned and e-mailed, but you were nowhere to be found. I knew something was wrong, so I went up to Brewster Drive with two of my guys. Angela Vasquez drove up ahead of us. Just like you planned, she wore a maid's uniform and knocked on the neighbors' doors. They told her where the guy with the old Jag lived. Then she drove back to the end of the street and watched for the security patrol while my boys and I went into Faraday's house. When we saw that cute Asian chick run into the back yard in her pajamas, with a gun in her hand, I knew you had to be nearby."

Lilith called at seven o'clock. "How are you feeling? Do you need anything?"

"I'm okay. The hospital releases me tomorrow at eleven. How about a lift?"

"I can pick you up, and we can buy food and take it to your place."

I suggested we also spend Saturday and Sunday night together, and that's exactly what we did. To make a logical distinction, that wasn't all we did, but it was exactly what we did.

41

Early Monday morning, my leg woke me. I rearranged myself on the bed, adjusted the covers, and tried to go back to sleep. No luck. It wasn't the leg that was bothering me now. Something was in the back of my mind, something just beyond reach. I eased out of bed, lifted my cane off the floor, and made sure Lilith was tucked in. Diffused moonlight painted her face luminous white, compelling me to stand and watch. I flashed on one of her kitchen bulletin board photos, in which a teenaged Lilith displayed a beatific smile on her face and a white poodle on her lap.

I went to the more distant bathroom, dialed the light halfway up, and examined the dressing on my leg wound. It looked okay, but a wayward idea was rattling around my brain. Back in the bedroom, I looked at Lilith again. Her kitchen photo display came to mind, especially the photo of her and the poodle. That reminded me of the hand-printed phone list at the center of the display. That reminded me of the hand-printed phone list on the wall next to Del Hoffman's desk.

I put on a robe, fired up my home computer, and opened the photo of Hoffman's phone list. Most of the numbers were five-digit internal Culver Aerospace extensions. No surprise there. There were nine ten-digit numbers, all of them external to Culver.

Five of the ten-digit numbers were other companies who could have a business relationship with Culver. Two were area code 661, Bakersfield, California, which made sense since Hoffman grew up there. The other two were noted as companies for which I could find no listing, and both numbers had invalid area codes. Fake phone numbers.

841-967-1102

368-943-8660

That wasn't necessarily suspicious. I've known cops and security professionals who disguise padlock combinations as phone numbers. For example, the first phone number might contain the six-digit padlock combination 84-19-67. You just ignore the last four digits.

A tiny silver bell tinkled in my head. In my laundry room, I found the hospital bag containing my bloody clothes, which I had dumped on the floor about thirty seconds after I arrived home. The notecard from Darcey's purse was still wadded in my pants pocket. Three phone numbers and three less obvious pieces of information were hand-printed on the card. I got back on my computer. The phone numbers were for Malaysia Airlines, Cathay Pacific, and Korean Air. I don't know what all was going through Darcey's mind during her final hours, but she was certainly thinking about leaving the country. These were the other lines:

(+41 55) 416 30 77

CH84 1967 1102 3689 4386 6

WW90024E

I tapped on my keyboard and learned a few things. The first line was the phone number for a Swiss bank. The second was in the format of a Swiss bank account number. The third appeared to be a password. I smelled money.

The bank's automated phone system provided more information. The password was valid. The account in question contained a little over two million dollars. That squared with what Faraday had said about Darcey's payoff being "twenty million reduced to two million." She probably received an advance up front, then the eighteen-million-dollar balance would be paid upon her delivering the data from the Paladin program. She only delivered a blank tape cassette, so her account was never credited with anything beyond the $2M advance.

I looked at Del Hoffman's fake phone numbers again, and a battleship klaxon sounded in my head. I converted the two numbers to a simple sequence with no dashes or spaces. I did the same to Darcey's bank account number and printed them in the alignment I wanted:

Del: 84196711023689438660

Darcey: CH84196711102368943866

Hoffman's fake phone numbers were a disguised version of Darcey's Swiss bank account number. All he had to do was drop the final zero and remember "CH." He could find the bank's phone number on the Internet. The password was either memorized or recorded somewhere else. If it weren't for my leg, I would have kicked myself for not examining Hoffman's phone list more carefully on Monday night when I was distracted by the news coverage of Sierra McCoy's murder.

The compulsion to kick myself subsided, and I slept soundly next to Lilith for three hours.

42

I pulled into the Culver Aerospace lot at about ten-thirty, parked as close as possible to the building, and poked my cane across the asphalt. My right leg was already getting sore from favoring my left. Lilith had called the security department and arranged for my visitor badge to be waiting at the front desk.

Before I left my condo, I told Lilith about Hoffman's involvement in the espionage scheme. She wanted to come with me when I confronted him, but there was no way I was going to put her in danger again.

During the two days she had been staying at my place, she didn't want to talk about the events in Laurel Canyon. She frequently sat on my patio alone, perfectly still, keeping her thoughts to herself. When we were watching TV, she would go several minutes without speaking. That wasn't the real Lilith. Normally, she had a wisecrack or a pithy comment for any occasion. The real Lilith was always observing something, talking, thinking, reading, or pounding away at a computer. I've never had any training in psychology or psychiatry, and I don't speak psychobabble, but it was clear to me that she had withdrawn from reality. She needed professional help, and I didn't know how to approach her on the subject. I was worried.

After I picked up my badge at the lobby, I limped down the hall toward Hoffman's office and tried to put myself in his shoes. By now he would know something had gone very wrong with the espionage caper. Neither Lilith nor Darcey showed up for work Friday, and neither called in sick; that would be unprecedented. The mysterious shooting in Laurel Canyon was all over the news. Reporters were starting to sniff out the connection between the Laurel Canyon house and the Trousdale house. Authorities weren't releasing any names or anything about the espionage angle, but Hoffman would know. What he would not know was whether he was going to the slammer or whether he was going to skate.

When I stood in his doorway, he was at his desk talking on his cell phone. He saw me and ended the call. "What brings you here, Salvo? I'm sorry to say I heard about Darcey when I spoke with the FBI yesterday. I was certainly relieved to hear Lilith is okay." He pointed at my leg. "Have a seat. Get the weight off that leg. Shot myself in the foot once. Hurt like hell. Grab a seat."

I continued standing. "Hunting rabbits in Bakersfield?"

He squinted hard, unable to hide his surprise.

I pointed at the section of wall next to his desk. "I see you took your telephone list off the wall. You know the list I'm talking about. The one with the fake phone numbers. Two million dollars in a Swiss bank. It should have been twenty million, but what the hell, two million is better than nothing, especially since you don't have to split the take with Darcey. At first, you thought you were going to score ten million dollars each, didn't you? You let her take all the risks. She snagged the classified tape at the off-site data storage facility in South El Monte. She made the dead drop in Franklin Canyon. You were hiding behind your desk. Did it ever occur to you where all the stealth technology was going or how it might be used against us in a war? How it might cost American lives?"

Hoffman gave no reaction.

I kept talking. "You probably weren't heartbroken to hear that Darcey was dead. Now she can't rat you out. All you had to do was keep a low profile, wait for the investigation to die down, and work on a plan to launder the money. Two million bucks sitting in that Swiss account, waiting for you."

For at least a full minute he sat perfectly still and silent in his own little world. Finally, he made eye contact. "Did you come alone?"

I nodded.

"Have you spoken to anyone?"

"I thought I'd give you the opportunity to be the first." I stepped forward and set the business card of FBI agent Balcom on his desk and went back to the doorway and leaned on it."

I said, "Be sure to have the speaker on. I want to hear what you and Gil Balcom have to say to each other."

He read the card carefully. "I have an alternative for you, Salvo. You take the money. I'm not saying let's split it. I'm saying you take all of it. You set up an offshore account. Then you transfer the money to your account. I will never know your new account number or your password. Then we never see each other again."

I shook my head.

He said, "Two million clear," and stared hopefully, as though I might change my mind.

"I don't claim to be an angel, but that's not my kind of money."

He set two fists on the desk. "I was thinking over the weekend something like this could happen, and I prepared an alternative." A grim smile clenched his mouth shut.

He slowly stood up, took off his tie, and folded it neatly on his desk. He moved slowly in my direction. I backed into the hallway, giving myself room to use my cane as a weapon. Suddenly, my leg hurt like hell.

Hoffman came out and said, "Follow me, Salvo. I'll take you to the end of your investigation." He marched swiftly, steadily leaving me behind. We went through three hallways, finally into the gigantic space in the center of the building. When I staggered into the room, Hoffman was already near the Paladin UAV display, at the other side of the room. I looked up at the overhead walkway Lilith and I had used in my first visit to Culver Aerospace.

Hoffman approached the security door at the entrance to the Paladin program area. He unclipped his badge from his shirt pocket, turned toward me, and shouted, "I'll be right with you, Salvo . . . in a sense." He badged himself into the door and vanished.

I stood in the middle of the room and waited. I got tired of waiting, hobbled over to the security door, and tried my visitor badge in the badge reader. It didn't work. My next move would be to piggyback behind the first employee who tried to badge through the door.

A voice shouted, "Salvo!"

I limped away from the door, leaned on my cane, and looked up at Hoffman on the walkway above. He held a coil of rope over his shoulder. One end was knotted into a large, shiny snap hook, maybe a piece of nautical hardware. The other was tied into a hangman's knot, tied with five or six coils. He snapped the hook over the railing and looped the noose around his neck. He pulled the noose tight, the coils just behind his right ear.

Several employees had gathered, looking up at Hoffman. A woman carrying a stack of computer printout gave out a shriek, dropped everything, and pointed toward the spectacle above. An older man in a dark suit crossed himself. A heavy-set young man wearing a shop apron turned and ran.

Hoffman folded the middle section of the rope back and forth across the railing. He climbed over the railing, held on with one hand, and adjusted the knot again.

I cupped my free hand and shouted up to him, "Come on, Hoffman. You didn't kill anyone. You're not gonna get the needle. All you have to do is cooperate. At Leavenworth you can get three squares every day and learn a new hobby!"

Hoffman announced, "I'm giving myself a nice long drop, Salvo. I'm not going to prison, and I'm not going to put on a dance show for you."

A uniformed security guard came out onto the walkway and slowly approached Hoffman. The guard held his hands out and said something in a soft tone.

Hoffman hit the end of his rope with a loud snap. His detached head banged off the Paladin UAV and came to a stop against the wall. The rest of him thudded onto the floor and lay in a heap. There were screams and shouts. Then silence.

OTHER JACK SALVO NOVELS BY JESSE MILES ARE AVAILABLE

THE MIDDLE SISTER

A wealthy woman hires Jack Salvo to find her wayward daughter Lillie, who has been missing for a week. Salvo figures the girl is probably hiding out with her friends. All he has to do is interview the friends, bust their stories, and deduce the missing brat's location. Salvo soon learns that her "friends" are somewhat parasitical. When he finds Lillie, she is hosting different kinds of parasites — the little ones that help rid the world of rotting corpses. Salvo is then pulled into a maze of murder, arson, and blackmail. During his high-speed-run down L.A.'s fast lane, he spars with grifters and gangsters, dodges the cops, and digs up a dark, deadly family secret.

The Middle Sister has a flair of 1940's style private detective novels . . . set in modern-day L.A.

The Tom Sumner Program — Old Fashioned Radio for a New Generation — KFOV 92.1 FM — Flint, Michigan

Written in the style of a true detective novel. Smart, sexy, intriguing.

Doris Vandruff (NetGalley Reviewer)

The characters seem absolutely alive and real, and the dialog is smart, hard, and often quite funny . . . Miles' descriptions of LA ring so true (and I know, I've lived here for 40 years), that if the city burned down tomorrow, it could be rebuilt just from his descriptions of it . . .

Leland Douglas (Kindle Reviewer)

The Middle Sister . . . a deliciously entertaining private investigation mystery that has every seedy element a reader could ask for — murder, arson, blackmail and more. The author offers Salvo as a dogged, but not always on the up and up, savior of sorts. All the juxtaposition is a thrill to devour.

Katherine Michael (Kindle Reviewer)

Being married to a homicide detective, *The Middle Sister* had me engaged from page one. The main character, private detective Jack Salvo, is hired to find a wealthy woman's daughter Lillie. Salvo finds himself in a world of murder, arson, and blackmail. *The Middle Sister* is a fast-paced suspenseful read.

Danielle Gould (Realm of Vibes)

CHURCH OF SPILLED BLOOD

When a group of world-class Russian ballet dancers visits L.A., Jack Salvo signs on as a bodyguard. It's a piece of cake. All he has to do is hang out with beautiful women. Then one of his charges is kidnapped from under his nose. In pursuing the kidnappers, he evades the FBI, finds bullet-riddled bodies near the Hollywood Sign, and dodges bullets. Drawn into a web of deceit and maniacal revenge, he finds himself in Saint Petersburg, Russia. Now he's a fish-out-of-water, an L.A. private eye in a strange land. The most popular historical site in town is called The Church of Our Savior Built on Spilled Blood. When Salvo tries to save the life of a ballerina with whom he has developed a close personal relationship, the church lives up to its name.

"The action is non-stop and the characters are fascinating."

John E. Flatley Jr. (Kindle Reviewer)

". . . hits it out of the park on all accounts."

Shay (NetGalley Reviewer)

". . . reminiscent of Elvis Cole in the books by Robert Crais . . ."

Nicholas (Kindle Reviewer)

". . . interesting characters . . . written in a style that enhances the presentation of the story."

Jay (NetGalley Reviewer)

"This is the 2nd book by Jesse Miles that I have read. Having recently been to St. Petersburg, I could visualize exactly where the events took place. I live in the southland and can say the same about his knowledge of the LA landscape."

Pat D (Kindle Reviewer)

". . . I will be looking for more Jack Salvo's books. . . This was a story with a good plot and enough twists to make it interesting but not confusing. . . Jack has an innate sense of honor that serves him well. The depiction of the ballerinas as the current Russian aristocracy was very interesting. The plot moves well, there was the requisite tension and good resolution."

Pick of the Literate